HE WAS TOTALLY WRONG FOR HER.
WHY DID THIS FEEL SO RIGHT?

He was already in her bed. Asleep, if she could believe his soft snoring.

His hair was dark against the snowy pillow. A hint of dark stubble shadowed the lean contours of his angular face. Dark, heavily fringed lashes drew her attention to the movement of his eyes beneath their lids. He was dreaming.

But she wasn't.

He was a sensitive, sexy man.

He was also her captor.

Was she just a victim of the Stockholm syndrome, falling for the man who held her hostage? Was she being incredibly foolish? A silly woman?

She'd never thought of herself as silly, and wasn't prepared to start now. For whatever reason, she trusted this man—believed he was telling her the truth when he said he had her safety at heart.

It was a big risk to take.

She could pay for that risk with her life, if she was wrong about him.

The more she thought about it, the more scared she became. And the more appealing sharing a bed with him seemed to her. With a sigh, she gave up her internal battle, tossed back the covers, and climbed in.

¤ ¤ ¤

Raves for *Sweet Amy Jane*

"Fast-paced, humorous, and suspenseful!"

—*Romantic Times*

"A light-hearted work of romantic suspense, filled with ever-growing tension, reminiscent of *Remington Steele* and *Moonlighting*."

—*Affaire de Coeur*

SOMETHING WILD

ANNA EBERHARDT

PINNACLE BOOKS
KENSINGTON PUBLISHING CORP.

PINNACLE BOOKS are published by

Kensington Publishing Corp.
850 Third Avenue
New York, NY 10022

Pinnacle and the P logo Reg. U.S. Pat. & TM Off.

First Pinnacle Books Printing: November, 1995

Printed in the United States of America

Acknowledgments

A special thanks to P.O. Robert Woods of the East Hampton Police Department.

Thanks to Jerry Julian, Al Rosenberg and Bill Mathews for their assistance.

Thanks especially to the following writer friends who took my calls, whatever the hour: Wendy Haley, Donna Julian, Bonnie Jeanne Perry, Nancy Dumeyer, Susann Batson (who brought food), Carla Neggers, Barbara Vosbein, Cindy Gerard and bad girls Olivia Rupprecht and Suzanne Forster.

Appreciation and thanks to my agent Denise Marcil and editor Denise Little for their continued and valued support.

One

Libby Gelman-Waxner was the only person who'd be more lost in the country than she was, Chloe Pembrook decided as she drove cluelessly down another unfamiliar street. The only difference was that Libby Gelman-Waxner would have asked the first really cute guy she saw for directions.

The calico cat curled up asleep atop the old-fashioned red Coca-Cola vending machine made up Chloe's mind to stop at the ramshackle garage to ask directions. When she'd passed the same garage for the second time a half-hour earlier there had been an attractive dark-haired man slouched on the machine slaking his thirst with a bottle of soda. Despite the fact that he'd looked so at ease, he'd looked out of place.

A stranger in town. The same as she.

He wore a cinnamon-tobacco brown vest and French walking shoes, with pleated khaki shorts, Fort Knox pilot sunglasses and a straw Borsalino hat—none of which exactly shouted small town middle America.

To her he'd looked like trouble on the hoof. Verbally adroit trouble to boot she'd surmised, noting the battered thick paperback beside him.

Now that he was gone, she was ready to admit she was lost.

Even if only to a cat.

Pulling her MG roadster off the cracked asphalt road to the gravel lot in front of the grey weather-beaten garage, she threw down her useless map in a fit of pique. The map landed on the leather seat with her accompanying epithet. The epithet was unseemly, considering her ladylike appearance.

In concession to travel she'd worn a matching linen shorts-suit of palest ballerina pink. Her antique blouse and Swiss lace pocket handkerchief were from her vintage collection. Upon seeing her, one imagined Chloe as the kind of woman who wrote thank-you notes instead of phoning—in fountain-pen black ink—her handwriting elegant and stylized, her stationery watermark with matching tissue-lined envelopes.

Not fussy. Particular.

And sensual. The kind of woman who would stop to stroke a cat dozing in the sun while the sleepy town seemed to be dozing too.

Gravel crunched beneath her low-heeled pumps as she walked to the long wooden porch covered by a tin roof fronting the garage. Searching through her wallet she came up with change for the old-fashioned Coca-Cola machine. A cold bottle of pop was just the ticket to soothe her nerves, frazzled from the frustration of driving in circles for the past hour.

Pleasantville was a small town, after all. How hard could one gingerbread house be to find? Trouble was, all the houses in Pleasantville were gingerbread, none of them on a street named Maple. There was not, as near as she could discern, a street named Maple in all of Pleasantville.

Tucking her wheat-colored hair behind her ear in an unconscious gesture, she took a sip of the cold pop. She had come tracking a trend. As a lifestyle expert with her own column in *Chicago* magazine she prided herself both on reporting the latest style trends in living, and on influencing them. Chloe was in Pleas-antville to meet a professional ribbon sculptress, want-ing to feature the woman and her ribbonwork in her column.

Ribbonwork had returned to adorn dresses, shoes and hats with the return to femininity in the 90s. Women who had fought in suits for their rights in the workplace were now secure enough to indulge their taste for frippery once again.

While Chloe quenched her thirst, she studied the calico cat dozing on the Coca-Cola machine.

"So tell me . . ." She checked the silver tag on the cat's collar. ". . . Rosemary . . . *Is* there a street named Maple in this town?" A vibrating purr was Rosemary's only response when Chloe began stroking her absently.

Chloe smiled. The field of tasseled sweet corn, across the cracked asphalt road, swaying in the occa-sional breeze seemed to be the only thing moving for miles around. If the town got any sleepier, it would be comatose.

With a sigh, she set down her empty pop bottle and made her way around a pile of dusty hubcaps, going inside the garage in hope of finding someone to give her simple directions that didn't involve the words north, south, east, or west—as she'd been born without an internal compass.

A quick glance about the front office of the garage showed that the place was empty. The proprietor was no doubt taking a nap, she surmised, poking about the brutally masculine room. Quarts of motor oil sat stacked haphazardly in cartons, assorted tires were jumbled against one wall and tuneup parts littered the entire space. She trailed a manicured fingertip and knew the place had never seen a dust rag.

Upon hearing a noise behind her, Chloe turned with a start, and snagged her pastel hose. She shook her head and fingered the runner creeping up her calf as she gave Rosemary a look of admonishment.

Unadmonished, Rosemary wound her way between Chloe's feet, nearly tripping Chloe.

Putting out her hand to steady herself, Chloe managed to get a glob of black grease on it. She looked around for a rag to wipe it off, but there didn't seem to be one, at least not a clean one. Studying her linen suit and snagged hose, she came to the rather obvious conclusion that the garage was no place for pastels.

The cat meowed and jumped up on the counter. Chloe looked up and her eye caught sight of the calendar on the wall. It was a flagrant cheesecake variety; the model appeared to be a nubile farmer's daughter, with improbable proportions. She was sprawled immodestly on a haystack. Chloe's mood brightened considerably as she approached the calendar and she reached out to wipe the black grease from her hand across it.

Men.

No, there was no such thing as men, she reminded herself with a resigned sigh. There were only women and boys.

Rosemary lay stretched out on top of the cash register and Chloe reached out to stroke the cat again.

"Put down the gun."

Chloe's hand froze in midair at the barked command. The voice uttering the command had been deadly serious. She looked in the direction from which the command had seemed to come—toward an open doorway leading into the bowels of the dark, cavernous garage.

What should she do!

The choice was taken from her by the *pop* of the gunshot shattering the breathless air around her.

A body fell backwards into her line of vision.

And then the man holding the gun loomed over the body. A man wearing a vest, pleated shorts and a hat. Chloe's scream was silent.

Two

"I can't faint, I can't faint, I can't faint," Chloe repeated mantra-like beneath her breath trying to banish the dancing fuzzies before her eyes. Her legs had become a curious and inconvenient mixture of lead and jelly. As a result her mad dash for her roadster looked more the ballet of a flustered injured goose than the speedy exit she'd demanded of her body. Nevertheless, she made it to the roadster without becoming bullet-riddled, even if she was wobbly, shaken and still faint.

"Please start, please start, *damn you*, start!" she begged her temperamental roadster while turning the key and tapping the gas pedal till she nearly flooded the engine. When she heard the combustive response, she blurted out a thankful, "Yes!"

Spewing gravel, the roadster obeyed, and ran peeling away from the grimy garage. Though she could feel her heart racing, Chloe was too frightened to look behind to see if she was being followed.

Everything had changed in an instant. One moment she'd been worrying about getting grease on her pale pink suit and the next thing she'd known, her concern had advanced to matters of life and death.

She'd just seen a murder!

Worse, she'd just seen the *murderer*.

This was nothing like the murders in the mysteries

she was so fond of reading. There was no safe distance. Driving one-handed, she placed her left hand
over her pounding heart. Oh God. What to do? She
didn't know anyone in Pleasantville. Where was the
police station?

Think. She had to think. Farm land whizzed by in
a blur as she racked her mind for the location of the
police station.

And then she recalled something helpful. She'd
seen a police car parked outside an official-looking
red-brick building in the center of town. If she could
just make it there, she'd be safe. And if she wasn't
mistaken, the road she was on led right past it. Floor-
ing the gas pedal, she prayed a policeman would come
along to give her a speeding ticket.

"Fat chance," she muttered to herself. The most
exciting thing she'd seen while searching the town for
Maple Street had been a hot-rod rally being set up on
the way into town. The bright primary-color paint jobs
on the hot rods had been jarring in the mellow-firefly,
front-porch-hammock, pastel-quilts-airing-on-a-wash-
line countryside.

Braving a sneak look in her rear-view mirror at last,
Chloe sighed with relief when she saw only a hay
wagon following in the distance. Maybe if she kept
going, no one would ever know . . . perhaps the murderer hadn't seen her at all, hadn't even known she
was there. When he'd stepped into her line of vision,
he'd been looking down at the body of the man he'd
shot, not at her. Sure he'd probably heard her drive
away in her roadster, but unless he'd actually seen her,
it could have been anyone at all.

Should she take the risk that he'd indeed seen her?
After all, if he had, it was a good possibility he might
come after her. A man who'd killed once would certainly find it easy enough to kill again to get rid of

an eye witness to his crime. She shook off a shiver at the thought.

She was sorely tempted to flee.

To pretend the murder had never happened.

She hated getting involved in what would surely be a mess, to say nothing of the danger she'd be placing herself in.

But then she remembered.

Taking her eyes from the road for a brief moment as she neared the red-brick building she was searching for, she glanced down at her stockinged left foot, *unshod*. In her haste to get away, she'd stumbled and stepped out of her shoe.

She had been too frightened to turn back for it. There was really no doubt that the murderer knew she'd been there. He had her pastel pink pump for proof.

Or worse.

He may have left, leaving her shoe at the scene of the crime. A siren wailed to life and Chloe looked up in time to see the police car pulling away from the curb, racing past her in the direction she'd come from. Now it was certain. If the murderer didn't have her shoe, the police would. And she didn't know which would be worse.

Taking a deep breath to calm her wild imagination, she pulled her roadster into the spot the police car had vacated in front of the police station. When she got out, her pink suit clung to her, damp with the clammy sweat of fear. No matter how afraid she was, the decision to go inside and report what she'd seen had been made for her—by her absent shoe.

As she hobbled through one of the tall glass entry doors of the police station, the hay wagon that had been following in the distance on the road behind her caught up. It slowed in front of the building long enough for a young man in a hat to jump off and hurry out of sight unseen.

"Ma'am! Are you all right?"

"No," Chloe answered the wiry young policeman who came to assist her. His grey eyes were full of concern over her disheveled appearance.

"You haven't been—" he asked, his eyes taking in the grease stains on her pale pink jacket and the torn stocking and missing shoe.

"No!" She pushed her hair back. "No, I haven't been . . . ah . . ."

"Good."

"I do need someone to talk to. I need to fill out a report or something," Chloe said when the policeman just stood gawking at her.

"Oh, right. Sure, ma'am. Here sit down and I'll ah . . ."

"I'd like a glass of water—" Chloe interrupted, in a raspy voice. She swallowed dryly. Her throat was parched from fear.

"Sure thing. You wait right here. I'll be back with your water and the necessary forms to fill out for . . . ah, what did you say it was you wanted to report?"

"A murder."

The policeman stopped in his tracks, turning to look back at her. "Did you say a *murder?*"

Chloe nodded.

"Stay put. I'll be right back, ma'am." Seconds later he was back with a dixie cup of water, and the needed paperwork. While she took a drink of water, he rolled one of the forms in his typewriter.

"Are you sure you're okay?" he asked, looking over at her.

"I'm . . . I was very frightened."

"Well you're safe now. I'm Zeke Francis. We'll take

good care of you. You're . . . ?" he asked, looking back at the form.

"Is that really necessary? I'd rather not get—"

"Oh, yes, ma'am," he insisted.

Chloe sighed, reconsidering the wisdom of what she was doing. It was too late to do anything now, but continue, so she gave him her name.

"Chloe Pembrook," he repeated, having her spell the unfamiliar name. "You're not from around here."

"No."

"You do realize you have to stay here until we go out and have a look. You are sure the victim is dead?"

"Yes. Well, I think he was . . . he fell when the gun was fired."

The deputy looked at her with sudden suspicion. "This isn't a confession, is it?"

"What? No, of course not! I saw the murder. I didn't commit it."

"Calm down, ma'am. You're not a suspect yet. We have to send someone to examine the scene of the crime and inspect the body."

"Of course I'm not a suspect. I saw who did it. That's why I'm here." Chloe closed her eyes and tried to reclaim her temper. Not an easy chore since she was known to throw a tantrum to do Scarlett O'Hara proud. Counting to ten, she tried to reassure herself that this hadn't been a terrible mistake. That it wouldn't have been better just to have kept going, putting the town and the murder behind her.

"Okay. Where did you say the murder took place?" Zeke asked, aligning the form in the typewriter.

"At a garage. I'd stopped to ask for directions. It was on, um . . . Elm Street, I think."

A puzzled look crossed Zeke's face. He turned in his chair, and called to the dispatcher, "Where'd that call the chief went out on come from?"

"Zimmerman's Garage on Elm."

"That the place?" he asked, turning back to her.

Chloe shrugged. "It had an old-fashioned cola machine. And there was a . . . a cat. The name on the tag said, Rosemary."

"That's Zimmerman's cat. Zimmerman lives down the road from the garage. But his garage has been closed down for the past week. He's on crutches with a broken leg."

"It was open when I stopped. At first there didn't seem to be anyone around the garage. But then I heard someone in the back say, 'Put down the gun.' "

Zeke turned to the dispatcher again. "See if you can get the chief on the radio. Tell him we got us a witness, if he's got a body."

The dispatcher nodded. Zeke turned his attention back to Chloe. "Now I want you to tell me in your own words exactly what happened in the garage. Take your time and don't leave anything out. You never know what little detail will turn out to be important."

Chloe proceeded to relay the murder with as much detail as she could recall. When she was done she waited for Zeke's hunt and peck typing to catch up.

Finished at last, he looked up at her. "I assume you didn't know the victim?"

Chloe shook her head no.

"Can you describe him?"

"He was young, in his twenties, I'd guess. I didn't get a very good look."

"What about the murderer?"

"I got a much better look at him."

"Okay, I want you to describe him to me. Take a minute to think. Now close your eyes and take a mental photograph and tell me what you see. Begin when you're ready."

Chloe closed her eyes, then blinked them open. She didn't want to see. She didn't want to remember him.

"What's the matter?"

"What if he saw me?" she asked, with fright edging up her voice.

"That's why I need you to describe him to me as accurately as possible. If he saw you, you're an eyewitness and he's not going to be real happy about that. So for your own protection, you're going to want to give us a good enough description to pick him up as quickly as possible."

"Right," she agreed. Taking a deep breath, she closed her eyes again. After a few moments she began. "He's tall; six-one or so. His hair is black. He needed a haircut. His eyes were . . . I couldn't see the color of his eyes, he wore sunglasses. He was on the lean side but in good condition."

"What was he wearing?"

"Khaki shorts, a vest, a cap, and, oh yes, he had on a bracelet." She remembered it on his gun hand.

"A bracelet? You sure it wasn't a watch?"

"No. No, it was a bracelet. One of those kind people wore for POWs or something."

"Ash Worth."

"What?" Chloe asked, looking puzzled.

"You've just described Ash Worth. He's new in town. Only been here a few weeks. He wears a bracelet like that."

"The chief wants you," the dispatcher called, motioning Zeke to his desk.

"I'll see what's up, and be right back with you. Don't worry, we'll be picking up Ash Worth before he can bother you any," Zeke assured her as he rose.

True to his word, he was back in a few minutes. "We got us an I.D. on the victim."

"Already?"

Zeke nodded. "Peter Blakemore, Jr., oldest son of the guy who owns Blakemore, Inc., and coincidentally the chemical plant where Ash Worth has been working."

"Was there some sort of grudge between the two of them?" Chloe asked, hoping it was a crime of passion—that Ash Worth wasn't a cold-blooded killer, the kind who would come after her.

"Nope. Doubt they knew each other more than to say hello. The Blakemores aren't the kind to mix with the plant people."

"Oh."

Zeke pulled the report from his typewriter, and had her sign it. "Come on, let's get you situated. Once we've got you tucked away, we can start hunting Ash. The chief said to put you up at the motel."

"Where is the chief?"

"On his way to tell Peter Blakemore, Sr. his eldest is dead. I wouldn't want to be around for that one."

"He and his son were pretty close then?"

Zeke shook his head no. "But it don't matter. Peter Blakemore, Sr. doesn't take kindly to anyone crossing him."

"I see."

Zeke took her suitcase from the roadster, and escorted her to the motel. When they arrived, he went into the office to make the arrangements. He got a key for the bungalow in sight of the manager's office. She hobbled ahead of him while he followed, carrying her suitcase. Chloe was looking forward to changing into something comfortable and a pair of sneakers.

Once they were inside the bungalow, Zeke set her suitcase on the bed and checked out the small space. "Okay now," he said when he was done. "You don't open the door for anyone but me, understand?"

She nodded.

"You get suspicious of anything, call the manager. He knows how to take care of any problems. So you just relax, and freshen up. We'll have Ash in custody before you know it."

Handing over the key to the bungalow, he left.

Chloe went to the door to make sure it was locked, then sank down on the bed, kicking off the remaining pink pump. For the first time since she'd stumbled on the murder, she allowed herself to relax. Everything was going to be over soon. The chief, whoever he was, knew who the murderer was. They would pick him up shortly. She was out of danger. All she wanted was a shower and fresh clothes.

Peeling off the pink shorts-suit, she opened her suitcase. She pulled out a T-shirt, pair of shorts and underwear. After packing her shorts-suit and pink pump, she headed for the shower.

Making use of the small bottle of shampoo, she even washed her hair. After she toweled off, and dressed, she picked up a fresh towel, carrying it back to the other room. Bending from the waist, she began fluffing her long, brown hair dry.

All she wanted to do was drive her roadster back home to Chicago. She'd find some other trend to feature in her column. In a matter of hours, this nightmare would be over, and she'd be safe.

That thought was followed by the thrust of a man's hand beneath the towel to cover her mouth, while his other hand went around her waist. As she struggled, he pulled her back toward the bed.

Chloe continued to struggle, but she was no match for the height and steely determination of her captor. A captor who kept the towel over her head while he bound her hands. When he was done, he pulled the towel away from her face. He covered her mouth preventing her from making a sound.

It was him!

Mustering every shred of will power she had, she tried to avoid letting him see any sign that she recognized him. If she kept her head, perhaps she could bluff her way out of danger.

He took the gun from the waistband of his khaki shorts, gaining her full attention by pointing it at her.

"You aren't going to scream," he ordered.

She nodded her agreement.

He removed his hand from her mouth carefully, watching her.

"Don't be coy. You know exactly why I'm here."

She shook her head in denial. "Don't hurt me, please. Just leave. I won't tell anyone."

"I think it's a little too late for that."

"No, really. I've never seen you before."

"Oh, but I think you have." He reached behind him, picking up a pink pump while keeping the gun trained on her with his other hand.

Her gaze flew to the bed where her locked suitcase still rested.

He lowered the pink pump to her bare foot, his green eyes impaling her.

"If the shoe fits, Cinderella . . ." he said, slipping it on.

Three

"Well, what do you know, Cinderella—looks like we got us a perfect fit."

Chloe felt weak. The jig was up. Her missing shoe had put the kibosh to her hasty lie. There was no longer any doubt in the killer's mind, if there ever had been, that she was the one who had witnessed the murder he'd committed; the one who could identify him as the killer. The one who could put him in prison for a long, long time. Or worse.

There was no longer any doubt in her mind that she was in deep, deep trouble.

Her voice cracked. Fear was closing her throat as she asked the inevitable, "What now?"

Her captor tugged her with him to the window overlooking the parking lot, where he bent a blind with his forefinger. He peered out, and she followed suit. As the motel manager's office had a clear view of the bungalow they were in, so did they have a clear view of the manager's office.

"We wait," her captor clipped, pulling her close. Holding her firmly at his side, he continued his surveillance at the window.

"For what?" she asked, squirming. He didn't have to hold her like *that*. He was taking undue advantage, the jerk.

"For a customer to show up and distract the motel

manager," he answered, continuing to hold her firmly at his side, despite her squirming. "The manager's keeping a close eye on you. I wonder for who? Jealous husband?" he guessed, tugging her bound hands up to glance at her marriage finger, which was ringless. "Nope, no husband. Must be the police then. Bet you gave them a real good description of me, didn't you?"

"Apparently not good enough. You got past the motel manager."

"Oh, he didn't see me. I had a friend call the motel, and keep him occupied on the phone for a while so I could slip past the office without notice."

"You've got a friend?" Why did she find that disturbing?

"Yes, now will you shut up, and quit trying to distract me," he ordered.

Chloe did as she was ordered, filling the time by mentally running through all the horrible ways in which people were found murdered in mystery novels.

She might just have lost her taste for reading them.

She looked at her captor, watching him in profile. It was true, this guy didn't look like a murderer. But then, she supposed neither had Baby Face Nelson. It didn't matter that this guy was the sort of guy she would have looked at twice under different circumstances.

She had to keep reminding herself of just what his crime was. She had plenty of evidence that this guy was indeed a murderer. It was knowledge gained with just one look.

One fateful look—when she'd been in the wrong place, at the wrong time.

Not more than two hours ago, she'd watched him point a gun, killing a man in cold blood. It was imperative she keep reminding herself of what her captor was capable of doing; capable of doing to her!

Though he apparently wasn't going to harm her until she served her usefulness as a hostage.

Watching through the kinked blind with him, she saw two teenagers get out of their convertible, and approach the motel office. Assessing the situation, Chloe wondered what her chances were of escaping if she created a disturbance.

Feeling her captor's grip on her tighten, she decided her chances were zip. Her best hope of staying alive was to do exactly as he said. There was no way he was going to take his hands and eyes off her long enough for her to try to foil his plan, whatever it was.

Questions began racing through her mind at a furious pace. Where was he planning on going? Was he planning to kill her as soon as he gave the police the slip, or was he planning to take her along to his destination as insurance against them catching up with him.

"Let's boogie," he said, interrupting her morbid thoughts, pulling her towards the door. "And don't be getting any crazy ideas about trying something fancy either. Not if you want to stay alive." He shot her a quelling glance, then tucked her behind him. Inching open the bungalow door, he guided her outside. At his urging, they set out in a dead run for the cover of brush behind the motel, covering a distance of maybe twenty yards.

They reached it without anything untoward happening. There hadn't been any shouts of discovery, nothing. Her heart was in her throat when he pulled her down beside him in a crouch. Her face felt hot, flushed. She gulped deep breaths of air while he kept his eye on the manager's office. From beside him, Chloe could see that the two teenagers were trying to convince the manager they were of age. They weren't having any success, but they continued in earnest.

"We've got to make tracks, before anyone discovers you're missing. Come on," he ordered, "just follow my lead, and stay low."

"Wait!" she cried, pulling back.

"What is it?"

"We forgot my suitcase."

"Oh for heaven's sake. Forget about your suitcase. It's not important," he said, frustrated and impatient.

What did that mean? Chloe wondered, trying to keep her hysteria at bay while she let him pull her along behind him. Oh God, was he planning to kill her shortly. Was that the reason her suitcase wasn't important?

Maybe she could make some sort of bargain with him that would keep her alive a while longer. The longer she stayed alive, the better her chances of escape and survival.

She wasn't ready to die.

Ten minutes later she was voicing her fears.

"I don't want to die!" she wailed, twisting her wrists. "Please untie me," she begged, when they stopped to catch their breath on the outskirts of town. They'd made their way to that point by cutting through backyards and such. They would have stood out like a blueberry in an apple pie, on the quiet streets. Chancing that, would have meant instant capture.

He was too smart for that. She didn't know much about her captor; just two things. He was a killer and he was smart.

Her clothes were sticking to her again. She was sweaty and panicked . . . and might as well not have taken a shower.

"Listen, if I get caught, I promise you you're going to die. Your only chance is helping me get out of this town fast. We need a car. Where'd you leave the roadster? We can double back and get it."

"I don't think so."

"Why not?"

"It's still at the police station."

"Damn." He rubbed his temple.

"Maybe we could hitchhike . . ." Chloe was surprised to hear herself suggest.

"Looks like we're going to have to risk it," her captor agreed, his voice resigned, as they rounded a curve in the road. "Whoa, what have we here? Finally a break in this beastly day."

Chloe followed his gaze to the hot rods sitting in the open clearing.

"Oh, no, you aren't going to steal a car, are you?"

He glared at her.

She wanted to kick herself. After all, once you've committed murder, stealing a car was kid stuff. She groaned. The beastly day might be getting better for him, but it was going distinctly down hill for her. And that was before he reached in his pocket and withdrew the pocket knife.

"That's exactly what we're going to do."

"We're?" she repeated, her voice quavering.

"That's right. I'm going to cut your wrists free, and you're going to help me."

"How?"

"You're going to distract the fellows while I hot wire one of their cars."

"You know how to do that?"

"I hope so."

"I want him dead," Peter Blakemore vowed, his voice muted by shock and grief. His hand shook as he took the stopper off the exquisite crystal decanter of fifty-year-old scotch.

Darrow Smith stood in the library of the Blakemore

mansion watching the toll death took on the tall, elegant man, who could buy anything he wanted; except his son back from the dead. Now, all his money could buy was the death of his eldest son's murderer. Peter Blakemore handed Darrow a whiskey, then tossed back his own, closing his eyes as if to blot out the shattering news the Chief of Police had brought him.

Most of the time Darrow Smith enjoyed being the Chief of Police, enjoyed the power it brought him. But not today. He knew the bad news was only starting with Peter Blakemore, Jr.'s death. His gut told him this was the start of things unraveling.

He was very much afraid that Peter Blakemore's evil empire was about to go to hell in a handbasket, and that his own career as a lawman was going to be one of the casualties.

An outsider had killed Peter Blakemore's son. An outsider named Ash Worth.

They had positive identification of the killer, an eyewitness to the crime. At least there was that. He'd witnessed Peter Blakemore's terrible temper on more than one occasion, and he'd been glad to be able to tell him they knew who his son's killer was. It would have been better, of course, if he could have told him they had Ash Worth in custody. But you had to be thankful to get the breaks you got.

Ash Worth was a dead man. Didn't matter if it took them a few minutes or a few hours to find him. They would find him. And then someone would find his body.

Hell, even if they hadn't had a witness, anyone would know that only an outsider would dare such a thing. Only an outsider would underestimate Peter Blakemore's wrath at the death of his son.

Darrow Smith took in the opulence of the library. It smelled like money. The lemony oiled wood paneling, the wool oriental rugs, the mustiness of shelves of leather-bound volumes and the fragrance of fresh flowers on the credenza.

It must be nice to have everything you ever wanted, Darrow thought, not for the first time. The lust for material things had drawn him into Peter Blakemore's employ.

Money couldn't protect you from life, as it hadn't protected Peter Blakemore or his son today. But it sure as hell could soften life's blows. Fifty-year-old scotch didn't burn on its way down like rotgut did.

"Don't worry, sir. I've got Zeke taking care of things. He and a few of the boys are out combing the area right now as we speak. Ash Worth isn't going anywhere," Darrow assured him. He hoped to heaven what he'd just promised Peter Blakemore was true. Nervously, he braced his hands on the back of a straight-back chair to one side of the massive walnut desk that was the focal point of the room. He gripped the chair as if by so doing, he could hold on to everything he feared he was going to lose.

Peter Blakemore was not a forgiving man, though he was in church every Sunday morning.

"Oh, I'm not worried, Darrow. I pay you a great deal of money to assure you'll do what I want, when I want. I own you."

"Yes sir." Darrow Smith couldn't argue with the fact. Peter Blakemore did own him; lock, stock, and soul.

Setting his empty glass on the bar, Peter Blakemore turned his glittering dark eyes back to Darrow. After a long moment of reflection, he asked, "Who found the . . . my son?"

Darrow reached into his jacket pocket, withdrawing a small yellow note pad. He, of course, knew who had found the body. His actions were only a stall for time.

Before he left the Blakemore mansion he wanted to get a phone call from Zeke saying that Ash Worth had been found— and dealt with. That was the best case scenario; to have everything over with before things started to unravel.

He began flipping the pages in the small notebook slowly until he found the name he sought.

"Here it is. The person who found the . . . your son, was a Miss Chloe Pembrook, sir."

"A woman!"

"Yes, sir."

"Pembrook, did you say? That name isn't familiar to me," Peter Blakemore said, sinking into the plush leather chair behind his desk. Even sitting, he looked tall. He looked imposing behind the massive desk. It was a fact he was well aware of, and one he used to intimidate others to do his bidding.

"She's not from around here, sir. Not local—she's from Chicago. And just in town today on business apparently."

"What kind of business? Was my son dating this Chloe Pembrook? Were they involved?"

"Oh, no. No sir. I'm sure they weren't involved. Miss Pembrook is some sort of lifestyle expert."

"A lifestyle expert? What the hell is that?" Peter Blakemore shoved his fountain pen in the brass holder on his desk, impatient with his inability to do anything about what had happened to him. Impatient with having to wait.

"She has her own column in *Chicago* magazine. It's about living with elegance in the 90s. I recall seeing something on her when she was on one of the morning network talk shows. Anyway, she says she was lost, and stopped in at Zimmerman's garage, according to Zeke. Instead of getting directions, she walked in on the murder."

"She saw this Ash Worth shoot my son?"

"That's right."

"Just a minute," Peter Blakemore said, picking up the telephone receiver and punching a number.

Someone must have come on the line, because Darrow listened while he asked for the person to pull Ash Worth's personnel file.

"Did you know this Ash Worth?" Peter asked while he waited.

"No. I've seen him around town a few times in the week or two he's been working for you, but I never paid him much mind. I figured he would be moving on."

"Why's that?"

"He didn't exactly fit in with the plant workers. Something about him seemed to say he was more of a city boy. I figured he was just traveling around and ran out of money. That he was only working at the plant to finance his next trip."

Peter listened as someone came back on the telephone, then began firing questions; age, references and where Ash was from.

He hung up a few minutes later, looking up at Darrow.

"Are you sure Miss Pembrook isn't involved?"

"Pretty sure. She's not the type. Seemed plenty scared for one thing."

"Hmmmm . . ." Peter Blakemore steepled his fingers, staring at the photograph in the silver frame on his desk; it was of him and his two sons. "Children aren't supposed to die before their parents."

"No sir."

"Where is this Miss Pembrook? I'd like to talk with her."

"With Miss Pembrook? Why?"

"Seems that scum Ash Worth is from Chicago as well."

"But Mr. Blakemore . . . she's sort of a celebrity. We can't—"

A discreet knock sounded at the library door, and then a servant begged Peter Blakemore's pardon, but there was an urgent phone call for the chief.

"He can take it in here," Peter Blakemore said, dismissing the servant, who closed the door.

Standing, Darrow picked up the receiver from the phone on the desk.

"Hello, this is the chief . . ." he answered, his stomach souring.

"Chief, we've got us a problem!"

"Shit, Zeke, I don't want to hear this," Darrow said, his voice clipped and impatient.

Peter Blakemore's head shot up. He waited expectantly as Darrow took the bad news.

"What's wrong?" he demanded to know when Darrow replaced the receiver.

"Chloe Pembrook is missing."

"What?"

"Zeke went back to check on her, and found her missing from the bungalow where he'd stashed her."

"I thought you were handling things—" Peter Blakemore shouted, pounding his fist on the desk.

"I'm sorry, sir. Ah, the news gets worse. A stolen auto report was just called in."

"I don't care about any . . ."

"I think you will, sir. It seems Ash Worth stole a hot rod from the rally. He was reported having a woman in tow—a woman who meets Miss Pembrook's description."

Four

Ash Worth hated secrets.

He hated that the pretty woman he held captive was terrified of him.

But there was no time to make explanations. He was fairly certain she wouldn't believe them anyway. He knew what she'd seen, she just hadn't seen what she thought. He'd tell her he was one of the good guys as soon as they reached safety. For now, his more immediate concern was escape. If the chief and Zeke caught up with them they'd be on the six o'clock news posthumously.

He had the goods to put Peter Blakemore, Sr. out of business and behind bars and the chief and Zeke were in Blakemore's pocket. The trouble was he didn't have the proof on him. He had to get his hands on the proof, get the proof to an honest cop and keep Miss Powder Puff from escaping.

But first things first.

They had to ditch the hot rod fast. It stood out like a beacon on the highway.

A solution presented itself when they passed a truck stop. The lot was crowded with eighteen-wheelers. With any luck, they'd find one unlocked and catch a ride with the trucker being none the wiser. With great luck, the truck would be making a return trip to Chicago instead of heading south.

Less than a mile past the truck stop, he turned off the highway onto a dirt road and drove far enough down it to hide the hot rod in a grove of trees and overgrown brush.

He turned to his captive who was cowering by the door.

"Don't even think about trying to escape. I've still got the gun, remember?"

She nodded, her blue eyes intelligent and wary.

Damn, he hated that she was scared, that he was having to scare her to insure her safety.

"Now here's the drill," he instructed. "We're going to high-tail it back to the truck stop we just passed and we're going to sneak us a ride. And you're not going to make a sound or do anything to draw attention to us. Just do as I tell you and you won't get hurt, I promise."

His promise didn't have her turning handsprings. Though she was near tears, she managed a glassy glare. But she did as he instructed; letting him take her hand when he came around the car to let her out. Tugging her along after him, he prayed his plan would work as they ran through the cornfield, hidden amongst the tall stalks.

They reached the gravel parking lot of the truck stop, where the big rigs were parked, in less than ten minutes. The siren that had wailed from a police car speeding on the highway had spurred his real fear of what would happen to them if they were caught. They were breathless and sweaty from their exertion as they knelt behind one of the oversize tires of a truck. Powder Puff looked more delicate than she was; she'd kept up with him as he ran, only stumbling once.

At the sound of approaching voices, Ash slapped his hand over Chloe's mouth and signaled her to behave with his eyes. She tried to bite his hand anyway, but to no avail. He'd cupped his hand slightly to avoid her sharp little teeth.

"You must be smoking some of that wacky tabacky, Wilbur, if you think Becky Ann would go out with a trucker," one of the male voices said in derision.

"What's she doing waitressing in a truck stop then?" Wilbur demanded.

"She's just passing through. She'll be gone before they flip up the calendar page. I'll bet you ten bucks she won't even be here on our return trip back."

"I'll take that bet, George. Only let's make it twenty," Wilbur said as the men passed by on their way to their rigs.

Ash kept Chloe hugged up tight against him with his hand clamped tightly over her mouth until the truckers pulled their rigs off the parking lot. Damn, but she smelled good.

"Will you stop manhandling me," Chloe demanded when he removed his hand.

"I'm sorry if you fancied Wilbur over me, but I couldn't allow it. This isn't a game. This is serious and you're in danger. As soon as we get . . . well, what have we here . . ." He smiled, reading the door of the black truck next to them. It read: Jones Transport, Headquarters . . . Chicago, Ill.

After a quick, careful survey of the full parking lot, he pulled her along to the back of the truck.

It was unlocked.

His bad day had ceased its downhill slide for the moment. When they got inside the truck, they saw why the trucker hadn't bothered to lock it. The trailer was empty. There wasn't a return load. It was empty, but for the two of them.

"Oh no, I'm not riding in this. It's . . . it's . . ."

"It's safety," Ash countered, pulling down the over-head door on the back of the truck.

"It's pitch dark in here!"

Ash hated that there was a tremor of fear in her voice, that he was responsible for it. He couldn't put off telling her any longer. He had to tell her the truth now. They were as safe as they were going to get for the moment. Hopefully the trucker would finish his meal and leave soon.

"Come here, let's sit down and I'll explain what's going on. You'll feel better, I promise. You don't have to be afraid of me." His voice echoed in the empty cavernous trailer.

"No?"

"Keep your voice down. We don't want to be discovered," he warned, needlessly putting his finger to his lips in a shushing manner. Neither of them could see anything in the darkness.

"Maybe you don't," she snapped, "but I do. I don't happen to like this at all. I've never been kidnapped before."

"And I've never killed anyone before. Now will you sit down and let me explain what you really saw instead of what you think you saw."

"No. I'll stand. I can't see where or on what I'd be sitting in the dark."

"You're a real priss, you know that? Tell you what, come on over here and I'll let you sit on my lap."

"No thank you."

He knew from the tone of her voice that arguing with her would be pointless. She was a woman who knew her own mind. One with more confidence than sense. Determined and willful, she was probably an only child like himself. Maybe if he knew her name, he could put her at ease. "It occurs to me in all the rush that we haven't been properly introduced. Your name is . . ."

"Chloe Pembrook," came the reply in the darkness.

She looked like a Chloe he recalled; all pink and pretty and sophisticated.

She'd said her name like he should recognize it.

He didn't.

He eased his lanky body down to the relative comfort of the floor of the tractor-trailer rig. Just because she was being stubbornly uncomfortable didn't mean he had to suffer.

"Aren't you going to ask me my name?"

"I already know it. Ash Worth. The police identified you when I described you to them."

"That must have been *some* description. My name isn't Ash Worth. I used Ash Worth for my cover. My name is Ace. It's really Ashley Clayton Ellsworth, but everyone calls me by my initials."

"Your cover . . . ?"

"You haven't heard of me then?" he asked, his vanity pricked.

"Should I have?"

"Not to be immodest, but I'm the *Trib*'s star reporter."

"A journalist."

He couldn't miss the way she'd said his occupation with the same inflection in her voice she would have used if he were a bug.

"You don't like journalists?"

"My parents are journalists; photojournalists. If it's ugly, they've taken a picture of it."

They must not have taken a picture of their daughter, Ace thought. "You don't approve of my career, I take it? Don't you believe the world needs to know the truth?"

"I think the world needs beauty, something to aspire to."

"Just my luck, I'm on the run with an ostrich."

She ignored his snide remark and fell silent.

"Well, since you're in a listening mood, let me explain what really happened back there in the garage. And before you start objecting, yes, you *did* see me shoot a man and as it happens kill him. But it was in self-defense."

He noticed she wasn't leaping to believe him. So he went on. "I've been here in Pleasantville working under cover on a story. I've been working for a chemical plant called Blakemore, Inc. The man I shot was Peter Blakemore, Jr., the oldest son of the man who owns the company."

"Why would a rich boy want to kill you?"

"He probably didn't. But his father wanted me dead and he was afraid of his father."

"I don't understand."

"Peter Blakemore, Sr. owns more than Blakemore, Inc. He owns practically the whole damn town, one way or another. He'd paid off the officials to look the other way while he dumped drums of toxic chemical waste."

"That's the story you were working on . . ."

"Right. And I think I've gotten proof; samples from the drums that were illegally dumped. Peter, Sr. got wind of it somehow and ordered his son to make sure the evidence didn't come to light."

"If you knew this, why did you meet Peter, Jr. at the garage. I mean you had to have arranged to meet him there, because there isn't anything else around for miles."

"I got a note telling me to be at Zimmerman's garage at a specified time if I wanted some incriminating evidence on the company."

"But there was no evidence, it was just a ruse on Peter, Jr.'s part to get you alone somewhere isolated so he could kill you, is that what you're telling me?"

He nodded, then realizing she couldn't see him, said, "Yes."

"Do you always carry a gun when you're investigating a story?"

"No. Oh you mean this gun. It's not mine. I took it away from Peter, Jr. before he could use it on me."

"If what you're telling me is the truth, then why did you run instead of telling the police what happened?"

"Like I said, Peter, Sr. owns the whole damn town. The police are in his pocket. Do you really think I stood a chance of getting out of town alive after killing the son of the most powerful man in these parts?"

"Just to be sure you did get out alive, you took me as your hostage then, I take it."

"No. I wouldn't do that. What kind of man do you think I am?"

She let her silent answer hang in the air between them.

"I kidnapped you for your own protection," he advised her. "They'd have killed you the same as me to hush up what was going on, what is going on in their town. They had no way of knowing what you might have seen or overheard. It wasn't worth risking leaving you alive, I promise. If I hadn't snatched you, you'd be one more person who disappears without a trace."

"Are you trying to scare me? Because if you are, it's working."

"Of course, I'm trying to scare you. I'm trying to keep you from doing anything foolish until I can clear my name and get the evidence I need to put Peter Blakemore behind bars where he belongs."

"Where is this evidence you claim to have?"

"I sent it to Jane."

"Jane . . . ?"

"She's a reporter for the *Trib*, too. We work together

on stories sometimes. I asked her to have it analyzed for me. That's why we have to get back to Chicago before the chief and Zeke catch up to us. I'm doing this for your own protection. Just listen to me and I'll take care of you. Nothing will happen to you if you do as I say."

"Trust you, right?"

"That's right, trust me."

"You must really think I'm stupid."

"No, I'm really hoping you're not."

A sound caught Ace's attention and he shushed Chloe. "Did you hear that? Listen . . ."

"What?" she whispered.

"Someone's coming. I heard footsteps crunching on the gravel parking lot. Hush, be quiet. If we're in luck it might be the driver and not the chief and Zeke."

As they listened intently, the footsteps kept approaching.

Zeke let out a sigh of relief when the footsteps passed the back of the truck and continued towards the cab. The door squeaked as the driver opened it to climb inside the cab and turn over the ignition.

As the truck pulled out of the parking lot, it turned right onto the highway, much to Ace's satisfaction. They were headed north to Chicago and safety.

And not a moment too soon. A siren had wailed past them onto the parking lot as they were pulling out.

That would be the chief, his deputy Zeke and with any bad luck at all, Jon Blakemore.

Five

The police car screeched to a stop in front of the truck stop, its siren silenced but its red light still flashing. A foreign luxury car pulled in right behind the police car. The chief and Zeke got out of the police car and Jon Blakemore emerged from the luxury car.

Jon barreled his way into the truck stop with Darrow Smith on his heels, the voice of reason. "Let me handle this, Jon."

"My brother is dead and I'm going to make sure Ash Worth pays."

"Your father instructed us to see what Ash Worth has on Blakemore, Inc. first. Just stand back with Zeke while I do the questioning."

Jon reluctantly followed Darrow's order, hanging back with Zeke.

Darrow didn't get any information from the first waitress he questioned, but he hit paydirt when he got to Becky Ann, the new girl with the bouncy ponytail, figure and personality.

"Hi Chief, what can I get you?" she asked.

"We're looking for an escaped murderer. He's taken a woman hostage. We found the car he stole abandoned just down the road and thought he might have doubled back here. You see anyone suspicious like that around here?"

"Maybe. What was the woman wearing?" she asked, setting the coffee pot down on the counter.

"Zeke, come over here. What was the woman Ash Worth kidnapped wearing?"

"Well, when she came into the station she had some kind of pink outfit on. Shorts and a jacket," Zeke recalled.

Becky Ann shook her head no. "Nope. The woman I saw had on white shorts and a blue T-shirt."

"What woman?" the chief asked.

"The woman I saw crawl up into the back of a truck on the parking lot. A tall guy with black hair stowed away with her. I saw them sneak into the truck when I was taking a smoke break a while back."

"Black hair, that sounds like Ash," Jon said, unwilling to stay in the background. "Did you notice if he was wearing a silver bracelet?"

Becky looked over at him. "You know, I did. I remember seeing it on his wrist when he gave the woman a boost up into the truck."

"That's them!" Jon insisted, excited.

"Can you show us the truck?" Darrow asked. His hand moved to rest on his gun.

"Sure. You can see it from the back door. I'll point it out to you."

The three men followed her.

"It's gone," she said, when she opened the back door and looked out. "Pete must have headed out for his return trip to Chicago when I wasn't looking. I've got to get back inside and get my tip."

"Are you sure the truck is gone?" Darrow asked.

"Yeah, I'm sure. I know Pete's truck when I see it. Besides he was finishing up a piece of pie so he was getting ready to shove off."

"Then you know who Pete drives for . . ." Jon urged.

"Of course I do. Pete's a heavy tipper and comes through here regularly. I've only been here a few weeks and I've seen him several times."

"So who's he work for—" Jon asked impatiently.

"Will you let me handle this Jon?" Zeke interrupted. "Who does Pete drive for?"

"He drives for Jones trucking out of Chicago. It's a silver bed with a black cab. You can't miss the lettering on the side."

"Come on, let's go," Jon said, turning.

"The police car is too conspicuous," Darrow said. "Zeke you go with Jon in his car. Just locate the truck and follow him and the woman. And don't lose them. Your daddy wants to know what Ash has on him. Nothing is to happen to Ash until your daddy gets it, you hear?"

"Yeah, I hear. Come on Zeke, we're wasting time."

"You two keep in touch with me and let me know what's going on and where you are. Your daddy's going to want to be kept posted."

"Sure thing, Chief," Zeke agreed, hurrying to catch up to Jon.

Darrow was on the phone reporting back to Jon's father as the two men sped out of the parking lot heading north.

"Do you think the coast is clear?" Ace asked.

"I don't hear anything," Chloe answered. "We've been here ten minutes or so I'd guess and the driver hasn't come back. I think he's parked the rig and gone."

"Are you with me, then?"

She was. On the five-hour ride to Chicago he'd convinced her he was telling the truth. Convinced her that both of them were in danger and the best thing she could do was stick with him until he could get the evidence of the story he was working on to prove he'd been set up to be killed by Peter Blakemore's son.

But she didn't like it.

She didn't like being affected by someone else's demons.

Ace slipped the flat rock from beneath the edge of the truck door that had kept it from locking them in and shoved the door up just enough for the two of them to slip out.

He took her hand and kept it after helping her down from the trailer of the truck. At the first public phone he saw he stopped to make a phone call to Jane.

Chloe watched as he listened to the phone ringing on her end. He shook his head and hung up. "She's not home and she forgot to put her answering machine on. She's always doing that and it drives me nuts."

"Now what?" Chloe asked, hoping it was going to be food, as she was starving.

"We put distance between us and the truck, just in case."

"Do you think we were followed?"

"You never know. I can't take any chances. You don't know Peter Blakemore like I do. He's a real cool customer. Doesn't seem to have any heart, rumor has it. Not even a soft spot for women. He's single, rich and powerful and that's the way he likes it. He's avoided marrying since his first wife ran off with her lover twenty years ago, leaving him with two young sons to raise."

"And he loved his sons."

"No, he owned them like he does everything else. And like all greedy men he doesn't like losing anything he thinks is his; even his son."

They caught the first bus they came to.

"Where are we going?"

"We can't go to my place. That's the first place they'll look. And your place is the second."

"I know a place we can go," Chloe said, suddenly remembering the key ring in her purse. They were in the back of the bus and the bus was only half full. No one was close enough to them to overhear their conversation.

She took the key ring from her purse. "A friend of mine asked me to water her plants while she was on vacation. We can go there until you connect up with Jane."

"You wouldn't be trying to pull a fast one on me now would you, Chloe. Remember I've still got the gun."

"You aren't going to use it on me, so give up threatening me with it, Ace. I believe what you've told me. You're like my parents; idealistic and blind, but you aren't a killer."

"You decided that, by spending five hours alone with me in the dark. I must be better than I thought."

The look she shot him was one he'd been getting from teachers since kindergarten.

He got down to business. "Where's your friend's place?"

"In Edgebrook. She inherited it from her parents. We should be able to get there in . . ."

"I know the area. Come on, let's get off at the next stop up ahead. We'll take the Metra."

They were in Edgebrook in twenty-five minutes. The Metra stopped in the heart of town and they got off to walk to her friend's house. It was a two-story white frame with a small detached back garage. As they walked up the steps to the porch, the scent of white lilac was sweet on the air from the tall flowering shrub near the railing.

She slipped the key in the lock and they went inside

to a warmy, homey atmosphere. The house had hard-wood floors throughout with area rugs in warm pastels. Soft, cushy furniture was informal enough to invite plopping down and putting your feet up.

"Would you look at all the plants? It'll take you a half hour just to water them," Ace said, looking around at the potted plants in every sunny nook.

"I know, Julie has a green thumb. Her husband keeps threatening to throw them all out, but he wouldn't dare."

"Husband. How big is he?"

"Don't worry, he's with her."

"I was thinking of taking a shower and borrowing some of his clothes."

"Oh." Chloe picked up the watering can. "Well, the shower's upstairs and his stuff would probably fit you okay. We'll just leave Julie a note that we've borrowed what we need. I think a shower and fresh clothes sounds good myself. Why don't you go ahead and I'll water the plants."

She didn't have to ask him twice. He was heading up the stairs as she filled the watering can.

As she walked around Julie's place watering the plants she could hear the shower running. It wasn't a familiar sound. Living alone, she'd gotten a little set in her ways. And her career had taken over her life. She preferred her life to be as pretty and serene as a Sargent portrait. In the space of an afternoon, her life had taken a definite turn. Never in her wildest dreams would she have believed she'd be involved with a man who loved courting danger by digging in life's messes. Her parents would be absolutely thrilled with Ashley Clayton Ellsworth. All the more reason why she wasn't.

She'd help him, and help herself in the bargain. And then she'd go back to reading mysteries, get-

ting her thrills vicariously. Today had been scary,
thrilling, exciting and exhausting. She was suddenly
tired and she sat down for a moment, turning on the
television.

The game show that was on WGN barely held her
attention and she was about to turn off the show when
a news bulletin flashed on the screen.

There was a picture of Ace, and one of her as well,
on the screen as the announcer read the bulletin that
Ace was being sought for the murder of Peter Blakemore, Jr. and for kidnapping her.

She quickly flicked off the television, shocked.

She'd let the events of the day recede to the back
of her mind, but the news bulletin had brought it all
crashing down on her. Anxious, she headed for the
kitchen to do what she always did when she was upset;
cook.

The shower had stopped, so she knew Ace would
be down in a few minutes. She needed to cook something that was quick.

A search of the pantry and refrigerator turned up
comfort food. By the time Ace joined her in the
kitchen it was filled with the fragrant aroma of bub-
bling soup and the buttery aroma of toasted cheese
sandwiches. She was sliding the golden brown sandwiches onto the plates when Ace came up behind her
and nuzzled the back of her neck.

"I think I'm in love," he growled.

"No, you're just hungry," she answered, slipping
away from him and returning the hot skillet to the gas
stove.

Ace took a seat at the table and a bite of the hot
sandwich as he watched her ladle the thick vegetable
beef soup into bowls, bringing them to the table to
join him.

While swallowing, he informed her that he'd called

Jane again, and there still wasn't any answer. It looked like they were going to have to spend the night.

"There's something you should know." Chloe took a spoonful of her soup and blew on it before sipping it.

"You're married."

"I think I'd have told you that on the five-hour trip, don't you?"

"That depends on how much you liked me," he countered, polishing off the rest of the toasted cheese sandwich.

"This is serious, Ace."

"What?" She had his full attention, immediately. He was a natural flirt in a pair of jeans a size too small, but he was all business when the occasion called for it.

"I had the television on and there was a news bulletin. They flashed our pictures on the screen, Ace."

"I was afraid of that. Wait a minute, you said *our* pictures. They'd have mine because I'm a celebrity, sort of. How did they get yours so fast?"

"I'm a celebrity, sort of, too."

Six

"What is it you do?" Ace rested his elbows on the table and his chin in his hands. She was pretty enough to be a model or an actress, he thought absently, waiting. But she didn't seem self-absorbed enough. She was in good shape, so she could be an athlete; a figure skater or in some other sport he didn't follow.

"I'm a lifestyle expert."

"A what?"

"I write a monthly column on lifestyle in *Chicago* magazine. I've had several lifestyle books published. And a fifteen-minute weekly spot for a morning TV show is in the works."

"You *do* want to decorate the world."

"And you want to destroy it," she countered, more than a little annoyed.

"How do you figure that? I uncover the truth."

"I'll give you that. But then what do you do? You report only the bad news. You inundate your readers with a dark and grim picture of the world. In effect you terrorize the public on a daily basis."

"What in the hell are you talking about?" he demanded, shoving his elbows from the table to rest on the arms of the chair.

"I'm talking about solutions. Solutions to problems—and hope. Journalists are short on supplying that. And I think it's irresponsible, that's all."

"Oh, I bet your parents found you a real joy to be around."

"They were photojournalists, so they weren't around. They were off . . . never mind."

"Sorry, I didn't mean—"

"That's all right. I shouldn't take out my childhood baggage on you. Besides we have more important things to talk about, like what are we going to do next. What if you can't contact Jane? Does she have a boyfriend she might be staying over with?"

"No, Jane isn't involved with anyone. But you're right, we do have to concentrate on what to do next. I have a pretty good idea where Jane is, now that you've told me about the news bulletin being on television."

"You do?"

"Yes, we've got this prearranged system that kicks in just in the case of something like this happening." He tucked into his food.

"Are you going to tell me what it is?" Chloe said, waiting.

"First we'll go by Jane's in the morning just to be sure."

Chloe began clearing the table. "We can use Julie's car if you want to go now. Her car key's on the same key ring as the house key."

Ace brought the rest of the dishes to the sink where Chloe stood. "What's the matter, afraid to spend the night with me? I thought you'd decided to trust me."

Chloe took the dishes from him and set them in the sink. "Trust you? No, that wasn't what I said at all. I said I'd help you."

"And I'll help you with these dishes. Then we'd better turn in early. We need to get up before the sun in the morning and check out Jane's place."

"Where does she live, is it far from here?"

"Old Irving Park. It won't take long to check out to see if Jane's flown the coop."

"Where are you supposed to meet her? I can wait here while you connect with her."

"That's not going to be possible, if Jane's already gone, we've got a long drive ahead of us."

Chloe looked back over her shoulder at him. "Long . . . how long? I've got a column to write and turn in and then I've got meetings—"

"You've got nothing until this is over. Zeke and Jon Blakemore aren't going to let either of us live if they can get to us before we can prove what was going on in Pleasantville."

"Quit trying to scare me . . ."

"I'm not trying to scare you," he said, pulling her around to face him. "The gun that Peter Blakemore tried to use on me was real enough to kill him. We may be safe for now, but we aren't out of danger."

He didn't like the fear he'd had to put back in her eyes, but he couldn't let her be lulled into feeling safe enough to do something foolish. "Come on, let's turn in. You need a shower after riding in the back of that truck and you'll feel lots better in the morning."

"But—"

He took the dish towel from her. "You go on ahead. I'll finish up here and be up in a minute."

She didn't argue with him.

Alone in the kitchen, he let down his guard and allowed the events of the day to catch up with him. His body slumped, weary from tension. Where the hell was Jane? Had she already left after seeing the news bulletin alerting her he was in trouble?

He trembled, thinking of actually killing another person even though it had been in self-defense. With any luck Jane was still in town and this would be over soon.

He wiped the last dish and went upstairs carrying that hope with him.

Chloe was still in the shower, he could hear the water running. He wasn't too tired to imagine her naked under the steaming stream of water, her smooth body covered with a foam of white suds. Suddenly he wasn't quite as tired. He shook his head at his erotic thought and went off to turn in for the night.

Stripping down to his Calvins, he slipped beneath the fluffy comforter that was little more than a sheet and closed his eyes.

A lifestyle expert.

All blond hair, blue eyes and pink and white porcelain skin, she looked like she couldn't be involved in anything more serious than a tea party. But he had to give her credit. She had been a real trooper today, holding up pretty well in a scary situation. Once she'd decided he was telling her the truth, she'd stopped giving him trouble.

Now the only trouble she was giving him was in his fertile and very active imagination. It was time to turn off. One look at him and she'd know for certain where his thoughts were wandering. He was a real hound to be such a male animal when he should be thinking thoughts of protection, brotherly thoughts.

The shower stopped.

He didn't have much time to fall asleep. He wanted to avoid talking anymore, wanted to avoid telling Chloe there were questions he didn't have the answers to.

Chloe dried off with an oversized peach bath towel. Reaching for the flowered cylinder of body talc on the vanity, she dusted it over her damp body. The scented talc perfumed the humid bathroom as well as her body. Picking up the clean T-shirt she'd found in Julie's husband's dresser drawer, she pulled it over her head. It flowed over her body, loosely skimming her thighs at a modest length.

Glancing in the mirror on the door she saw that she looked suitably covered even if she did feel vulnerably naked beneath the soft T-shirt.

After running a comb through her hair, she went to the master bedroom hoping to talk Ace out of the king-sized bed. She was exhausted, totally drained by the emotional roller coaster she'd ridden all day.

Upon entering the bedroom she was brought up short by the sight that greeted her.

Ace was already in bed.

Asleep.

If she could believe his soft snoring.

She could try to wake him on the pretense of asking if he'd checked all the locks on the windows and doors, but that would be petty. And then he'd know she was really afraid.

Standing at the foot of the bed, she drank in the sight of him.

His hair was dark against the snowy pillow. A hint of dark stubble shadowed the lean contours of his angular face. Dark, heavily fringed lashes drew her attention to the REM movement of his eyes behind their lids. He was asleep, dreaming.

But she wasn't.

His full lips and sinewy biceps disturbed her in ways she'd not been stirred before. She'd felt his masculine strength when he'd pulled her into a sort of embrace while they were doing dishes. He'd insisted on finishing them alone, giving her a chance to go upstairs alone in privacy.

A sensitive, sexy man.

Was she just a victim of the Stockholm syndrome,

falling for her captor? Was she being incredibly fool-ish? A silly woman?

She'd never thought of herself as silly and wasn't prepared to start now. For whatever reason she trusted Ace—believed he was telling her the truth when he said he had her safety at heart.

It was a big risk to take.

She could pay for that risk with her life, if she was wrong about him.

But he was a journalist. Whatever their faults, jour-nalists were idealistic. Her own parents had cared about her, they'd just cared about the whole world more.

She turned away from the tempting man in the bed and went in search of an empty bed to claim for the night. The guest room provided it in the form of a single bed. She was tired and emotionally drained so she thought sleep would claim her as soon as she crawled beneath the cool smooth sheets.

She was wrong.

Tossing and turning, she found sleep eluded her. She kept going over and over the events of the day in her mind. And the more she thought about it the more scared she became.

And the more appealing sharing a bed seemed to her. With a resigned sigh, she gave up the battle and tossed back the covers.

If she was lucky, Ace would still be asleep and she could join him, sleep soundly—clear over on her side of the king-sized bed and wake before him, without him ever being any the wiser that they'd shared a bed.

Without him knowing what a chicken she really was.

Feeling like a kid afraid in a thunderstorm, she crept in the master bedroom. Standing beside the bed in the dark she listened to the even sounds of Ace's breathing. How could he sleep so soundly, so easily?

Taking great care not to disturb him, she lifted the sheet and slipped between the covers of the bed, holding her breath, least she wake him.

But her worst fears weren't realized and his sleep went undisturbed.

She lay in bed beside him mentally preparing herself to wake early in the morning so she could be up before he awoke. She was normally a very early riser so she had faith she could pull it off.

Feeling safer sharing a bed, even though she'd taken great care that no part of her body touched Ace's, she finally drifted off to sleep.

"Why don't we just go in and get them," Jon demanded, shifting uncomfortably in the front seat of the luxury car as they sat parked down the street from the white gingerbread house Ace and Chloe had gone to when they'd left the safety of the over-the-road truck they'd stowed away in.

"You know we can't do that. The chief said your daddy's instructions were that we were just to watch them, to see where they went and if they had any evidence on them."

"How in the hell are we supposed to know if they have the evidence on them, if we don't get close enough to them to check."

"That's easy," Zeke said from the back seat where he was resting comfortably. "They don't have the evidence on them, if they did, they'd have contacted the Chicago police right away."

"So we just wait?"

"We just wait until they go to sleep and then we plant a homing device on the car in the garage. I'm betting they're going to use it instead of public transport from now on. After that we keep our eyes open the rest of the night."

"How are we supposed to do that all night?" Jon shifted his large athletic frame uncomfortably.

"Simple," Zeke answered. "We sleep in shifts."

"You go first," Jon offered.

"Generous of you—" Zeke looked at Jon suspiciously. Peter Blakemore's son reminded him of a bear with a thorn in his paw and a disposition to match.

"Who can sleep when it's this uncomfortable. I feel like a damned sardine packed in here."

Zeke shrugged. "I've slept in worse places . . ."

"Trouble is, being uncomfortable makes me want to shoot someone."

"See that you don't . . ."

Seven

Ace opened one eye to survey the unfamiliar room.
His survey stopped short when he came to the
blonde in bed with him. He racked his memory. She
hadn't been there last night when he'd went to sleep.
Had she?

No. He'd have remembered.

He remembered everything else about yesterday.

The murder. That he'd killed Peter Blakemore's
son even if in self-defense. The blonde sleeping peace-
fully beside him who'd walked in just in time to witness it. Their escape—so far.

He reached for the bedside table and tilted the face
of his watch so he could read the time; seven-thirty.

Time to try calling Jane again.

A smile ghosted his lips as he gave one more glance
to Chloe who'd kicked off the comforter, exposing a
dangerous length of thigh. When, he wondered, had
she gotten daring enough . . . or afraid enough . . .
to join him.

A lifestyle expert, he mused—whatever the hell that
was. His grandmother would get a kick out of that.
She'd even approve of Chloe, probably, which would be
a first, when it came to the women he usually took up
with. Not that he and Chloe were . . . He resisted the
urge to push an errant strand of hair from where it

had strayed over her face. He didn't want to wake her until he had to.

She deserved the sleep, the rest. Who knew what today would hold for them. Maybe he'd get hold of Jane and everything would be cleared up quickly, neatly. His gut, however, which was usually right, told him he was just whistling Dixie. He'd bet Jane had lit out when she'd seen his picture on the news bulletin. Grass never grew under Jane's feet—it was what made her such a good journalist.

Slipping from the bed taking care not to disturb his willing hostage, he pulled on a pair of borrowed jeans and left them comfortably unbuttoned as he headed downstairs shirtless and barefoot.

As soon as his bare feet hit the cold tile floor in the kitchen, he called Jane's number, letting it ring and ring. The peals had a lonely sound to him.

He hung up the phone. There was nothing to do now but go by Jane's place and check it out. It would be a mistake to assume anything. A grave mistake. Jane had what he needed to clear himself and pin the guilt on Peter Blakemore, Sr. where it belonged.

He flipped on the television set to see if they were still a news item. There was nothing. A drug deal gone south during the night with the involvement of a prominent politician's nephew in the body count had supplanted their celebrity.

That was a piece of luck—not for the nephew of course. It was time to wake Chloe. They needed to get moving, get a course of action going based on what they discovered when they checked out Jane's place.

He took the stairs two at a time. The good night's sleep renewed his flagged energy. Not wanting Chloe to see that he was worried, he pasted a carefree look on his face before reentering the bedroom where she still slept with the innocence of a baby.

Apparently she'd moved in her sleep because the cover lay bunched at the foot of the bed. She'd managed to kick free completely. Lying sprawled across the bed all pink and golden, all legs, she looked like a Barbie doll come to life.

He closed his eyes and tried to recall why he'd come back upstairs.

Food, yeah that was it, he finally remembered. He was hungry, and running out for donuts this morning wasn't a risk worth taking.

He remained in the doorway, not trusting himself to get any closer to her. Attempting to wake her, he cleared his throat.

Then again, louder.

She stirred, mumbling something in her sleep about not fainting.

He called her name.

Her eyes blinked open and she sat straight up in bed. A look of confusion crossed her face when her gaze fell on him lounging in the doorway. She rubbed her eyes with her fists. When she looked at him again she was fully awake and aware. Reaching for the bunched cover, she tugged it to her protectively.

He wondered if the light of a new day had given her a change of heart. He had to put her at ease. And maybe get the gun from the night table where he'd stashed it last night before nodding off.

Returning his carefree look to duty, he asked, "Do lifestyle experts cook?"

She sniffed the air. "I take it journalists don't?"

"At least not this one."

"What about Jane?"

"I already called. Still no answer."

"No, I mean, does she cook?"

"Not anything anyone would want to eat, believe

me," Ace answered with a laugh. "She could burn toast to the most interesting charcoal lumps."

"I think I can manage toast," Chloe said, moving to the side of the bed to get up. "And maybe, if you're lucky, French toast."

He got French toast with a side of a lot of questions. The toast was delicious, almost worth the interrogation.

By the time he'd finished his toast she knew almost as much about him as his grandmother. He wasn't sure he liked it. He was sure he'd not had any choice if he wanted her to continue to be cooperative. She was reassuring herself that she'd made the right choice—that the adrenaline of yesterday's events hadn't colored her decision.

He laid down his fork and pushed his sticky plate away from him.

"Okay, you know I'm single. I'm a journalist for the *Trib,* my grandmother is the only person in my family who speaks to me since I was disinherited, and that I sleep in my Calvins," Ace said, looking up at her. "How about forking over some information about yourself."

Chloe picked up their dirty dishes and carried them to the sink to wash, keeping her back to him. "What is it you want to know?"

"For starters do you have a boyfriend who's going to come looking for you?"

"No boyfriend."

"Why not?"

"That's not an acceptable question."

"Oh, touchy subject, huh? What'd you do, just break up with him—or get dumped."

"No."

He let the silence force an explanation.

"I've been too busy with my career to—"

"A dry spell, eh?" he interrupted. "Been through a couple of those myself." He saw her hand clench the plate she was washing and wondered if maybe he ought to duck. Instead he came up with another question quickly. "What about family? Are they . . ."

She turned and glared at him.

"Oh right. They're off somewhere picture-taking. Bosnia probably, I'd guess."

This time it was she who let silence hang between them.

"How about we switch to a safer topic. You know I sleep in my Calvins, you bold woman. What do you sleep in? Can't be a man's T-shirt like last night since you claim to be without romantic attention at the present."

Silence.

"Oh, I get it. You sleep in the buff—"

"No! No, I do not sleep in the buff. If you must know I have a charge account at Victoria's Secret. I like silk and satin."

"Me too. And just my luck I made you leave your suitcase back at the motel where ol' Zeke had stashed you. Oh well, you can't win them all."

"We'd better win this one," Chloe said, pointedly getting the conversation back to the predicament they found themselves in.

"And we will," he assured her, getting up from his chair.

Chloe placed the last dish in the wooden drainer on the counter, then turned to look at him. "Are you ready to leave for Jane's place."

Ace nodded. "Just let me call one more time." He placed the call, but was met with the same lonely ringing and hung up.

"You said something about a car . . ." He held out his hand for the keys.

"I can drive."

"I'm driving."

"Whatever," she grabbed her purse and tossed the keys she removed to him.

The drive in Julie's Cougar to the Northwest Side neighborhood didn't take long. Jane's was a lovely old house in the middle of renovation. It was on a tree-lined block and there were no signs of life.

"It doesn't look like she's home," Chloe said, stating the obvious.

"No, it doesn't. Come on, let's go have a look inside."

"What are we looking for?"

"A note or something, so I can be sure that she's headed out to our meeting place."

Climbing the steps to the front porch, she reminded him that he hadn't told her where that meeting place was.

"Let's make sure Jane's gone first. I wouldn't want to give away . . ."

"That's rich. I'm trusting you with my life and you're not prepared to tell me—"

"Shush . . ." He held up his hand to hush her. "I hear someone. A man talking. Wait out here. If I don't come back out soon, run to the car and get to the police and don't stop for anyone."

He inserted Jane's spare house key in the lock, and went inside the brick two-story to investigate.

Chloe waited on the porch as instructed.

For about a minute.

She glanced around nervously. A black luxury car sat parked across the street and down the block a ways. No one appeared to be inside. Still, she felt vulnerable standing out on the porch with the wind buffeting her.

Trying the door, she found it still unlocked, so she slipped inside. She inched along the living room wall following the sound of the man's voice. It was muffled and she couldn't make out what he was saying.

Suddenly it stopped.

And so did she.

She froze as she heard footsteps coming toward the living room. What should she do? She couldn't call out. Moving quickly, she hid as best she could behind the long striped sofa.

The footsteps drew nearer.

She held her breath, waiting, listening.

"Ace!" she cried out, jumping up from her hiding place when he entered the living room. It had been his footsteps she'd heard.

"What are you doing? I thought I told you to stay on the porch and wait for me."

"I decided—"

"Let's get that straight right now. If I tell you to do something you do it. Your life could depend on it. Do you understand?"

She nodded, feeling dumb.

"Who was talking?" She moved from behind the sofa to join him.

"The radio was playing."

"But Jane's not here . . ."

"Right."

"Isn't that unusual?"

"She probably left in a hurry and was distracted enough to forget to turn it off." Ace's glance roamed the living room as if he was still searching for something.

"What are you looking for?"

"A message from Jane. She always leaves me a message. A particular message." Spotting something, he moved to the mantel and picked up the card propped there.

"Is that it?" she asked as he read the card.

"Yep. We're outta here."

Chloe had come up behind him to read over his shoulder.

"The coast is clear?" she read. "That doesn't sound like she's gone to me."

"She is. It's our code. Come on, let's get out of here."

Ace shepherded her out to the car.

"I don't understand," she said, when he started the car. "Why are we leaving if the coast is clear?"

"Because the coast is clear means Jane has gone to my grandmother's with the evidence for safekeeping. We're to meet her there."

"But why didn't she just wait for you here?"

"Because it's well known that Jane and I sometimes work as a team on stories for the *Trib*. If they're looking for me, they'd head straight for her place."

"Who would, the chief and his deputy?"

"I'd guess his deputy, Zeke, and maybe Jon Blakemore. The chief will stay in Pleasantville to keep Jon's daddy informed."

Chloe noticed as they pulled away from the front of the house that the luxury car that had been parked across the street was gone. She'd been spooked over nothing.

Eight

Back at Julie's place they went upstairs to borrow a few items of clothing to get them to the coast.

"Just grab enough for two days," Ace instructed. "The drive shouldn't take much more than that, with any kind of luck."

Chloe looked over at him. "I don't think either of us is having any kind of luck of late, do you?"

Ace grabbed another shirt. "Right. You'd better make it three days."

"Why don't we just fly?" Chloe asked, hesitating in her packing of one of Julie's soft satchels. "That would only take a couple of hours."

Ace shook his head no. "We can't chance getting stopped at the airport. Driving is safer."

"Julie is not going to be thrilled to come back and find out I've taken her car to the coast."

"We haven't got any choice. My license plate would give us away and we certainly can't rent a car."

"Aren't you going to call your grandmother and warn her?"

"No, she's used to my being in trouble of one sort or another. And she likes Jane. Jane will just tell her we're working on a story that's sensitive. Well I'm all packed. Finish up here and join me downstairs. I'm going to check over the car and make sure it's up to the trip. The last thing we need is a breakdown on the way."

When he was gone, Chloe's thoughts turned to Jane.

For someone who wasn't involved, he seemed to have a closer than close relationship with Jane. She'd noticed a picture in a silver frame on the mantel at Jane's house when Ace was reading the note next to it. The picture had been of Ace and Jane. She assumed it was Jane, because it was on her mantel. Ace had had his arm around the woman and both had been smiling happily into the camera.

Chloe dismissed the picture from her mind. It was none of her concern. She had a life, a column to write and now it looked like fax to *Chicago* magazine. And she had to help Max keep both of them safe.

Looking for some hand cream, she pulled open the drawer on the bedside table and jumped back with a start.

Lying next to the hand cream was a gun.

Julie hated guns. She wouldn't allow one in the house.

This one belonged to Ace. She recognized it as the one he'd pointed at her. She leaned forward and picked it up.

"I forgot—"

Chloe swung around at the sound of Ace's voice, the gun in her hand, pointed at him.

"Ah, so you found it. I'll take it." He started toward her.

"Stay where you are," she commanded.

He stopped at her command and looked at her strangely. "What?"

"I said stay where you are."

"Don't fool around, Chloe. Give me the gun."

"Not so fast. Maybe I'm not sure I want to go with you to the coast. Maybe I'm not sure I don't want to pick up that phone and turn you in to the police. I don't have any proof that what you've told me is true. You could be stringing me along."

"Now why would I do that?"

"A willing hostage is a lot more easy to deal with than one who isn't willing."

"You aren't a hostage. I explained that to you already. I'm keeping you with me for your own protection. On your own you're expendable."

"Says you."

"It's the truth."

"Is it?"

"What kind of men have you been involved with?"

"None who've picked me up at gunpoint."

"Is that what makes you nervous?" he asked.

"Doesn't it make you nervous to have the shoe on the other foot, to have me be the one holding the gun on you?" The gun in her hand wavered.

"No, not really. Keep it if you want, but we've got to get going," he said, dismissing her. "We've got a long drive ahead of us." He turned then and started walking back toward the door.

"What are you doing pulling some big macho act of bravery?" she accused, sputtering because she was so angry at his dismissal of her as a threat.

He looked back over his shoulder. "No, not really. I don't particularly like guns. That isn't my gun, if you recall. I took it away from Peter Blakemore when he tried to shoot me. I'm uncomfortable carrying a gun. Why do you think I left it in the drawer?"

"I could shoot you," she insisted.

"No, you couldn't. For one thing your fingerprints are now on the gun so it would be your word against mine over who shot Peter Blakemore."

She felt herself blanch. The blood draining from

her face made her feel faint. "You mean you'd set me up—"

"No, the main reason I'm not afraid you'll shoot me is because I've got the bullets for the gun in my pocket. I unloaded the gun last night before I went to bed."

"Why didn't you tell me!"

He grinned wickedly. "You seemed to be having such a good time, I didn't want to spoil your fun."

"Here." She shoved the gun at him as she walked past him in an embarrassed rush.

His rich laughter followed her down the stairs to the kitchen where he joined her a few moments later, the satchel she'd left behind in his hand.

"Write a note to your friend telling her you're okay and you'll explain everything later," he instructed.

"Can't I at least tell her where—"

"No."

"Why not? No one will—"

"No."

She wrote the note as he'd instructed.

He took it from her, read it and nodded his approval. "That's it," he said, putting the note by the phone. "Let's go."

Chloe took a deep breath, picked up her satchel and headed out the door. Until now she'd been able to tell herself she was headed for Chicago and safety. Now she didn't know where she was headed and her safety was in the hands of a stranger she had to trust.

Because she couldn't dismiss his story that once she'd reported the crime, she'd put herself in danger. If she believed part of his story, she had to believe all of it.

And if she believed all of it, she had to believe they were being hunted by someone who wanted both of them dead. Someone who'd already tried to kill Ace, and had sacrificed his son trying.

Peter Blakemore, Sr. was a powerful man, used to getting what he wanted, and according to Ace he wanted the two of them dead so his illegal activities wouldn't come to light and put him in prison.

And she was supposed to turn in a column.

Like *Chicago* magazine was going to want to publish a column on how to pack when on the lam.

"You wanted to see me?" Darrow Smith said, entering Mayor Billy Whitehouse's office.

The mayor ate almost as excessively as he drank and was therefore a stocky man with a florid complexion. And at the moment he wasn't a happy man.

"Hell yes, I wanted to see you. Would you like to guess what about?"

"I think I can guess."

The mayor pulled a bottle and two glasses from his bottom drawer. After pouring them both a shot, he handed one to Darrow.

It was a little early in the dawn for Darrow to be tossing back liquor but he did, since he didn't want to stir the mayor up any more than he obviously was.

The mayor set his glass back down on the desk and stared at the almost empty bottle. "Blakemore's been on the phone again. He wants to be kept informed on an hourly basis. He wants progress and he wants it now."

"Then he's not going to like what I have to report to you," Darrow informed him, setting his glass on the desk next to the bottle.

"Damn it, Darrow, what's gone wrong—"

"Evidently whatever Ash Worth has on Blakemore Chemical wasn't in Chicago. He and the woman have left the city and headed east."

"East? Where east? Where in the hell are they going?"

"Zeke didn't seem to have figured that out when he called. Just said he and Jon were still on their tail. Those are Blakemore's instructions, aren't they? To follow them until they find the evidence Peter, Jr. was supposed to when he got himself killed instead."

The mayor nodded. "That's still the plan. You know what to do once the evidence is recovered."

"I've got some more news Blakemore isn't going to like, as long as you're reporting back to him."

"Now what?" The mayor's hand caressed the bottle of liquor.

"Ash Worth's real name is Ashley Clayton Ellsworth III. He's not just any snoopy reporter. He's an award-winning journalist for the *Tribune*."

"Shit." The mayor upended the bottle again, looked at Darrow who refused, then tossed back another drink.

"The word is he's known for being good at turning over rocks and exposing what crawls out from beneath them to the light of day. I'd say Blakemore has reason to be worried."

"So do we."

"I know."

"Maybe Jon will make it easy for us."

"That would be nice and tidy, wouldn't it?"

The mayor stared off into space. "I just hope this whole nightmare is over by the funeral."

Darrow hoped so too. But he wouldn't bet money on such a flimsy hope. The odds were way against that happening.

When things turned ugly like they had, they had a way of getting worse.

Darrow had a feeling that in a not very long time Billy Whitehouse was going to be the town drunk . . .

which he already was . . . he just wasn't going to be the town drunk *and the mayor.*

"Where in the hell are they going?"

"East," Zeke answered the cranky Jon Blakemore.

"Damn, I know that. But why? He's from Chicago. She's from Chicago. Why would they head east?"

"Probably because they didn't find what they were looking for. Or maybe Ash Worth didn't have anything on Blakemore Chemical after all. Maybe your brother's information was wrong."

"All I know is my brother's dead and Ash Worth killed him." Zeke noticed the fierceness with which Jon's big hands gripped the steering wheel. Zeke had no doubt about the violence Jon was capable of. He wished the chief had insisted Jon stay in Pleasantville. This was one job he'd rather do alone.

Jon was a loose cannon.

And that, he knew, was exactly why the chief hadn't balked at Jon joining the chase. The chief's job was threatened and he'd do most anything to hang on to it.

Zeke turned on the radio and found a country music station. He stopped on a station playing Reba's latest hit. Boy that woman had a set of lungs on her. She could belt a song out. He wondered if she even needed a microphone for her concerts. She wasn't bad on the eyes either.

Jon reached over and turned off the radio.

"What'd ya go and do that for?"

"I hate hearing chicks sing."

Zeke sighed. It was going to be a long trip no matter how short it was.

"We could kill the woman."

"What?"

"I said we could kill the woman. Daddy didn't say nothing about her."

"What are you talking about? The woman is an innocent hostage."

Jon snorted in derision. "Women are never innocent."

Zeke wasn't surprised at Jon's statement. Jon had a reputation for knocking women around. It no doubt had something to do with his own mother abandoning him. It had only been with the chief's intervention and Jon's father's influence that Jon hadn't landed in jail for his proclivities.

Nine

"Now will you tell me where we're going?" Chloe asked as they headed east on highway 90 out of Chicago in Julie's blue sedan.

"Cleveland."

"Cleveland! That's not the coast."

"It's our first stop on our way to the coast. I checked the map before we left. It's about 343 miles to Cleveland and should take us about eight hours. That will put us there by five-thirty or six this evening."

"Fine, but where are we going?"

"After Cleveland? Philadelphia."

"You're being purposely obtuse."

"I just figure the less you know the better off you are."

"No, you figure the less I know, the less I can tell."

"Same difference."

He wasn't going to tell her.

Giving up, she occupied herself with watching the scenery whiz by as she tried to come up with a subject for her column.

Her columns usually consisted of reports on the current trends on everything from the style with which one lived, to the nuts and bolts of how to do it.

She'd had a lot of new experiences to inspire a column. She had only to choose one. Perhaps she should do a column on making sure a gun was loaded when you wanted to make a point, or one on how to pick up a drop-dead gorgeous man who wouldn't dream of letting you out of his sight. All you had to do was see him murder someone . . .

She glanced over at Ace.

Was she being foolish trusting him? How much of that trust had to do with his good looks? She'd read the studies and knew it was natural for people to attribute qualities to people who were handsome just because they were handsome. Probably a really scary-looking guy would have had a harder time convincing her. Still the ride in the back of the big rig to Chicago had been in total darkness.

It was there that she'd bought his story. But again, how much of that had to do with adrenaline?

No, she'd made the right choice. After all he could have shot her with the same gun that had killed Blakemore's son and he'd unloaded it instead.

A niggling voice reminded her however, that a dead hostage was useless to him. He needed her alive.

But did he also want her alive?

Maybe it was in her best interests to get him to want to keep her alive. Mostly she just seemed to amuse him. Perhaps she should up her entertainment value and make him think that if he played his cards right she might be inclined to . . .

Good grief what was wrong with her? She prided herself on being an independent woman of some intelligence. Trying to captivate her kidnapper was just dumb. The thing to do was try to find out as much about him and his/their situation as possible. That was how she'd built a successful and growing career.

She looked back over at Ace.

"What?" he asked, under her scrutiny.

"I was wondering. What brought you to Pleasant-ville in the first place. I'm sure you didn't suddenly decide to work in a chemical plant for the hell of it. You must have had a reason for picking Blakemore, Inc."

"I got a letter tipping me off that toxic chemicals were being dumped by the plant."

"Who sent it?"

"The letter was unsigned."

"Do you always go off on investigations on the flimsy substance of an unsigned letter? After all there are lots of crackpots and just plain nasty people out there who love to stir up trouble and make everyone in general as miserable as they are."

"You mean journalists?" he asked, on a grin.

She ignored his wise-ass remark.

He swerved the car over a lane to get around a truck that was dropping hunks of fresh topsoil from its over-loaded bed. "The answer is no. I don't go off investigating every tip I get willy-nilly. I follow up on the tips that interest me and that feel right. You get so you have a gut feeling about things that you learn to trust when you're in my business."

"Your gut feeling kinda let you down when it came to meeting Blakemore's son, didn't it?"

"I got careless because I got greedy. I should have known it was a setup."

"Did you ever discover who sent you the tip while you were working in Pleasantville?"

"No."

"Any ideas?"

"It was probably someone with a grudge against the family for some reason. Maybe a plant worker who was fired. Just because the reason someone rats isn't altruistic doesn't mean good can't come from it."

"But you did get some sort of evidence that the tip was on target . . ."

"I did. Luckily I sent off the samples to Jane before

I went to meet with Peter Blakemore, Jr. Let's just hope that the samples turn up to be toxic. Otherwise, we're in deep doo-doo."

"Where are they dumping the waste and how come no one has noticed?"

"On plots of land on the outskirts of town. They're fairly isolated."

"They aren't dumping it all in one place?"

"No. They spread it around so the drums of the stuff aren't so noticeable. It's fortunate that they did it that way because the samples I got were from one of the first places they started dumping the stuff. They keep a closer eye on the current site, so it would have been harder for me to go snooping around without getting caught there."

"Isn't it illegal to ship—"

"I took every precaution . . . but sometimes you have to do something that skirts the edges of the law if you want to get results."

"So the laws don't apply to you."

"Hey, am I going the speed limit?"

She glanced at the speedometer. He was.

"That's because there isn't a good reason to break it. But if you were hurt and I had to get you to the hospital, you can be damn sure I'd break the speed limit."

It was hard to argue with his line of reasoning. It was harder to want to.

"So we know what I was doing in Pleasantville. What were you doing? Was it all business or were you visiting an old beau or someone?"

"It was strictly business."

"Don't you ever have any fun?"

"Of course I have fun. In case you were wondering, this isn't it."

"So what is?"

"I like to go out to restaurants, movies, gallery exhibits and to the ballet."

"Oh you're just going to love this road trip—"

"There isn't going to be camping, is there?"

"You hate the outdoors, right?"

"No, I like to bike ride."

"You're a biker chick?"

"Ten speed."

"No wonder you didn't have a problem keeping up with me running through the cornfield to the truck stop. I would have figured you for aerobics."

"I do take a low-impact class. But sometimes I like to feel the wind in my face."

"Then you picked the right city to live in."

"And I wish I were there right now. Which reminds me, we're going to have to stop somewhere along the way so I can get a notebook to write my column up in."

"What are you smoking?"

"I've got to get my column in—if I fax it, I can make my deadline in time."

"Get over it. You're not faxing anything."

"Why not?"

"Because a fax will leave a paper trail and it's a risk we can't afford."

"Don't be ridiculous. *Chicago* magazine is located in a big city. How would anyone know if I sent them a fax?"

"Simple. You can be sure Blakemore and Billy Whitehouse have run a thorough check on you. They'll know everything there is to know about you, including the fact that you write a column for *Chicago* magazine. All Billy Whitehouse has to do is call the magazine, tell them you're missing if they don't already know, and ask if they've heard from you. The magazine will remember the fax, check it and give them the information on it that tells where the fax was sent from. It won't pinpoint us exactly, but it will tell them more than I want them to know."

"You're right. No column."

He looked at his watch. "It's almost the top of the hour. Turn on the radio and see what the news has to say. With any luck we won't be on it."

She did as he requested, tuning in a station. Rush Limbaugh was gleefully wrapping up his hour, still delirious over the big Republican upset over the Democratic congress. The news followed a minute later. The lead story was unfortunately an airplane crash. A 747 had gone down in a thunderstorm in Florida. A sports figure had died in the crash, and the spot focused on his career. The next item of news dealt with a serial killer loose on the West Coast. It was a relief to finally get to the weather segment.

Sunny and mild the weatherman reported, predicting more of the same for the next three days. The traffic was also benign.

Rush Limbaugh returned after the news spot and Chloe switched the station to one that played classical music. She expected an argument from Ace on her choice but she didn't get one.

"We may be news in Chicago, but looks like we're way down on the list in Indiana," Ace said, showing his relief. She hadn't realized how tense he'd been while listening to the news report.

"You don't think we're being followed, do you?" she asked, suddenly more nervous with the realization that he was.

"I don't know. I don't think so, but we could have screwed up somewhere without knowing we've tipped them off. I just know I'll feel a lot better when we get to—"

She waited for him to say where, but he recovered nicely with, ". . . the coast."

"Should I be watching for something?" she asked, turning to look out the back window at the heavy traffic behind them on the highway. Sometimes she thought people were like ants. No matter what time of the night or day there were always strings of traffic scurrying back and forth on the highway, always in a hurry.

But none of them were in as much of a hurry as they were.

Unless, of course, they were following them.

She shook off a chill in the warm car.

"I couldn't even begin to tell you what to be looking for," Ace answered. "Besides, if they see us, they won't be trying not to be seen. Zeke's police car is way too conspicuous to chance using it to track us out of state. If Zeke and Jon Blakemore are together, they'd be in Jon's car I imagine."

"What kind of car?" Chloe imagined every car she saw behind them as the one. Especially the cars she saw where she was unable to make out the driver.

"I don't know. I heard he wrecked his fancy sports car a few days ago. I don't know what he's driving in the interim. It could be anything."

"Well, then I guess I'm not much help as a lookout," she said, turning back around.

"You could be. Keep your eyes peeled for a gas station. We're running low on fuel."

She pointed out a Texaco station a few miles down the highway and he began easing the sedan over to the exit lane to get off the highway to refuel.

She was anticipating stretching her legs and getting a cold soda.

"Sonovabitch!" Ace cut the wheel of the car sharply. A car had come out of nowhere to cut them off, and went sailing past them down the exit ramp at high speed.

Their sedan went into a tailspin and the two of them saw only a blur.

"Are you all right?" Ace asked, looking to her when he'd regained control of the car and righted it.

"I think so." Her heart was in her throat, but it was beating, pounding was more like it.

"Did you get a look at the car or who was in it?"

She shook her head no. And then she realized what he was asking her. "You don't think—"

"Nah. It was probably some joyriding kid starving for a burger."

He was trying to reassure her.

And wasn't completely successful.

Ten

Ace watched Chloe get out of the car to stretch her legs as he stood at the pump fueling the car. Since they were in a small town, he didn't insist she stay in the car so no one would recognize her. Besides he was enjoying the view.

She was lithe and very feminine. Her blond hair was pulled back in a ponytail which made her look like a teenager. Her long legs, tanned to a light biscuity color, were coltish. The shorts she wore that she'd borrowed from her friend were a little baggy, but she'd belted them with a kerchief that showed off her narrow waist. Her friend's T-shirt was a little small, and showed off a gorgeous pair of sweater puppies.

When she got back in the car, he was embarrassed to see the tank was already full. He wondered if she'd noticed. Maybe that had been the reason for the half smile she'd given him.

Feeling a little foolish, he didn't look at her as he replaced the fuel hose at the pump and went inside the station to pay. In cash, of course; he couldn't take the chance of a credit card. Not unless they got desperate. The wise thing to do was make it to the coast with the little cash they had.

He splurged for two cans of cola and a pack of gum, and headed back to the car.

Within a few miles they'd left Indiana and the northern countryside dotted with Amish buggies, beaches and back roads behind them.

"My parents are out of the country, so they won't be worried about me," Chloe said, making conversation to break up the monotony of the long drive. "But what about you? Isn't there anyone else besides your grandmother who you should call to tell you're all right?"

"No. When a family like mine disinherits you, to them you cease to exist. It's like being shunned. They wouldn't talk to me if they saw me face to face."

"What was it you did that—"

"I don't want to talk about it."

She tried more angles but she finally got his drift and gave up on the line of conversation.

Feeling guilty, Ace tossed out another conversational gambit. "A lifestyle expert—that sounds like a career that would involve a husband and children. How come you're not married? Would the reality be less than your ideal, too messy?"

Had she squirmed just a little?

She wouldn't acknowledge it, he'd bet, but clearly he'd come close to the mark. Chloe Pembrook wasn't the sort of woman to settle for less than perfection. And why should she? Everything about her was perfect.

Or so it appeared.

If it wasn't, any flaws would start to surface on the long trip. First dates were easy to make a good impression on; it was relationships that were hard. And they were thrown together in a relationship for survival whether either of them liked it or not.

"Everyone doesn't have to be married." Her tone was defensive, and it gave away her perhaps unconscious desire to be.

"That's true," he said, agreeably enough. "But you do."

"What?"

"You need to be married," he repeated, smiling. He was poking her, getting a rise out of her, and darned if he wasn't enjoying it. His grandmother would say it was what he enjoyed most; stirring things up. He'd always been that way . . . inquisitive, never settling for surface appearances if he suspected something hidden. He wanted to know every secret.

At any cost.

"I was married. I didn't like it."

Well, he certainly hadn't expected that. She'd rocked him back on his heels and *almost* left him speechless. Married, huh? Why had she kicked him out? He knew with certainty that she'd been the one to want out. Why he knew that, he didn't know. Gut instinct was all.

"You tried it once and that's it? Not very adventurous are you?"

"At least *I* tried it."

"You must have been young. What were you thirteen?" He was still poking at her, unsettling her, provoking her.

"Eighteen," she sniffed.

"What happened?"

"It didn't work out—"

"For you . . ." he coaxed.

"He was ah, . . ."

"Let me guess, no match for you."

She turned and looked at him.

"You are a handful you know. It would take the right sort of man to be able to handle a package like you. Cut you down to size, let some of the air out of your airs."

"He was a lot older than I was," she said, not taking his bait.

"Worse, a father figure. You don't need a daddy, you need—"

"No one," she bit off.

There was a determined look on her face as she'd made the vow, a vow he thought had the echo of a lonely childhood to it. This was a woman who longed for something she'd accepted she would never have.

"I am perfectly capable of taking care of myself," she glanced at him, ". . . unless I'm being pursued by murderous goons."

"I'm convinced. You're a rock. But tell me honest, don't you sometimes just long to have your wrists kissed?"

He heard her sharp little intake of breath.

And he grinned. He still had it. He'd liked women all his life. A little too much, maybe and a little too indiscriminately maybe, but even he could see that Chloe Pembrook was special. The kind of woman who'd need wooing, anticipation and just plain ol' fun. She had been seriously deprived, marriage or no.

And this time he had left her speechless.

The prospect of wrist kissing hung in the air between them. It beat the hell out of wondering if they'd almost been deliberately run off the road a ways back.

They passed a road sign listing the miles till Fremont, Ohio, and Cleveland. A few more hours' drive and they'd be looking for a place to spend the night.

It wasn't going to be to her liking he knew.

A cheap motel wasn't Chloe Pembrook's speed, but it was what the budget called for. She'd have to get used to it. They would be sharing a room and a bed.

And this time it wouldn't be a king-sized bed they'd be sharing.

If he hadn't needed a good night's sleep so desperately, things could get interesting. But as it was, sleep was high on his list of priorities. There was a lot of hard driving ahead of them. He had to be alert and watchful. Just because things had gone their way so far, didn't mean their luck would hold.

Murphy had a way of showing up sooner or later. It was in the fine print of his law.

"We can't stay here." Chloe stood in the middle of the room and refused to put down her satchel. "Anything would be better than this."

"The only thing better would be cheaper, but we don't have camping gear. I'm sorry if the accommodations aren't to your liking Miss Pembrook, but we not only can, we are staying here for the night.

"And yes it's a cheap motel. That's precisely the point. So get over it."

"But there are waterstain marks high on the wall, the place reeks of mildew and you could put saddles on the roaches and ride them out of town," Chloe objected, more than a little horrified at the room they'd been shown to at the Vista motel with what she was sure was a permanently lit pink neon Vacant sign.

She dropped her satchel on the bed, seeing his mind was set.

"Good. You're being sensible. We've got to get some sleep after we eat. We have another long drive ahead of us tomorrow."

She wasn't smiling when she turned to him. "And we're going where tomorrow?"

"East."

"I had to ask." Turning away she went to splash some cold water on her face before they went out to find something to eat.

At least since they were scrimping on accommodations, Ace might spring for a decent restaurant.

A fast-food drive-thru restaurant named Buns wasn't what she'd had in mind, but it was what she got. Burger and fries for him, chicken and salad for her. They ate the food in the room to avoid undue exposure.

They didn't know how far the television news bulletin had been broadcast last night or if Zeke and Jon were nearby lurking. She kept trying not to think about them, but Ace kept reminding her of the danger they were in. Apparently he wasn't completely sold on her.

He was afraid to trust her not to bolt.

And not without good reason, she thought, looking around the shabby room as she cleared the paper trash from their meal.

She picked up a booklet titled *Calendar of Ohio Events.* Someone had left it on the Formica desk. Leafing through it she found a baseball schedule. "We could go to a baseball game. The Cleveland Indians are playing at Indian's Park," she read.

"We're staying in. The only baseball we're going to see is if it's on the TV."

She noticed the TV for the first time and laughed.

"So it's not a big screen TV, get used to it," he said.

"That isn't what I was laughing at."

"What then?"

"You're right. The TV is primitive. It *might* be color. But for sure it doesn't have a remote control . . . get used to it," she lobbed back.

He scowled. "I'm going to bed."

Suddenly the bed he was lying on with his hands stacked behind his head was the biggest thing in the room, although it was twin-sized.

"I'm going to take a shower," she said, practically bolting with her satchel to the bathroom.

"Intelligent, feisty, and scared of her sensuality," he

ticked off on his fingers. Oh yeah, he was in trouble in more ways than one. And she was sensual, though she'd deny it, not realizing her sensuality went past fabric textures, smelling good, and gracious living.

And right now he didn't have the time to show her, darn the luck.

To distract his masculine inclinations, he picked up the *Ohio Calendar of Events* Chloe had dropped, and he began leafing through it.

An ad for the Raptor caught his eye. Too bad they didn't have time for a little side trip to Sandusky, Ohio either. A ride on what was billed as the world's highest, fastest, steepest inverted roller coaster wouldn't be bad foreplay.

Reading the ad for the looping, twisting, ride that promised untold excitement wasn't distracting him from thoughts of the woman who'd soon be sharing the small bed with him.

The indifference which he needed so he could pretend to get through the night was bogus, but necessary. Undressing quickly down to his underwear, he crawled under the sheets. Then swearing, he climbed back out of bed, realizing there really wasn't a remote control for the TV.

A baseball game was on.

He tried watching it but couldn't concentrate. His mind kept insisting on focusing on the woman he was on the run with. All this wasn't really fair to her.

It only gave her added reason not to like journalists. He hadn't purposely brought her to his problem, but he'd surely involved her. Now it was his responsibility to keep her safe.

He had to keep his wits about him.

And his Calvins *on*.

Eleven

When Chloe came out of the tiny bathroom he wasn't asleep.

And she wasn't wearing silk and satin.

Instead of borrowing something from her friend Julie, she'd snitched a couple more of her friend's husband's T-shirts for sleepwear. What she didn't know was that the soft cotton T-shirt made her look just as sexy as the silk and satin would have. Ace looked away, back to the baseball game on TV.

She turned out the light and crossed to the bed, bending one knee on the edge. "You're on my side of the bed, move," she ordered him.

"Not tonight," he answered without looking away from the TV screen.

"You weren't sleeping on that side of the bed last night."

Taking hold of the nearest pillow, she threw it at him.

"Hey, what are you doing?" he said, blocking the pillow.

"What am I doing? What are you doing? You're being a bully," she answered without waiting for him to. "You're taking that side of the bed just because you're bigger and stronger."

"You're right," he agreed smugly. "I take whichever side faces the door to protect you," he explained.

"Oh." The steam went out of her argument. She retrieved the pillow and placed it back on her side of the bed. Then slipping off the socks she wore to keep from walking barefoot on the grungy carpet, joined him in bed.

"Who's winning?" she asked, looking at the TV while taking great care to hug her side of the bed.

"The home team."

"I'm glad somebody is," she grumbled, giving him her back.

"Hey, don't lifestyle experts have manners?"

"Why?"

"You didn't say good-night."

"That's because it isn't one."

The baseball announcer's voice was bored as he gave the final score in the lop-sided game the locals won by seven runs. Ace got out of bed and turned off the TV, banging his shin on the bed in the dark in the process when he returned to bed.

"Are you okay?" Chloe asked when he stopped swearing.

"Just ducky," he mumbled.

The silence in the room echoed between them for a while until he finally broke it with his, "So how come the marriage didn't work out?"

She didn't answer him at first, and for a few minutes he didn't think she was going to. Finally she said, "I thought because he was older than me by a good several years that he was wiser than me. So I let him talk me into marrying him. I was too young to be married, to know what I wanted. It's the last time I ever let someone talk me into something."

"You mean until now."

"And I'm probably going to regret this too."

* * *

"Can you hear anything?"

Jon shushed Zeke with his finger and listened intently at the connecting wall of the motel that joined their two rooms.

"Not even bedsprings squeaking," Jon answered.

"They're probably asleep," Zeke surmised, getting ready for bed. He wasn't thrilled with the prospect of sharing one with Jon Blakemore. Zeke was certain there wasn't going to be much restful sleep gotten, by him anyway, either way you looked at it.

They had to be certain Ash Worth and Miss Pembrook didn't get an early start in the morning and leave them sleeping unaware that they'd lost their quarry until it was too late. Tailing the two of them as they did, meant they had to be extremely careful about their car being suspicious. To that end they'd parked their car on the other side of the mostly vacant motel. It wouldn't do for the two of them to notice it on the highway behind them and then begin wondering if they were being tailed.

It was bad enough Jon had pulled that reckless stunt back at the exit ramp nearly getting them all killed. Jon just couldn't seem to resist bullying. He was angry at the world because his mother had abandoned him. His older brother had been his only soft spot because he'd physically resembled their mother, Zeke assumed, having seen a picture somewhere. Now with Peter, Jr. dead, Jon's explosive rage had grown hair-trigger explosive and dangerously close to going off. Zeke sorely wished he were handling this one for the chief alone.

Jon was going to screw things up. Zeke had a sick feeling in his stomach about that. Even Jon's father was going to have a hell of a time deterring his son from exacting revenge before it was wise.

Bored with listening at the wall, Jon frowned at Zeke

who'd already taken the right side of the bed. "I wish I were sleeping with that pretty little blonde next door instead of you."

"If it's any comfort, I wish you were too," Zeke grumbled, rolling over with his back to Jon.

Chloe was still awake an hour later, her eyes wide open and staring at the shabby motel room. Even the grey-shadowed darkness didn't improve it. But her mind wasn't on her surroundings. She was thinking back to her failed marriage.

Failure wasn't something that came easily to her lips to admit. She should have bailed out on the honeymoon. But she had been a shy child with no knowledge of males. The sex was tepid. Her professor husband performed only barely adequately. She hadn't known that of course until later. She'd been a virgin when she'd married him.

It had probably been a large part of her draw for him.

She'd celebrated getting her freedom with a trip to Cancún. And on that trip a vacationing architect with a surfer's body had shown her what physical passion was all about. She hadn't left the room long enough to get a decent suntan. She could almost feel herself blushing thinking about it. It had been a fling she hadn't repeated. Perhaps in a way it had been too disturbing.

It had been almost twelve years since she'd taken over control of her life and she hadn't looked back. She hadn't for a minute regretted divorcing a man she hadn't loved.

There was no guilt. Once her husband had realized he'd misunderstood that her delicate appearance disguised a strong will, he'd exposed a cruel streak she hadn't known he had. Like some brainy men, his specialty hadn't been physical abuse, but mental abuse. He became the king of the put-down, angry that she didn't live up to his idea of a perfect wife; obedient, submissive and ornamental.

Ornamental hadn't been a problem for her, she loved to accessorize. Loved being a woman. But the obedient and submissive qualities she'd shown as a student of his, were ones she grew out of very quickly.

It took tremendous drive and determination to build a career as she had. A career based on nothing more than her eye for beauty, her knack for knowing what would make people feel better about themselves and their lives.

But she had done it, and her career was still growing. It gave her a great deal of satisfaction to know she could take care of herself. To provide for her own needs. The way she'd grown up with her parents dumping her with relatives whenever their career took them away had forced her to become independent after all.

She'd married and it had been a false start because she'd married for the wrong reason . . . fear. Fear that she couldn't take care of herself.

But she could and did, and yet when Ace had explained he'd taken the side of the bed closest to the door to protect her, it had touched her.

His words were sincere, she knew instinctively, and they had warmed a very needy part of her. Those words were keeping her awake.

Although she was happy, she worked too hard.

She'd neglected parts of her that weren't tough, weren't part of the super-woman facade of the 80s when she'd begun her career. Then it had been the slogan that a woman could do everything a man could. And they could. But in the process some women, herself included, had made sacrifices they were only just becoming aware of.

Now, as the mid-nineties approached, balance was becoming the button word. Everyone was too busy to be a real friend or lover. And they were suffering because of it.

Was she so desperate for nurturing and affection in her life that she looked for it in a killer? She was taking a chance believing him. But it was nowhere near the chance she'd be taking if she let down her personal guard and believed they were together for any reason other than mutual survival.

Still it felt good to hear someone else's breathing besides her own in the bed. She'd kept herself too busy to notice how lonely she was. Had she done it purposely? Or had the sudden disruption in her normal life merely pointed it out to her?

When this was over she was going to examine her life, her priorities. Her work would still be important to her, but it could no longer be the only thing to her. Because if it was, she'd become like her parents when she wasn't looking.

She wondered if Ace was sleeping.

Or was he lying awake like her, too keyed up to sleep.

She punched her pillow trying to get comfortable. She drew her knees up, then stretched them out. Raised her arms, then lowered them. She turned. The turn brought her closer to Ace. Real close—she could feel his breath on her cheek.

She held her own breath.

Just when she released it, deciding she hadn't woken him, he spoke.

"Want me to tell you a story?"

She pretended not to be unnerved by him lying there almost naked, almost touching her. "If you mean the one about the big bad wolf, I already know it."

"How about Goldilocks?" he said, playing along, but tugging a long curl near her cheek.

"I know who's sleeping in my bed."

"You real sure about that?"

"Maybe not," she admitted.

"So ask me anything . . ."

"Okay, where're we going?"

He laughed. "Nice try. Anything but that—"

She flipped over on her back. He was too close. She couldn't think with him . . . "Do you find this exciting?" she finally asked.

"I like women, if that's what you're asking. And yes I find this exciting—why do you think I can't sleep? Same reason you can't."

"I meant your story. Do you find the idea of writing a story on what you've uncovered exciting. Does it give you a rush?" she said, sidestepping the subject he'd brought up . . . the obvious subject.

"Don't you think people like Blakemore who are breaking the law because they are rich and powerful belong in jail? I do. And I get a lot of satisfaction exposing the truth to the light of day."

"Are you ever wrong?"

"I try very hard not to be. I check and recheck everything before I put it in print."

"But what if you're wrong about Blakemore?"

"I'm not wrong. He didn't send his son to kill me because he had nothing to hide. Blakemore has something to hide all right and I'm going to expose him."

"How are you going to do that if the samples Jane has turn out not to be toxic?"

"I don't know. But I promise you if that's the case, I'll go to the police and try to prove my innocence and get you the protection you need."

"You'd turn yourself in when you know that I'd have to give evidence that could incriminate you. Are you telling me that you'd sacrifice yourself to protect me?"

"Yes."

Twelve

Ace wasn't nearly so chivalrous in the morning when the two of them exited the motel to begin the long day's drive.

"I don't friggin' believe it." He kicked the flat tire they were confronted with and turned his back to the car. After stomping around and swearing, he turned back to the tire, glared at it and kicked it again for good measure. "Damn."

His mood didn't improve when he went around to the trunk and popped it open to get out the jack and the spare. He found the jack right off. But after lifting the trunk carpeting, he discovered there wasn't a spare, not a donut, nothing.

"Women . . ." he grumbled, staring at the empty well where the spare tire should have been.

"What about women?" Chloe demanded, standing beside him.

"This is your friend Julie's car, right?"

Chloe nodded.

"I rest my case. Only a woman would drive without a spare tire."

"Maybe she didn't know—"

"More like she didn't think."

Chloe knew arguing the question was pointless. Especially since that was what he so clearly wanted to do. Lashing out at her about the tire vented his frustration even if it only served to inch hers up.

"So what do we do now?" she asked, moving away from bickering to the heart of their immediate problem.

"I think I saw a service station across the street last night when we pulled in. Let's go see if it's open."

She tagged along to the station, where he bought her breakfast from the vending machine. The station didn't have a repaired tire at a reduced rate so they had to pay the station's inflated price for a new tire.

Back at the motel she watched while he easily jacked up the car, made short work of the lug nuts with a muscular dexterity his leanness belied, and replaced the flat tire in less time than it would have taken her to repair a broken nail.

When he was done he went inside to wash up and she waited in the car. When he came back out it struck her how it looked. It looked like they had spent a night together in a seedy motel. Well, they had, of course. But there had been nothing salacious about it. The stories she had to tell her grandchildren were going to be pretty boring.

Ace wasn't in a talkative mood as they headed back out on highway 90 along Lake Erie on their way to Pennsylvania. Off to her right over the rolling farmland she spotted a speck in the sky. As they ate up the miles of highway the speck became bigger and bigger until she could make out what it was. The hot-air balloon with its bright zigzag pattern added a distracting bit of colorful whimsy to the morning.

It would be nice, she thought, to be floating high in the air above your problems letting the wind carry you along at a carefree pace. She wondered who was in the balloon. A pair of lovers maybe . . . or perhaps a couple celebrating an anniversary, the husband having surprised the wife with the romantic gesture.

Snap out of it, she told herself with a shake of her head. There was no hot-air balloon, no lover, coming to carry her away from the situation she found herself in.

She turned to Ace. "Are we going to reach our destination today?" she asked, anxious to know how soon this was going to end.

"No." He didn't elaborate, still uncommunicative.

Must not be a morning person, she surmised. "Great," she said dryly, ". . . another night in a seedy motel. I can hardly contain my excitement."

"No seedy motel," he quipped.

"You mean we get to stay somewhere they have soft sheets, hot water, and room service!"

"Last time I looked, the back seat of this car didn't provide any of those luxuries, so don't go getting yourself all excited."

"What are you talking about. What's the back seat of this car got to do with anything?"

"The back seat of this car is where we're sleeping tonight."

"That's not funny, Ace." She had a sinking feeling he wasn't trying to be funny.

"It might not be funny. But it's true. I spent tonight's motel room money on the flat tire I had to replace. If you want to eat anytime before tomorrow, we sleep in the back of the car tonight."

They were sleeping in the back seat of the car, her stomach told her, signaling that the candy bar she'd had for breakfast wasn't going to hold her to tomorrow.

Tonight was going to be a very long night.

* * *

"Where the hell are they going?"

"I don't know, Chief," Zeke answered, trying not to let his boss's frustration get to him. "We're just along for the ride right now. You told me we were to follow and see where they go, not to do anything yet."

"That's the way Blakemore wants it. He wants to make sure he gets Ash Worth for killing his son, but not at the expense of letting any evidence of his illegal dumping surface to ruin him. Where are you calling from right now?"

"We took highway 76 across most of Pennsylvania. Right now we've stopped in Philadelphia at a fast-food place that specializes in Philly Cheesesteaks. They aren't exactly taking a luxury trip. The Vista motel we put up at last night was a dive. They must be short on cash."

"Are you spending the night in Philadelphia?"

"I don't think so. They didn't book a motel before they hit the restaurant. I expect they may be planning on making up some time because they had to replace a flat tire this morning. Jon's idea of fun. Can't you find some reason to call him back there?"

"If he's not coming back for his brother's funeral, I think you're stuck with him. I know he's a loose cannon, so watch him."

"I'll call you when I'm sure we've stopped for the night."

"Do that. Blakemore's on my case constantly wanting to be informed about what's going on. I keep having to tell him nothing. It would be nice if you could get some information for me."

"I'm doing the best I can, Chief." He hung up the phone, wishing this were over so he'd know how bad it turned out. It would turn out bad, it was just a matter of how bad.

* * *

"Chief, it's me."

"Zeke, I didn't expect to be hearing back from you this soon."

"And I didn't expect to be calling you so soon. It appears we are staying in Philadelphia after all. The two of them seem to be settling in for the night."

"What motel are you staying at?"

"We're not. We're sleeping in the car."

"Right. I'd buy tickets to see Jon Blakemore sleep in his car."

"I'm serious, Chief. After Ash Worth and Miss Pembrook ate, they went to one of those dollar movies and now they're parked on a residential street. I think they plan to spend the night in the back seat of the car. At least that's where they are now."

"You said it's a residential neighborhood. Maybe they're waiting for someone to come home. Have they gone up to any of the houses?"

"No."

"Okay, well keep watch in case they do. I don't envy you sleeping in the back seat of a car."

"That's not the worst part, the worst part is sleeping in the car makes Jon feel uncomfortable—and when he feels uncomfortable, he feels like shooting someone."

"See that he doesn't."

Ace hadn't been kidding.

They were spending the night in the back of the car. The front with its console in the middle dividing the seats was impossible for sleeping. And the car seats didn't tilt back. So they found themselves in the back seat.

"Tomorrow night should be interesting," she ventured trying not to feel his legs wedged against hers.

He shifted his legs, still trying to get comfortably settled. "What do you mean?"

"I mean it will be interesting to see what you come up with. First we started with a king-sized bed, then it was a twin-sized bed last night and now we're reduced to the back seat of the car. I don't see how you can find anything smaller and more uncomfortable." And more intimate, she thought, but didn't say.

It didn't help that she could still recall quite clearly how masculine and sexy he'd looked, changing the flat tire. There was something sexy about a capable man.

Or maybe she was just finding Ace so attractive because of the element of danger surrounding them. The knowledge that their pursuers could be out there anywhere.

"You don't have to worry," Ace said, interrupting her thoughts. "Tomorrow night you'll have clean sheets and your own bed."

"You mean—"

"Yes. We should arrive at our destination by tomorrow night, barring anything untoward happening between now and then."

"Good, I was beginning to think this grandmother of yours and Jane were figments of your imagination. How much of an effort could it be for a writer like you to make up a story I'd buy."

"It's no story. Tomorrow this could all be over and your life could be back to normal."

"It can't be soon enough for me. While you might find all this terribly exciting, I don't. I like my life just fine, thank you."

"You haven't told me much about your life and hey, we've got all night. Tell me what a lifestyle expert does. Do you get up in the morning and make your bed with a dozen pillows placed just so? And then spend an hour deciding what to wear and getting your hair just so? And then making exotic tea and french pastry for breakfast with a table set just so with real silver and china and cloth napkins?"

"You're mocking me. It's not wise to mock someone who could put you in prison with their testimony, Ace."

"But you wouldn't do that, now would you? Not because you like me all that much, but because you know in your heart that I'm innocent."

Innocent. Premeditated murder of Peter Blakemore, Jr. was probably about all Ace was innocent of. She suspected he was a born journalist and would do most anything to get a story. He'd be relentless in his pursuit of what he wanted. He'd use guile, charm and his extraordinary good looks and do whatever it took to win.

He was a mental athlete, competing in a cerebral arena. Outmaneuvering was a skill he'd have honed to perfection. Was he doing that now? Were they really going to be off the road tomorrow night or was he lulling her with a false sense of security?

"You're not jumping to confirm my claim of innocence I notice," Ace said, taking her shoe off.

"What are you doing?" Chloe demanded when he started rubbing her foot.

"Giving you a foot massage. Try not to jump out of your skin, will you. It's just a harmless form of relaxation I thought might help you fall asleep."

Harmless? She thought not. Foot massage in and of itself might be harmless. But it wasn't harmless in his hands. It was as erotic as hell and she had a feeling Ace knew it.

But she wasn't going to give him the satisfaction of squirming. She steeled herself not to notice the skill in his touch.

"Is this one of your investigative techniques you use to get your subjects to tell you what you want to know?" she asked, certain it would be very effective.

"No, I use it to get my subjects to do what I want them to do." His tone was wickedly suggestive.

He was bored, and playing with her just for the sport of it, she knew.

She pulled her foot away from him. "Forget it Ace, it won't work. I'm not going to curl up and go to sleep with my head in your lap."

"How about just the your head in my lap part . . ."

She kicked him and he laughed, a deep pleasurable laugh.

Thirteen

Darrow Smith dreaded the early morning meeting with Peter Blakemore. Like most really successful men, Blakemore was an early riser. Darrow knew as he pulled up to the Blakemore estate that he was going to be called on the carpet. Was even more certain of it when he saw the mayor's car parked in the circle drive next to the fountain.

By the time he was shown to the library, Darrow had a pounding headache. He took a seat next to the mayor, who merely grunted at Darrow's greeting.

Blakemore was sitting at his desk staring at the framed picture in his hand. Darrow remembered seeing it. The picture was an old one taken of Blakemore's young wife and Jon and Peter when they were toddlers.

Darrow supposed he should cut Blakemore some slack as his son was being buried later in the day.

Blakemore looked up from the picture frame and set it back on the corner of his desk. "Jon is all I have left."

"If we had a decent Chief of Police maybe Peter's killer wouldn't have gotten away," the mayor offered, eager to throw blame away from himself.

"And maybe if we had a mayor who wasn't the town drunk we'd know who brought this Ash Worth to town to investigate in the first place. Maybe we could have prevented your son's death," Darrow countered.

"My son is dead and all the excuses the two of you can make are not going to bring him back. I want his killer, Darrow. What have you got for me on him?"

"Not a lot. All I've been able to turn up on him is that he's a crack investigative journalist for the *Chicago Tribune*. He's a bit of a ladies' man, but he's never been married. He lives alone and travels light. Doesn't seem to have any family that I could turn up. The closest person to him is a Jane . . ." he paused to flip open the small notebook he always carried, ". . . Jane Talbert. She's an investigative reporter for the *Chicago Tribune* too. They were involved romantically as an item a few years back, but now their relationship is strictly professional. They team up for stories sometimes."

"Did you talk to her?"

"No."

The mayor made a disparaging noise, and Darrow explained.

"Zeke and Jon followed Ash and Miss Pembrook to Jane's place, but she wasn't there. I tried calling several times but couldn't get an answer."

"Well keep trying. She might be the key to all this. What's the latest report on Zeke and my son? Where are they now?"

"Zeke called last night from Philadelphia."

"Philadelphia? Where the hell are they going?"

"The more important question is—why? Both of them are from Chicago," Darrow said, watching the mayor fidget with his vest where Darrow knew he kept a flask of whiskey hidden.

"Whatever the reason, the two of you had better find out. Because I promise you if I go to jail, the two of you are coming with me."

* * *

"Aren't you kinda bucking a major trend? Don't you find it ironic that when most women are relaxing the standards of domesticity you're raising them?" Ace posed, with his terrier-like determination to get to the heart of exactly what it was Chloe Pembrook did, the following morning as they drove to New York.

Both of them had slept better in the back of the car than either had imagined possible. And somehow when they'd awoke, Chloe had had her head in Ace's lap . . . something she took great pains not to notice.

He was finding it a great distraction to pester her. "Aren't you setting standards no woman can achieve?"

Chloe wasn't unaware of that argument. It had been used before on her by reporters and her feminist detractors who thought women's work as it used to be called was limiting to women. She didn't agree. It was her belief that the baby had been thrown out with the bath water when women gave up completely on the niceties of making a home.

"You make me sound like someone's mother-in-law showing up with white gloves to test for dust," she sniffed.

"Well, aren't you?" he nudged.

"No. I think I provide ideas, not standards. I try to inspire people to infuse their lives with the genuine pleasure of taking care of their homes, and the joy that comes from preparing a good meal. And I must be doing something that strikes a chord. My column in *Chicago* magazine reaches over a million women. My books are best sellers and I have the offer of a spot on a nationally syndicated television show."

"But don't you feel like you're keeping women in

their place? Don't you feel guilty, after all the struggle for women not to be kept down with domesticity?"

"I never said it was something only women could do. Lots of my fans are men. It doesn't matter if a man or a woman makes the home, or if they share the tasks. All that matters is that we start to take pleasure in what we do again. Speed is the demon that has taken over our lives. And all work has to be dead serious. Why can't some work be performed so that it's fun while you do it, instead of something to be endured and gotten over with as quickly as possible. Life has become oppressive, and we are partly our own oppressors. Slowly we've eliminated all the little human comforts until we're nothing more than sterile robots with lists to cross off to prove our worth, the pleasure all in the crossing off and not in the doing, the living."

"Bossy little thing, aren't you?"

"I am not bossy," she said, as a light rain began to dot the windshield of the car.

"Don't go and get all huffy on me. I never said there was anything wrong with being bossy. Anyway, it's not like you could have avoided being bossy. You're an only child just like me, wanting to be in control comes with the territory. We're the worst possible combination, you know."

"That shouldn't be a problem much longer. If Jane comes through for you tonight, you'll have your story and I'll have my freedom. Both of us will be happy."

"Jane will come through. You can count on it. She always comes through."

"Tell me a little about Jane. What's she like? I keep picturing her in tights, a cape and wearing magic gold bracelets on her wrists."

Ace laughed.

"Jane would get a chuckle out of that. Superwoman, she's not. Jane has a mouth that won't quit." He thought it politic not to mention that Jane had a body that wouldn't quit either. "Jane's her own woman, but she's a soft touch underneath all her bluster of a tough surface. She's blond like you, but with rougher edges, from having grown up on the street. She won't take nothing off no one—man or woman. And she's the best in a crisis. I think a lot of Jane. She's a peach."

"Sounds like the two of you might have more than just a professional relationship going for you. Are the two of you . . . an item?"

"Usta be. But Jane and I found out we were better friends than lovers. It was our shared excitement over getting a story that drew us together in the end. So we stopped being lovers and remained being friends."

Chloe wondered if Jane would tell the same story. If Jane shared the same view of their relationship or if instead Jane had settled for whatever piece of Ace she could have.

It was easy to see where a woman could get hooked on Ace. He had a physical magnetism that could cause painful withdrawal pangs, she was sure, if you allowed yourself to get hooked on it.

She'd been smart enough to avoid that when it would have been easy not to. The combination of close quarters shared, and danger, was combustible at the slightest hint of fire.

She'd felt the heat, there was no denying that.

But she'd withstood the temptation to find out what it would feel like to have Ace's lips conquer hers—and more.

"Tell me about your grandmother," she said, not wanting to linger on Jane and Ace, and why the thought of them together disturbed her.

"Grandmother will love you. She's the one responsible for whatever manners I have. She defines gracious living. There's always a project afoot with her. And she'll rope you into helping.

"Gardening season is the worst. She grows rows and rows of green and purple decorative cabbages with ruffled leaves just because she likes the way they look so pretty. And guess who gets to spade her garden if he's about. I try to visit in the off-season."

Chloe smiled, picturing the fanciful garden of cabbages. "It does sound as if we'll get on."

"Like ducks to water and that's what worries me. I don't want to think what a formidable pair the two of you will make. Lucky for me Jane will be there. She thinks gracious living consists of paper plates on hand for the take-out pizza."

"Guess Jane would have loved the Vista motel . . ." Chloe found herself snipping.

"Nah, she'd have bitched about that place too. She even complains about all the butterflies that swarm around grandmother's flower garden. I keep telling her she's too young to be a curmudgeon, but she goes right on complaining anyway."

Ace reached to straighten the rear-view mirror and the sunlight glinted off the silver bracelet on his wrist. It was an MIA bracelet and she'd been wanting to ask him about it from the first time she saw it. However, she'd sensed it was something he didn't want to talk about and so she'd refrained from asking until now. Since they were almost at the end of their journey, she was emboldened to ask.

"Can I see your bracelet?"

"I never take it off."

"I'm sorry. It's sentimental to you then?"

"It reminds me . . ."

"Of who?" she blurted, impulse overruling her natural good manners.

"It's not of who, but of what."

"I don't understand," Chloe said, puzzled.

"This bracelet reminds me that the truth is a very elusive commodity. That people will lie to you given half a chance. And that you will then make decisions based on misinformation—decisions that could affect your whole life. So I wear the bracelet, never take it off, to remind me to always question, always dig until I'm as certain as I can be that I'm being told the truth."

"Whose name is on the bracelet?" she asked, fascinated all the more by his explanation, even if she didn't fully understand what he was telling her.

"It doesn't matter." His tone of voice said the topic was closed to discussion and so she let it drop. There wasn't any point in pursuing it when he'd made up his mind.

"All in all, I guess you have to admit we have been very lucky so far, haven't we," she said, changing the subject.

"Lucky?" He turned to glance at her with a look of confusion on his face. "I wouldn't call spending the last couple of days running from a murder rap lucky by any stretch of the imagination. Whatever are you talking about?"

"What I meant was that Jon and Zeke haven't been able to follow us or they'd have burst in on us by now. And we haven't been run off the road, well, there was that one time at the exit ramp, but I'm sure that was just some reckless kid. And aside from the flat tire, our luck on the road has held up very well."

"I guess you're right about that. It could have gone worse for us, that's for certain."

"And we dropped from front burner to back burner news very fast. That was a break, a real break. Otherwise we'd stand the chance of someone recognizing us and turning us in. In fact, if only we were better fixed for cash this wouldn't have been so awfully bad."

Ace began maneuvering the car over to the far right lane. "We need to get gasoline. So if you need to use the ladies' room, please do it now."

They both saw the flashing lights up ahead at the same time.

Fourteen

Ace hadn't gotten any further than the middle lane, when traffic crawled to a congested standstill.

"Can you see, is it an accident?" Chloe asked.

"No, I can't see a thing but the flashing lights. I hope to heaven it is an accident, and of course, that no one was hurt."

"What else could it be?"

"A roadblock. And I've got the sick feeling that that is what it is. Yep, there's police cars sideways on the highway I'll bet, and they're checking cars for something, or someone or *two someones.*"

Chloe swallowed dryly. "You don't think—?"

"Maybe you shouldn't have spoken so soon about us being lucky on the road. Someone must have spotted us or your friend Julie turned us in reporting her car was missing. Someone may just have spotted the car. That's the downside of car phones. They can rat on you from the road."

"Do you really think Julie would have . . ."

"She's your friend, what do you think?"

"I don't know. We left the note. Of course, she couldn't know for sure if I wrote it willingly. She might be worried that I'm in danger. I mean, if she's heard about the murder and your kidnapping me, it would only be logical for her to report her car stolen and me missing. I'd do the same thing and so would you."

"Maybe," he conceded.

"Wait a minute. It couldn't be Julie. They went on vacation for a week. She wouldn't be back yet."

"Things happen, people get sick, they break legs, they change their minds. They could have come back early. We can't rule out anything."

"Maybe we're jumping to conclusions. Maybe it is an accident. Why don't you get out of the car and try to see if you can tell, or if the word is being passed back. We're not moving anyway."

He turned off the ignition and followed her suggestion without argument, surprising her.

Chloe didn't know how she felt. Part of her was hoping it was a roadblock and part of her was hoping it wasn't. The more time she spent with Ace, the more confused she became. It was more than sexual chemistry she tried telling herself. Her self didn't seem all that convinced.

Her self reminded her how vulnerable she was. Reminded her Ace was an oasis in a long dry desert that represented her love life. She was thirsty.

But was she dangerously thirsty?

Ace returned to the car.

"Is it an accident—"

"No such luck."

"It's a roadblock," she sighed.

"Bingo. Give the woman the prize money."

"What are we going to do?"

"Turn on the radio," he instructed, putting the car back in gear and inching forward behind the car ahead of them. Traffic was barely moving, when it moved at all.

"What am I looking for?" she asked, trying to find a static-free station. What had tuned in, in Philadelphia, wasn't working as they approached New York.

"The news. Find a top forty station. Maybe if we're

lucky the roadblock isn't for us. There should be some sort of bulletin if the police are looking for someone local."

She pushed the tuning button, going through stations until she got a strong signal, then left it on that station while they waited to inch up to the roadblock.

Chloe looked at the wooded terrain along side the highway. "How about if I drive through the roadblock and you circle around through the woods and I pick you up when I get past the roadblock and out of sight?"

Ace looked over at her. "Let me get this right. You drive the car up to the roadblock while I run through the woods and then you pick me up on the other side . . ."

Chloe nodded.

"I think there are a few flaws in that scenario. One, I'd have to trust you not to get up to the roadblock and turn me in, two I'd have to hope there were no officers combing the woods along side the roadblock, and three, I'd have to hope that if you didn't turn me in, the police at the roadblock didn't recognize you as the celebrity who's been recently kidnapped and missing."

"You don't trust me?"

The radio music was interrupted by a news bulletin distracting them.

"A roadblock has been put up on highway 95 as police search for the teenage boys who gunned down two police officers when they stopped them for a traffic violation. One of the policemen was pronounced dead at the scene of the shooting and the other is in critical condition. Traffic has slowed to a standstill so you might want to avoid the area. We'll have more news on this manhunt as it becomes available."

"They aren't looking for us," Chloe said. Her body relaxed.

"That's a break," Ace agreed. "But we're still not out of this yet."

"What do you mean?" Chloe asked, as Ace inched the car forward again.

"I mean there's a warrant out for my arrest for the murder of Peter Blakemore, Jr. and the kidnapping of Chloe Pembrook, remember?"

"Yikes." Chloe grimaced, rubbing her temples. It was hot in the car even with the windows down. They couldn't turn on the air conditioning because they were low on fuel.

"And," Ace said, wiping the perspiration off his upper lip and eyeing the fuel gauge, ". . . if we run out of fuel, we're toast."

"I think this is where we pray."

"Like I haven't been doing that all along."

"I've got an idea," Chloe said after each had sat in silent prayer and reflection while the cars ahead of them moved ever so slowly forward.

"I'm not going in the woods . . . and neither are you. We're even easier prey on foot."

"No, I'm not talking about the woods. I'm talking about trying to make the odds work a little better in our favor. Switch places with me and let me drive. I'll put my dark sunglasses on and pull my hair back in a ponytail so I won't be easily recognized. You put my reading glasses on and pretend to be dozing with the map in your hands. I'll pass you off as my shiftless older brother."

"I've got a better idea."

He was a man, of course he would. Chloe listened patiently, unprepared for his improvement on her idea.

"Switching places is good, the sunglasses and all are

good, but I think it would be more believable if you pass me off as your husband. We're newlyweds. Hopefully it won't get as far as driver's licenses."

"Newlyweds!"

"Yeah, you'll do great at it. You're already blushing." Ace grinned—waiting for her to acquiesce to his spin on her plan.

Maybe she would turn him in.

Unfortunately, she did see the wisdom in his idea. They were from out of state on their honeymoon, it was a logical and easy explanation for the license plates on Julie's car.

"Okay," she agreed, and they got out of the car and changed places.

People up ahead were starting to get annoyed and horns were honking. Some of the drivers were climbing out of their cars to sit on the roofs so they could see what was going on up ahead. The guy next to them was talking on his car phone and doing business like he was at his desk. A few others like him were prepared to wait patiently, but mostly the crowd was hot and frustrated.

As they themselves were, with an added fillip of anxiety. Could they pull this off without getting caught, or was this the end of the line for Ace.

What would she do if they arrested him and took him off to jail? Would they impound Julie's car? Would they arrest her? If they did, what would it do to her career? That was a selfish thought and she felt ashamed, a moment after thinking it.

But she needed to think ahead, something she hadn't been doing. She'd been letting Ace lead the way and she'd followed in his wake. True, it wasn't as if she'd had a lot of choice, but still she hadn't acted so passive since her marriage.

"Are you nervous?" she asked Ace as she pulled her

hair back into a ponytail, her hands shaking from nerves over their predicament.

"What do you think?"

"Yeah, I guess that was a dumb question, huh?" She dug in her purse for her dark sunglasses and slipped them on when she found them.

"Don't be so hard on yourself. You've been quite a sport about all this. If we make it through, I'm going to owe you big time."

Chloe smiled. "Then I'll occupy myself with thinking of how you can repay me."

Ace lifted an eyebrow. "As long as it doesn't involve high tea . . ."

"You mean your grandmother hasn't instructed you in the joys of high tea?" It was Chloe's turn for a wicked grin, as she tried to diffuse some of the tension that was inching up in the car as they drew closer to the roadblock that the police had slapped up.

"Why do you think I specifically said, no high tea? Grandmother dotes on it and me and in that order, I do believe."

"You poor dear." Chloe couldn't help the giggle that escaped as she pictured Ace dutifully accompanying his grandmother to high tea.

"You must love her very much," she said, her opinion of him rising. Any man who'd accompany his grandmother to high tea had some redeeming quality.

"Grandmother is a real charmer," he admitted, with a warm smile in his eyes. "It's not like I plan to spade her garden or accompany her to high tea when I visit, I just find myself doing those things. It's like she casts some sort of magic spell on me."

Chloe knew that spell was probably called love.

It could make you do a lot of things you wouldn't ordinarily do.

It could make a loved little boy keep going home to the one place he knew he could always count on getting that unconditional love. Especially when he'd been disinherited and shunned by the rest of his family.

She and Ace had a lot more in common than she would care to admit.

They inched ever closer to the roadblock up ahead until they were only two cars away. The flashing red lights atop the police cars made Chloe's adrenaline race along her veins.

The policemen's faces were grim. One of their own had been killed and it brought home to each of them how tenuous their hold on life was in a dangerous profession in an increasingly unsettled culture.

The music on the radio stopped as a news bulletin interrupted them once again.

"This just in. A second policeman shot this afternoon has had his condition upgraded to serious after surgery to remove the bullet in his abdomen. A manhunt is being conducted by police for the two teenagers who shot and killed his partner. So far roadblocks and searchers have not turned up the suspects. We will keep you informed of any developments in this fast-breaking story with bulletins and news at the top of the hour."

"Can you tell what they're doing?" Ace asked from the passenger seat.

Chloe had the better view as she was just behind the car being stopped ahead of them. Ace's view was obstructed by the police car.

"The one policeman is talking to the driver, while the other one is directing traffic. He's looking in the back seat. And now he's waving them on."

"Well, I guess this is it," Chloe said, pressing her

foot to the gas and approaching the officer waving them forward.

"Not a great way of phrasing it," Ace grumbled, as he closed his eyes and pretended to sleep.

Fifteen

"Ma'am," the police officer said as he waved her forward and Chloe pulled the car forward to stop along side him.

Out of the corner of her eye Chloe could see Ace slouched down in the seat with the map unfolded across his lap. He'd put on her reading glasses, but his eyes were closed.

Chloe looked up at the graying police officer who had to bend low to see into the car. Infusing her voice with innocence, she asked, "What's going on officer? Are we in any danger?"

"A police officer has been killed and his partner has been wounded," he answered, his expression grim. "Hell of a thing to come back to on my first day after being off on medical leave for being shot myself. The worst of it is a couple of kids did the shooting. The whole damn country seems to have gone trigger happy. There's no respect for anything anymore." He glanced over at Ace who kept up his pretense of sleeping.

"I'm sorry to hear about the officers," Chloe said hastily, meaning to distract the officer. "My husband and I are on our honeymoon. We've come all this way to visit New York City. I want to see Niagara Falls, but he keeps trying to talk me out of it. He says it's too far to drive."

A hint of a grin tilted the corner of the police officer's thin lips as he noted, "You do seem to have worn him plumb out, ma'am."

Chloe didn't have to fake the blush that crept up her neck to her face.

"Go on through," the officer said, waving them on as an impatient motorist began honking. "Ah, keep your britches on, you're not going anywhere until we say so," the officer yelled out to the traffic jam as he motioned another car forward when Chloe pulled away.

Chloe felt the muscles in her back and shoulders untense as she floored the gas pedal to pick up speed and leave the roadblock behind. Their ruse had worked. She hadn't given the police officer any reason to become suspicious and check their driver's licenses.

"Don't," she warned, not daring to look over at Ace.

"What?" he asked, having difficulty controlling his mirth.

"Don't say it."

"You mean about your being such a voracious lover that you plumb wore me out?" He gave in to laughter, annoying her.

"It's not funny," she fumed.

"Right." And then he began laughing all over again. When he regained control of himself, he told her to pull off the highway at the next exit so he could take over the driving.

She told him no.

And made it stick.

"I can't believe we're stuck in this mess. What in the hell is going on?" Jon Blakemore asked, as Zeke stuck his head out the window of Jon's car stranded with everyone else in the snarled traffic.

"A roadblock's been set up ahead."

"You don't think—"

"I don't know. Why don't you mosey on up real casual-like and keep an eye out while you stay inconspicuous. I want to know if they detain Ash Worth and Miss Pembrook. Your daddy isn't going to like it if they do."

"You're right about that," Jon agreed, putting the car in park and letting Zeke slide over while he went to see what he could find out about the roadblock and the car they were tailing.

He'd missed his brother's funeral. Things had better not go wrong now. He had plans to make Ash Worth pay for what he'd done.

Plans to take Ash Worth out right now if the police decided to detain him. He'd deal with his daddy later, make him see that it was the only way. You couldn't let people get away, couldn't let them do you wrong and not pay.

Peter Blakemore, Sr. didn't hear any of the words the preacher was saying over his son's grave. The scent of flowers was sweet and overpowering. People had paid their homage to him because they owed their living to him. He owned them just like he owned every machine in Blakemore Chemical.

He wasn't numb with grief over his son's death as everyone thought. He was filled with rage over someone, anyone having the audacity to cross him. Ash Worth would not get away with his act of defiance. It would have been far wiser for him to have given the evidence over. Then he *might* have had a chance of staying alive. Now he was a dead man.

Peter Blakemore had every confidence his only surviving son and Zeke Francis would return with the

evidence Ash Worth had gathered against Blakemore
Chemical. And when they did, he would finish the
job, if Jon hadn't already.

The boy had a bad temper he hadn't yet learned to
control.

A bad temper could be a dangerous thing.

The preacher finished his words of solace and
stepped back to allow those gathered at graveside to
pass by the casket for the final time.

Peter Blakemore, Sr. stood watching.

Until he stood alone.

Mayor Billy Whitehouse's snoring woke him up to
a room filled with bright sunshine.

He sat up in bed, his head groggy from a hangover
from the binge he'd tooted on the night before. A
drinking binge meant to chase the demons away. A
binge that had succeeded in doing just that. He'd
passed out cold.

But now there was the devil to pay.

He'd miss the funeral.

And in so doing had arranged his own.

He reached for the bottle under his bed. The hell
with it.

He didn't have to answer to anyone.

He was the mayor.

Darrow Smith arrived at the cemetery just as Peter
Blakemore, Sr. was leaving.

"Sorry I missed the funeral, sir. I was on a call with
a private eye from Chicago I've engaged to see what
he can dig up on Ashley Clayton Ellsworth. Let's see
what happens when we turn over the rocks in his life.
You never know what might crawl out. I find it curious

that he seems to have no past. He's got to be hiding something. I'd bet Billy Whitehouse's liver on it."

"Not much of a bet," the older man said, crumbling the rose in his hand in his fist.

Darrow followed Jon's father as he walked to the black limo waiting on the winding cemetery path.

Before the older man got into the limo he turned to the chief and said, "I'll make it worth your while to find out who brought Ash Worth to town. Find out if he came here on his own or if he was tipped off."

Darrow stood watching as Jon's father then got in the limo and the driver closed the door. The window of the limo slid down as the driver went around to get in and drive.

Cold eyes were behind the order that came from the limo. "An example has to be made. No one crosses me. No one."

The limo window then slid closed and Darrow watched it pull away and travel down the winding path until it was out of sight.

He never should have taken this job.

But he had.

And it was too late now for regret.

Or too early.

When Darrow Smith was gone too, a lonely figure strolled to the fresh grave after the casket had been lowered and the cemetery workers had left.

"I never meant for this to happen. I promise you I never meant for this to happen."

The words were carried on the wind as a cloud passed over the sun casting the grave site in darkness as if someone had switched out a light.

* * *

"Well, what's going on?" Zeke asked when Jon returned to the car.

"Some kids shot a cop and so the place is crawling with cops looking for the kids. That's the reason for the roadblock tying up everything."

Jon inched the car closer, guesstimating they were about five minutes from their turn at the roadblock. "What about Ash and the woman?"

"They made it through. She's driving."

"She's driving? What do you mean she's driving? I thought she was his hostage."

"I don't know. But I tell you she was driving. Maybe they've gotten friendly, if you know what I mean," Jon said suggestively.

"Yeah, maybe. Or maybe he was holding a gun on her."

"I don't think so. He was asleep."

"What?"

"He was sitting beside her asleep."

"You got that close? You didn't let yourself be seen, did you?"

"She's never seen me before. She wouldn't be suspicious of me, if she did see me."

"*Jon*—"

"Calm down. Don't worry—I wasn't seen. I know what I'm doing."

Zeke seriously doubted that.

Or maybe he just didn't want to think about what Jon's plans might be.

It was their turn. The police officer was motioning them forward.

"Just keep your mouth shut, Jon. I'll handle this."

"You don't have anything to worry about. Neither of us has been carded in years. They aren't likely to suspect us of being teenagers. Besides, just flash your badge and we're through."

"We don't want to be noticed or remembered—"

"Oh, right."

"So are you going to tell me where your grandmother lives now?" Chloe asked as they entered the Holland Tunnel.

"She lives in the Hamptons."

Chloe whistled. "Very posh."

"Old money, not new," Ace informed her. "The place has been in the family forever."

"Is she your maternal grandmother?"

"How did you know?"

"Just a lucky guess."

"How about your grandparents? I thought you said you lived with them. Aren't you close to them?"

"They died. Within three months of each other. And like my parents, they didn't need a kid around. They were everything to each other. I guess relating patterns get passed down through families."

"Sometimes. Sometimes not. I got disinherited because I broke the unspoken pattern. How about you, Chloe? You planning on a kid?"

"Maybe. If I have one, I won't shut it out or shuttle it around the way I was."

"You mean you'd give up your career and stay home?"

"I haven't thought about it," she lied.

Sixteen

Chloe found herself fading in Queens.

"What are you doing?" Ace asked when she exited 495 in Queens.

"I'm falling asleep. I need some coffee to keep me going. We need to stretch our legs anyway. And you can drive, okay?"

"Coffee, yeah," he said, suddenly agreeable.

She stopped at the first place she came to. The sign outside said, Jake's Joint.

"At least it's not a fern bar," Ace grumbled, holding open the door for her to enter.

Chloe squinted through the smoky haze that greeted them, and headed for the bar to the left of the pool tables. Long rectangular lights hung over the pool tables to spotlight the games in progress.

"What'll you have?" the bartender with a small dangling gold cross earring and a gold-capped tooth asked.

"Coffee," Chloe answered, digging in her purse. "You do serve coffee here, don't you?"

The bartender nodded, studying Ace. "Yes, ma'am. We've got eighteen flavors. Would you like to see the list?"

"No. Just make it anything strong and black."

"How about you? You having the same thing as your sister? Or do you have other preferences?"

"Just bring me a coffee," Ace answered. "Me and

my woman have got a long drive ahead of us." Ace slid his arm around Chloe's shoulder.

"Can I buy you that coffee?"

"What?" Ace turned to his right to see a guy in an expensive, perfectly tailored suit smiling at him.

"No thanks, I think we've got it covered," Ace said as Chloe pulled some bills from her purse and laid them on the bar before them.

Ace turned back to Chloe and pulled her closer.

"What did he want?" Chloe asked, misunderstanding the reason for Ace's wanting her attention.

"He wanted to buy the coffee."

"You shoulda let him. I thought we were short on cash. It's not like he can't see I'm here with you. You don't have to be so protective of me."

The bartender returned with their coffee, and set two steaming cups before them. He set a bottle of Amaretto in front of Ace.

"What's that for?" Ace asked. "We didn't order any liquor."

"It's for your coffee from the gentleman cuing up to break balls," the bartender answered, nodding to the short blond body-builder in a jean jacket.

"Isn't that sweet," Chloe piped in. "Tell him I said thank you. You know, Ace, I really should get out more. Maybe you're right. Maybe I don't take enough chances." She took a sip of her coffee while Ace choked on his. "I don't give men a chance, and I need to if I don't want to be married to my job. I mean look at all the great-looking men in just this one bar."

"I think it's safer if I don't."

"Oh come on, Ace. No one is going to challenge you to a fight over me. This isn't high school. Just relax and drink your coffee and try not to show you're jealous while I enjoy the view."

"I'm not jealous," Ace bit off, tipping the Amaretto in his coffee in desperation.

"You're not jealous, right. That's why you put your arm around me when we first came in, to announce to all the men here that I'm with you so they don't get any ideas about poaching. But you needn't get so annoyed just because they ignored your warning and are flirting with me. It's just harmless, Ace. You know how men are. They have to prove—"

"Shut up and kiss me."

"What!"

"I said, shut up and kiss me, woman."

"Woman? What is this, you get around other men and you grow antlers and regress a species back? Really, Ace. I don't think it's necessary for you to—"

"Ah hell . . ." He cut off her rebuttal by taking her mouth with his in a thoroughly captivating conquest. The kiss was showy and obvious.

That was a fact she caught onto right away. The fact that she was part of a display put on for the benefit of the men watching.

She pushed him away.

"If I were you, I'd return my kiss with a little more enthusiasm, Chloe."

"Look, Ace. I refuse to be a part of your overt public display of affection. I don't know what's come over you, but I'm not dancing to this tune."

"You'd better if you don't want me to have to dance with the guy whose Amaretto I just drank. He's coming this way with 'dance with me' in his big brown eyes."

"You dance with—" Chloe looked to where Ace was staring and the reality of the place dawned on her. "Oh . . ."

"Yeah, oh."

She gave Ace tongue.

When Ace recovered, his friend had backed off.

"You're a real charmer Chloe," he said, his tongue licking at the blood where she'd bit his lip to punish him for not telling her what kind of bar they'd stumbled into right away, for letting her make a fool of herself prattling on about all the men flirting with her.

"I try," she answered, smiling, refusing to be chastised for drawing blood.

"What are they doing now?" Darrow Smith barked into the phone, frustrated as hell. His sixth sense was ringing bells. This whole mess wasn't blowing over quickly, wasn't showing any signs of resolving itself or ending at all well. Each day that went by worried him more.

"They're having coffee in a gay bar."

"They're what?"

"They stopped for coffee at a place called Jake's Joint. Wait a minute, they're coming back out. I guess they just needed to wake up. They must not have slept too well in the back seat of the car. It's not something I'd recommend, I'll tell you," Zeke said.

"Where are you exactly?"

"We're in Queens."

"Queens, where the hell are they going?"

"I don't know, Chief."

"Wait a minute. You don't suppose they're planning on leaving the country? Maybe they're headed to JFK airport. I want you to call me immediately, if it looks like that's the case," Darrow demanded, getting worked up at the very idea.

"Sure, Chief. Do you want us to detain them if they do purchase a ticket, or do you want us to catch the same plane? They're bound to spot us if we get on the same plane, don't you think?"

"I want you to detain them. Whatever you do, don't
let them leave the country, do you understand, Zeke?"

"I understand, Chief. And it looks like you might
be right," Zeke said, getting excited. "We're tailing
them now and they're picking up 678 which takes you
straight to JFK airport."

"Shit. Don't lose them whatever you do," Darrow
warned, popping an antacid tablet.

"Don't worry we'll find a way to detain them," Zeke
promised, ending the call.

"Damn, I forgot," Ace said, slapping the steering
wheel. "We need to get off the highway again."

"What'd you forget—to leave your phone number
etched on the bar at Jake's Joint?" Chloe couldn't resist
needling Ace about the misadventure of their last stop.

Ace just looked at her. "No, I need to try Jane at my
grandmother's."

They stopped at a deli when they got off the highway and Ace made his phone call while Chloe eyed a
tavern egg one of the customers was served. The spicy
breaded sausage wrapped around a hard-boiled egg
teased her nostrils making her salivate.

"Jane, good you're there," she heard Ace say and
was distracted from the food to his conversation.

"Do you have it?" he asked, a note of cautious anticipation in his voice.

"No, I came all this bloody way to smell the flowers
in your grandmother's garden. What do you think,
you putz? Of course, I have it. Where the hell are
you? Your grandmother has me weeding her garden
for heaven's sake. I may just kill you when you get
here if I break another nail. Do you know what a
French manicure costs?"

"I'm glad to hear you're so concerned about me. I almost got killed, you know."

"The way I heard it on TV, you killed someone and took a hostage. So lose the plea for sympathy, and tell me what the hell is going on."

"When I get there. Right now I need to know if the results were positive."

"The stuff was toxic, if that's what you're asking. Thanks again for sending me such a lovely package to unwrap. Next time I think you owe me flowers."

"Flowers are for funerals."

"Good, then I'll remember to send you some if you don't show up here soon."

"We'll be there in a couple of hours, I promise. All you have to do is keep grandmother from catching on to what is going on. I don't want her worrying about me, you understand. Just keep her focused on her flower garden."

"Easy for you to say, you're not the one digging around in manure. She claims it's the best thing for her prize-winning roses. I don't know how a flower that smells so sweet comes from—"

"Jane, I'd love to stay and listen, but I've got to get on the road if I'm going to get there by dark. We've already come up against one roadblock. Who knows what hurdles await us?"

"Will you stop with being a drama queen. You ran into a little trouble getting a story. It happens. Of course, most of us are smart enough not to take along a hostage to slow us down, but you always were a stubborn cuss, Ace. And I bet she's real pretty too, isn't she."

Chloe felt Ace look over at her and then she watched as he mumbled something into the telephone.

Was he talking about her to Jane?

A flood of questions swirled in her mind.

What would Jane think of her? Would Jane consider her a threat? Would she consider Jane a threat?

What was the real status of Jane and Ace's relationship? Had it ended badly? Had it ended at all?

Ace hung up the phone, ending her mental musing. He signaled he was ready to go.

"So does she have it?" Chloe asked, when they were back on the road.

"She has it."

"Then this is finally over soon."

"Just as soon as we get to grandmother's and get the evidence to the proper authorities."

"Maybe I'll still be able to get my column in. Maybe I can—"

"You're welcome."

"What?"

"I said you're welcome. You did say thanks for saving your life, didn't you?"

"Do you really think we've done it? That we're going to pull this off?"

"We seem to have so far. If our luck holds out, we should have Peter Blakemore, Sr. behind bars and you back to being whatever it is you are, very soon."

"And without luck . . . ?"

"We'll deal with that if it happens. But right now the sun is out, so don't be looking for any dark clouds to build on the horizon. Think positive."

"I thought I was the ostrich."

"You did pretty good, all in all," Ace admitted however reluctantly.

"Gee, thanks for the vote of confidence. Don't put yourself out."

"Chloe—"

"Okay, I'll be quiet and let you drive."

"No, that's not it. Is it me, or is traffic starting to back up . . ."

Seventeen

"You don't think it's another roadblock, do you?" Chloe asked, craning her neck.

"I don't know. I suppose it's possible. Turn on the radio and see if you can find something. How hard could a couple of kids be to catch?"

Chloe ran through the stations without luck. "Must be a breakdown or something up ahead," she suggested as the traffic slowed even more.

"Just in case, I'm going to start maneuvering over to the far lane. I don't want to get hung up again for hours. Jane's expecting us. What does traffic look like behind us? Can I make it over? I can't see past that blue van off my rear bumper."

"You're going to have to do it a lane at a time. I can't see that well either."

"Now?"

"Now."

Ace eased the car over one lane.

A black limo behind them honked impatiently and Ace glanced in the rear-view mirror. "Wait a minute, I think I might know the reason for the slowdown. I remember seeing a newspaper someone left lying on a table back at the deli. There was a headline about the president coming to New York to give a speech tonight."

Chloe glanced at the black limo behind them with

the darkened windows. "You think the president is behind you in that limo?"

"Of course not. We're heading toward the airport. He'd be going the other way. But I'll bet his flying in would snarl things up around the airport for security reasons."

Ace saw an inch or two opening and he forced his way over another lane. One more lane and he'd be able to exit if need be, Chloe thought.

"I like that song," Chloe said when the theme song from the *Lion King* came on.

"Figures," Ace mumbled. "You probably think Disney should run the world so it would be all nice and pretty."

"Not a bad idea," she answered positively, refusing to be baited.

When the song was over, the news at the top of the hour came on. The lead story was the bomb scare at JFK airport. Someone had called it in, and a search was being undertaken. Motorists were advised to avoid the area.

"You're a little late with your warning, pal," Ace said, turning off the radio and concentrating on finding his way over to the final exit lane.

"Be on the lookout for a motel. We're stopping at the first one we see and hiding out until traffic clears out. I don't want to get caught this close to the end of our journey."

The motel they pulled into had a vacancy and they got a room straight away on the second floor. A balcony ramp surrounded the second floor. It was metal and painted someone's idea of a festive blue.

The room itself was done in earth tones, if you considered dirt brown and bright orange earth tones. Evidently the new owner—the sign out front was made of canvas and slung over the previous permanent one—had only remodeled the outside of the motel to draw customers. Rightly, he figured most of the people who stayed at a motel near an airport were transient and he wouldn't have to worry about making an impression once he had their charge number. They wouldn't be repeat customers so why bother with the expense.

The room was ugly enough to make Chloe feel sick to her stomach.

Ace advised her to get over it, pointing out that at least it had a shower; an amenity they'd had to do without last night.

"If we're out of money, how'd you pay for these lovely accommodations?" Chloe wanted to know.

"I used my charge card. I figured we're close enough to our destination it won't matter. This time tomorrow at the latest we'll have everything straightened out and you'll be free of me."

"That long?"

"Go take a shower."

Chloe didn't argue. A shower was relief from the constant exposure to Ace's charms. He'd been growing on her—way too fast.

That bit of kissyface in the gay bar hadn't exactly helped cool things off either.

In the bathroom she stripped off her shorts, T-shirt and sneakers, then fiddled with the water until she had it a perfect temperature, before climbing into the shower stall.

As she stood beneath the stream of warm water she thought about how good it would feel to get dressed in something other than shorts, T-shirt and sneakers. Ace had yet to see her in anything else.

The soap the motel furnished wasn't the milled fragrant type she used. In fact she was fairly certain if the soap had a wrapper the first ingredient listed would be lye. The cloth she used to wash with was rough and thin.

She supposed she was spoiled.

Ace had called her a real charmer. It hadn't been meant as a compliment.

He didn't understand. A woman had to learn to stand up for herself. She couldn't afford to count on anyone or let anyone push her around. While she might look like a piece of fluff, she'd learned to hold her own.

Ace ought to understand that, being in a profession that entailed being shoved around.

She wondered again about the silver bracelet he wore on his wrist. He never took it off, so she couldn't get a really good look at it. It fit with the scruffy beard and mustache he'd allowed to grow during the several days they'd been on the run. He looked like the rebel he was.

What had she gotten herself into?

She'd bought his story without any sort of proof that he was who he said he was. Of course, there had been that news flash on television. But people changed. What if he'd covered one grim story too many and snapped, if only for that one brief moment when he'd killed Peter Blakemore, Jr.?

No, the trouble was, he appeared completely normal to her. Perhaps normal wasn't the right word, but he didn't appear loony crazy at any rate.

He only made her loony crazy.

She found herself imagining the most romantic—all the way to torrid—encounters with Ace. He had sexual chemistry to burn, of that one fact she was certain.

But she'd been cool.

She'd not let him get even a glimmer of his immense appeal to her. And that was the way she wanted to keep it. Just a little while longer and she could go back to her nice safe life.

Boring, her wicked mind edited.

She closed that mental door. That way led to trouble. Ace was not husband material.

Not that she was looking for a husband.

Or she hadn't been anyway.

Ace was the man you treated yourself to if you'd been married badly, or dumped. Any woman foolish enough to think he was serious about anything but his work was a foolish woman indeed.

It wasn't that he was one of the bad guys.

He wasn't.

As near as she could judge he had lots of fine qualities to recommend him. He was protective, sensitive (though he'd hate to hear that) and even honorable in his own way. He could have, after all, let her think he was one of the bad guys to get her to be his hostage. He could have held a gun on her the whole while they'd been on the run. He'd chosen instead to tell her he was one of the good guys instead of terrorizing her and he kept the gun in his carryall.

Thinking of bad guys, she wondered why they hadn't shown up. Was it possible that they'd made a clean getaway? The longer time passed without someone putting in a villainous appearance the more relaxed she became.

Danger did not fascinate her. She found nothing about it compelling. In fact she even liked her murder mysteries with the off-stage murders of the cozies.

Order, not the unexpected was what she appreciated. Order and justice. One should be held accountable for one's actions. Unfortunately the world around her had gone into a buck-passing frenzy.

Get a grip, she told herself, pulling a towel from the rack when she turned off the shower. Ace had her thinking politics and social change instead of lifestyle. She needed to put her mind back on business.

If she got the spot on television, she was planning to use her expanded celebrity to launch a series of lectures on lifestyle. After speaking she'd autograph her books. That would give her books a longer selling period, maybe she'd be successful enough to have a permanent back list that kept selling year round.

Hers were the kind of books people not only bought for themselves but as gifts to give to friends as well. Even busy career women were interested in entertaining, collections, decor, gardening and such. In fact they were some of her most loyal fans. While they didn't have time to garden, or for housekeeping, and cooking, they enjoyed reading about it and looking at beautiful pictures.

She smiled.

In a way, she supposed her books were, for women, comparable to *Playboy* for men. For many women the glossy pages were a fantasy. One they didn't expect to have, one that gave them pleasure just to look at.

Television excited her. It was a way to reach an expansive audience with her message that making small changes for the sake of beauty had a rippling effect. Television's negative images served a purpose, she supposed, but the power needed balancing with what could be right with the world.

No one seemed to know how to take care of anyone anymore, not even of themselves. Nurturing was important to well-being. So if the only way you could get the nurturing you needed was by doing it yourself in a very harried world, then she proposed to teach everyone how to do at least that.

A generation had been raised by women who'd abandoned the home for the workplace. They hadn't the time or energy to teach their children about making a

comfortable nest. And now everyone was suffering. At
the end of the day everyone was returning home to
homes that were houses. No warmth, no care, no love.
Had the world become a cold and unfeeling place or
was she fueled by the feelings of her own childhood?

No matter. She knew she was right about what she
had to contribute. She knew she could in a small way
make the world a better place—a more comfortable fit
for humans, who, if the news reports were any indication,
were feeling more and more stressed.

Balance was the key.

And it was the key even for her.

She hadn't followed her own beliefs, instead she'd
let her career take over her life. Spending time with
Ace had shown her how alone she was. How she used
being busy as a cover to hide the fact from herself that
no matter how much she tried, she couldn't provide
everything she needed for herself.

She needed a real man in her life. Not just a series
of long relationships that went nowhere.

And she needed to develop stronger friendships;
not just the sort like she had with Julie that consisted
of watering each other's plants when they were out of
town.

Julie!

She'd have to contact her first thing and explain
what had happened. They didn't have the kind of
friendship for Chloe to take the sort of liberties she
had.

Julie had a small nursery that specialized in bulb
flowers and herbs. They'd grown friendly because of
their shared love of forced flowers and fresh herbs in
their cooking. Each admired the other's work. Their
friendship centered around work. She realized she
knew little about Julie other than that she was married.

"Are you going to hide out in there all day?" Ace called, pounding on the door.

"I'm almost done," she called out, gathering up the towel and hanging it on the towel rack before opening the door to him. "It's all yours."

"I'll bet you used all the hot water, didn't you?"

She just flashed him a grin, and gave him her back.

He shook his head as he closed the door. A cold shower wouldn't be a bad idea, he thought, looking at the fogged up mirror that reflected his own heated state.

It was getting so the sound of her showering was almost too provocative for him to bear. His mind kept doing the darndest things. He kept imagining joining her and where that naturally led to wasn't hard to guess.

"You're a sad case," he admonished himself. "You don't even know how to keep your mind on business when your life is in danger."

So what's wrong with dying happy? his libido wanted to know as he stripped down.

He groaned and reached to turn on the cold water.

Eighteen

"So what have you missed the most these past few days?" Ace asked as they were trying to decide what kind of food to order. Chloe had vetoed pizza and Ace had vetoed Chinese.

Chloe considered a moment and was about to answer his question when Ace interrupted, "No, wait, let me guess. I know," he said, snapping his fingers and grinning. The scruffy beard only served to accentuate his, "come kiss me" mouth. "I bet you miss your laptop and your pinking shears the very most. Am I right?"

"Pinking shears?"

"Okay, your fancy sewing machine."

"Where did you pick up—"

"I recently did a story on sweatshops. You'd be amazed at all the stuff I keep up here when a story's over. You never know when you're going to need something—like now."

"I think it's time you had a garage sale," Chloe said, unimpressed.

"I'll tell you what I miss the most," he offered.

"Chicken," Chloe suggested, looking up from the phone book.

"No. I don't want chicken. I want something, I don't know, spicy maybe. Aren't you even a little interested in what I've missed the most these past few days?" he asked when she bent her head back to study the restaurant listings in the yellow pages.

"Female mud wrestling and tequila shooters, right?" she said, drily, not even bothering to look up to see if her insult had struck its well-aimed mark.

"You've wounded me sorely. At least give me a little credit for some taste. As it happens I prefer my liquor to come from micro-breweries."

"But I was right on about the mud wrestling, wasn't I?"

He made her look up to see his teasing nod. "What can I say?"

"How about Mexican?" Chloe suggested, giving up on her attempt to put down a man who already liked crawling on his belly when it came to entertainment.

"Mexican sounds good to me. Yeah, I could go for Mexican. Order something."

"Like what? Don't you want to select what you want to eat?"

"Surprise me. I'm not a picky eater. I like to eat with the same spirit of adventure that I make love with." He'd obviously meant to shock her.

She took the voltage and arced it back, "Oh then I was wrong . . . what you really missed was your trapeze."

"Why, Miss Chloe Pembrook, wherever did you hear of such things. You have only *heard* of such things, haven't you?"

She smiled way too sweetly as she dialed the number for the Mexican to-go order she placed, ordering extra jalapeño peppers on his order.

Twenty minutes later Ace had dozed off watching a game show on television and Chloe was making notes for her column on the back of an envelope she'd found in the desk drawer.

She rubbed her finger over her lips as she thought

about the right tone for her column after what had happened. Should she make note of it at all, or pretend it had never happened? Probably the latter. There were sure to be legal issues involved, so the less said was probably for the better in the long run.

Her hand smelled antiseptic, like the soap, instead of like vanilla which was the fragrance of her usual soap. Women had taken to wearing fragrance for themselves instead of to please men. CK—the new fragrance worn by both sexes—had been the most successful fragrance launch of late.

The bottle design would probably show up in the Museum of Contemporary Art. As would Calvin if he didn't start aging before his second wife.

Chloe's mind wandered to what Ace really would have missed most in the past few days, all kidding aside. She decided it would probably have been hearing some great live music—some blues maybe at Buddy Guy's Legends club on South Wabash.

From there her thoughts wandered to fantasizing a perfect date in Chicago with Ace. Here they both lived in the same great town and their paths had never crossed. She had to get out more—and apparently to nude mud-wrestling establishments that served Rolling Rock or Red Dog.

She wondered what Ace would think about her fantasy. Would he think she was a good date? She'd like him to take her to an intimate little theater on North Halstead for a Neil Simon play and then maybe a room with a queen-sized bed at the Richmont Hotel with a breakfast buffet for two.

No mud wrestling, no trapeze.

No games.

Well, maybe some consensual ones, she thought with a smile.

She looked over to where Ace lay asleep. He was a

complicated man, but he'd probably prefer a baseball game if one were to be had. A champion of lost causes, he'd be a Cubs fan for sure. A baseball hat would be the perfect topper to his outfit of T-shirt and snug jeans.

Concentrate. She really had to concentrate instead of mooning over her kidnapper like some lovestruck teenager. He wasn't courting her, she'd been thrust upon him by circumstance.

She looked away from Ace and down at her notes. While she had a savvy knack for predicting what would become a trend with regard to lifestyle, her knack still required the input of creativity and confidence. Now, when she was about to close her deal for television, was not the time for her to stumble.

Chloe couldn't allow her intuition to be colored by any fanciful romantic longing stirred up by danger, and forced proximity with an altogether too attractive man.

Sanity had to rule.

As did work.

She had to work hard to continue to solidify her image. It was important for her to present an image women could and would want to identify with.

Obsessive worked for her.

Or at least it had.

Her eyes strayed back to the man snoring softly on the bed. Was it uncommonly hot in the room? She went to fiddle with the air conditioner.

But she was only kidding herself. As long as she and Ace didn't act on the electricity that sparked by their rubbing against each other's psyches it was going to be hot wherever they were.

And, trouble was, she was dead certain acting on it would only up the wattage to mega-status. Acting on it would be a foolish impulse doomed to start something that held quicksand emotional pools sure to suck her under.

Besides who'd asked her?

Darrow Smith propped his feet up, ankles crossed, on his massive oak office desk. He admired the pair of dark-brown calfskin boots on his feet. A few months old and already they looked like old money. He smiled with satisfaction at the pleasure material things gave him. Growing up dirt poor had given him a love for what he'd been deprived of in his youth.

Maybe money didn't buy happiness, but it sure as hell brought a lot of smiles. If this damned mess with Ash Worth blew over, he had his eye on a new Chevy Blazer with sleek lines he planned to order loaded.

And if the damned mess didn't blow over, his boots would be pounding the pavement looking for work—if he was lucky.

The telephone on his desk rang, pulling him out of his worried musing.

It was the private investigator Darrow had hired to dig up information on Ash Worth or Ashley Clayton Ellsworth which was too big to get your mouth around, so he just thought of the fugitive as Ash Worth.

"Have you got something for me?" Darrow asked, trying not to sound over eager and failing.

"Sure do, Chief. I think I know where your boy is running to."

"Well, spill it man."

"He's going home to grandmother's house."

"His grandmother's house?" Darrow repeated, incredulous. "Are you sure about that?"

"Let's just call it a very expensive hunch, okay Chief. Your suspect belongs to a blue-blood old money family from East Hampton. They've been in the Blue

Book since forever. Ashley Clayton Ellsworth managed to get himself disinherited for some unknown reason and the only family member who didn't disown him is Sarabeth Ellsworth, his paternal grandmother."

Darrow rubbed his chin thoughtfully. "And you say this grandmother lives in East Hampton . . . that would fit as a possible destination. You got an exact address?"

"Is Tonya Harding trailer trash—of course I've got an exact address. It's a big old shingled place not far from Ralph Lauren's place I understand."

Darrow recognized the Tonya but was clueless on who Ralph was. He let it pass, though, as he wrote down the address the private eye gave him.

"Anything else you want me to find out?" the private eye asked, angling to drum up more business.

"No, you did good. Send me a bill."

"Glad to, Chief. Later."

Darrow hung up the phone and swung his feet down from his desk, feeling better than he'd felt in days. Maybe things would turn around.

He picked up the phone to call Peter Blakemore, Sr. For once he had news he wanted to share with him.

He wasn't at his office so he called Blakemore's home number.

The maid informed him that her employer had gone out to the cemetery.

Always glad of an excuse to get out, Darrow decided to relay the news in person. It was a warm day, but not hot. An afternoon thunderstorm right after lunch had cooled the air temporarily. He tuned in a country music station in the police car and relaxed for the first time in days, letting Wynonna Judd take him away.

He was in such a good mood that he even pulled into a GM dealership to check out the recreational vehicle he had a yen for. They had one in the color he wanted and it was tempting, but he decided not to count his chickens before they were hatched.

Zeke and Jonathon hadn't called in. He'd feel better about things once he'd talked to them and relayed the address he'd gotten from the private eye. The two men could scare the old woman into giving up whatever Ash Worth was going to East Hampton to claim. And they could destroy any evidence against Peter Blakemore, Sr. before her grandson even showed up.

Then he'd place his order for the exact vehicle he wanted. It'd be his reward.

Maybe even old Blakemore would be feeling magnanimous enough to spring for it because he was grateful.

Darrow laughed out loud as he got back in his car to head for the cemetery. Hell, what was he smoking? Blakemore was tighter than Silas Marner with his emotions. He expected Darrow to deliver.

And no one, no one smart anyway, disappointed Peter Blakemore, Sr.

Especially not when he already owned you.

Like he did Darrow.

Peter Blakemore signaled his driver to stop on the long winding road that sat above the site of his son's grave. It was a hell of a thing to visit your son's grave. Even worse when the person who'd murdered your son was out running free from justice.

Darrow had better not disappoint him.

The mayor was already history.

Darrow would be too if he didn't do the job he paid him to do.

His driver held the door open and Peter Blakemore got out and walked over to his son's grave. It was the last time he planned to visit it. He was only there to make sure the tombstone had been executed to his specifications. You couldn't trust anyone to do the job they promised.

No matter how well you paid them.

People just weren't to be trusted.

The sound of a car drew his attention and he watched the police chief park his police car and approach the plot where he stood.

"I've got some news," Darrow said when he joined him.

"You've got the evidence Ash Worth had on me?"

"No. Not yet. But I know where it is. I'm going back to the station now to wait for Zeke to call so I can give the information to him. I just thought you'd like to know I'm doing my job."

The cold look in Peter Blakemore's eyes said he'd expected him to be doing just that. There was no acknowledgment forthcoming.

Uncomfortable, Darrow looked at the new tombstone that had been set on Peter, Jr.'s grave.

"Those are beautiful," he commented on the dozen red roses laid against the tombstone, not knowing what else to say. "I'm sure Peter would have appreciated your bringing them."

Peter Blakemore's eyes turned frigid. "I didn't bring them. My wife was the one who loved flowers—red roses."

Nineteen

There was a sudden loud crash followed by the door to Ace and Chloe's motel room flying open to bang with a thud against the wall. A nervous Zeke Francis and a cool Jonathon Blakemore burst into the room waving guns they pointed at the both of them while barking orders.

"Leave her alone," Ace said, nodding to Chloe. "I'm the one you want. Just let her go."

Jonathon who was closest to Chloe, grabbed her and covered her mouth with his hand when it looked like she might scream. "Keep quiet, bitch."

Chloe's eyes were wide with fear and she followed Jonathon's order.

"And be still," Jonathon ordered when she continued trying to twist free of his grasp.

"Let her go, man. She doesn't know anything. I'll come with you, if you turn her free."

"You're not the one giving orders here," Zeke informed him, punctuating his words with the gun in his hand he had trained on Ace.

Ace glanced over at Jonathon. "Oh, let me guess who is—daddy, right?"

"Shut up," Jonathon bit off, twisting Chloe's arm behind her back and pushing it up high between her shoulder blades until she cried out in pain.

Ace started after Jonathon in a white-hot rage, but

Zeke's cool words and the point of a gun stopped him in his tracks. He didn't want to give the two men any excuse to rain a sudden hail of bullets on them.

"Where is it?" Zeke demanded.

"Where is what?" Ace asked.

"The evidence."

"What evidence?" Ace continued playing dumb.

"You were gathering evidence against my father's chemical plant. That's why you agreed to meet with my brother when you killed him."

"Who says I killed him?" Ace wasn't admitting to anything.

"She does," Zeke pointed to Chloe. "Gave us a real good description of you, too."

"He tried to kill me. Now I wonder why he'd do a thing like that if your family's business dealings were so squeaky clean?" Ace taunted, hoping Jonathon would make a tiny mistake that he could take advantage of.

"I'm not going to stand here and listen to the two of you argue." Zeke moved to the window and cut the cord on the window blind with a pocket knife he had on him. "Sit down over there," he ordered Ace.

"Why?" Ace asked, trying to buy time.

"The better to tie you up, dummy," Jon answered for Zeke.

Ace sat. There was no use arguing with two guns, not when he had Chloe's safety to consider.

Zeke jerked Ace's hands behind the chair back and began binding his wrists tightly. That done, he looped the blind cord around his chest several times and secured it. While Zeke was cutting another length of cord from the window blind Jonathon began working on Chloe.

"You'd better tell us what you know if you want us

to go easy on him. Where are you headed? He must have told you where he's taking you."

Chloe shook her head no.

"What does that mean?" Jon demanded. "He didn't tell you, or you won't tell us."

"He didn't tell me."

Good girl, Ace thought. She couldn't tell them what she didn't know. They'd leave her alone.

"You going to tie me up, too?" she asked, seeing the cord in Zeke's hand.

"No." Zeke bent to bind Ace's ankles together.

"Why are you tying me up? Why don't you just let the girl go . . . and . . ."

"And what?"

"I'll take you where I was going. I'll trade you that for the girl's freedom. She doesn't know anything, let her go."

"She was at the garage—" Jon interrupted.

"But she didn't overhear anything, I'm certain of it. We've been together night and day for days. She would have told me by now."

Ace could see the look of confusion on Chloe's face. What wasn't she supposed to know? he could see she was wondering. She had that look in her eyes again.

That look of distrust.

Her certainty that he was telling her the truth was beginning to crumble. She was wondering if Ace had been involved more than he'd let on.

She was wondering if he was one of the bad guys after all. Wondering if she'd been a fool.

He tried to catch her eye, but she wouldn't look at him.

"I've got a better idea for an exchange," Zeke said. "We take her with us. You go get the evidence you claim to have. And then we'll make us a little exchange. The girl for the evidence."

"No deal." Ace didn't want Chloe with Jon without any protection. Jon liked battering women too much. The least little excuse was all he needed.

"It's not like you have a choice," Zeke informed him, standing from his task.

"We're taking the woman with us. If you want her back, you know what to do." Zeke's words were final, brooking no further discussion.

"How am I supposed to find you to let you know I've got what you want?" Ace demanded, working his bound hands behind him, trying to loosen the cord.

"Easy. Call the chief. He'll let us know when you're ready to make the exchange. Once he sets up a time and place we'll do it. But if I were you, I'd not waste any time getting back to us. Jonathon isn't a patient sort, if you know what I mean." Zeke looked over to where Jon was holding Chloe, tighter than was necessary.

Zeke nodded to Jon and began making his way toward the door.

"No!" Ace cried out, knowing his demand was without hope. Zeke had made up his mind and Jonathon Blakemore was only too happy to follow Zeke's plan, tugging Chloe along with him.

"Wait—how am I supposed to go anywhere when I'm trussed up like this?" Ace demanded.

Zeke stopped at the door, reached in his pocket and pulled out a pocket knife. He opened the blade and tossed it end over end to land stuck in the floor a foot away from where Ace sat. "You're such a clever guy, I'm sure you'll find a way to free yourself once we've had enough time to stash the girl."

"If you so much as harm a hair on the girl's head, I promise you I'll—"

"Yeah, right," Jon smirked, pulling Chloe out the door of the motel room.

Ace squirmed in the chair, trying to get free to get to Jon to no avail.

"If I were you I'd concentrate on getting us what we want," Zeke warned, before going out the door and closing it behind him with a final thud.

Ace couldn't believe the strength of his anger didn't break the cord that bound him to the chair. He made a determined effort to calm himself so he could think straight and set about the task of freeing himself.

There wasn't a thing he could do for Chloe while he was incapacitated. Once freed, he'd rescue her one way or another.

Right now he had to put all his effort into freeing himself. Twisting his body, he tried moving the chair closer to the pocket knife imbedded in the floor near his feet.

His efforts were clumsy and fruitless. If he'd moved the chair an inch it was a lot. At that rate it would take him an hour or more to just get to the knife.

If he tilted the chair just so, it would fall near the knife, near where his hands were tied behind his back. Then he could grab the knife and begin the tedious task of sawing through the cord to free his hands.

Tilting the chair, he fell to the floor with a crash. His aim had been off a little so it was necessary for him to wriggle the chair several inches backward.

He bit his lip when his hand closed over the handle of the knife at last. It came out of the floor easily and Ace maneuvered the knife in his grip so he could slide the blade back and forth over the blind cord.

He concentrated so hard his teeth bit into his lip and drew blood. It reminded him of Chloe's kiss that had also drawn blood. And his complete attention. Where had she learned to kiss like that, he wondered.

Probably that surfer she'd treated herself to after her divorce. The thought didn't please him. From a professor to a surfer—there had to be a more reasonable choice somewhere in between . . . say, a journalist.

Chloe!

Thinking about Zeke and Jon having her made his hands saw faster, faster.

He dropped the knife. Damn.

He recovered it, and began again.

He had to quit and rest his hand when it began cramping from the continuous uncomfortable motion. Looking around the room while he rested, he tried to find a faster way to free himself, but no solution other than the pocket knife presented itself.

He began again. Twisting his neck, he tried to check on his progress. He couldn't see, so he had to judge how he was doing, hoping he was making progress because he felt a slight lessening of the tension of the cord wrapped around his wrists.

How had Zeke and Jon found them? Surely the credit card he'd used to check into the motel hadn't given them away that quickly.

Ace blamed himself for putting Chloe in danger. He should have been more careful. The truth was, when no one had shown up after a few days, he'd figured they were safe. He'd been wrong.

Now he had to free himself and get Chloe back before he could continue his quest to clear his own name and the murder charge against him while putting Peter Blakemore, Sr. in jail where he belonged.

His fingers were stiff from holding the knife so desperately tight, but he kept sawing at the rope. The knife wasn't all that sharp and the task was taking a lot longer than he'd hoped it would.

He kicked his legs, but they were bound securely. There was no loose rope. Zeke had done a very careful job when he'd tied him up, making sure there would be plenty of time elapsed before Ace could try to follow them.

By the time he was loose, Ace knew his only choice would be the one Zeke had given him. He'd have to get the evidence Jane had brought to his grandmother's and turn it over to Zeke, who'd give it to Peter Blakemore.

It was the only way to get Chloe safely out of their hands. But he'd have to be very careful. There was sure to be a trap. Peter Blakemore wasn't about to let either him or Chloe walk away with what he suspected they both knew about Blakemore Chemical's illegal dumping of toxic wastes from the plant.

He needed a plan.

If he ever freed himself from the freaking cord.

His hands were numb and he felt like yelling at the top of his lungs from sheer frustration.

Just when he was about to despair of ever cutting through the damn cords someone began pounding at the closed door to the motel room.

Someone must have heard the thud when he'd tipped over the chair and fallen to the floor. Renewed hope surged through him as he called out for whoever it was to come in.

There was the noise of someone twisting at the doorknob and then the pounding began again.

And kept going.

Loud and insistent.

Until Ace woke up.

He nearly rolled off the sofa, he'd been so deep in the nightmare he'd been having. He rubbed his eyes and called out to whoever was pounding on the door to wait a minute.

As he cleared his mind, he realized it was the Mexican take-out delivery. He answered the door and took the food Chloe had ordered on his credit card. After slipping the delivery boy a couple of singles, he closed the door and called to Chloe that the food had arrived.

She didn't answer.

Figuring she hadn't heard him, he went to the bathroom door to knock.

But the door wasn't closed completely and swung open at his knock. One look was all it took to see the bathroom was empty.

Where was she?

Spinning around, his adrenaline surging, he scoured the room with his eyes for any clue.

He saw it then; the ice bucket was missing.

Aw hell, she'd gone for ice without him.

That was a stupid thing to do. He swore, pulling on his shoes and heading down the hall to the ice machine.

Twenty

He was still groggy as he left the room to tell Chloe the food had arrived. That and give her a lecture about doing something so stupid as to go fetch ice by herself. The nightmare he'd had when he'd fallen asleep hadn't been real, though it had certainly seemed so—but the danger they were still in was real enough.

The nightmare had been a warning from his subconscious that he'd been getting careless, taking chances that could put both of them in danger. They weren't safe until they had Peter Blakemore, Sr. in jail where he belonged.

He was fully awake when he got to the little alcove at the end of the hall where the ice machine was housed.

The alcove was empty.

It took a few seconds for the fact to register, because his mind didn't want to accept it. Where else would Chloe be? She had to be—

And then he saw it . . . the ice bucket, lying on its side near the back of the ice machine with half the ice in the ice bucket spilled on the floor.

It hadn't been set there.

It had been dropped and rolled there. His eyes followed the sprinkling of ice cubes on the floor where they lay scattered.

In a heartbeat he knew what had happened.

Knew his nightmare had turned into reality.
They had Chloe!

He ran around the metal balcony overlooking the parking lot searching for sight of Chloe, his heart pounding in his ears, hoping that she hadn't been gone from the room for more than a few seconds before the food had arrived. If he were lucky he might still be able to catch up to them.

Luck was with him.

As he turned the corner he saw Zeke Francis shove Chloe into a black luxury car and then climb in the front seat as the car pulled out of the parking space.

Ace raced back down the metal balcony to where the sedan they were driving was parked. He vaulted over the balcony railing, not even bothering with the stairs as he ran at breakneck speed for the sedan. He was tugging the keys from his pocket on the way.

Opening the car, he jumped inside and started it, tearing from the parking lot on the tail of the black luxury car.

He couldn't lose them.

If he did, Chloe was dead.

Zeke looked in the rear-view mirror and swore beneath his breath. Ash was on to them, openly on their tail. He must have come looking for Chloe and seen them pulling out of the parking lot.

There was a good chance the kidnapping was going to be botched. He had to prepare for the fact that Ash might get the girl back.

But there was something he could do. He could work on the girl while Jon was trying to shake him; put doubt in the girl's mind about him.

He turned to her, trying to keep her from noticing the sedan behind them. Trying to keep her distracted from the fact that Jon was driving like a madman and why. He didn't want her trying to help derail them.

She tried to turn around to look anyway.

Zeke stopped her. "Don't be looking for your hero to rescue you. He's in this up to his ears."

"What . . . what are you talking a . . . about?" Chloe stammered, her cheeks glistening with tears. She'd struggled and cried, but nothing had stopped them from grabbing her and dragging her to their car.

Jon had wisely headed away from the airport thus avoiding the traffic that had been exiting the jammed highway in search of an alternate route. He pressed the gas pedal harder, speeding up while Zeke answered Chloe's question.

"He's trying to extort money from Blakemore Chemical. If Blakemore doesn't pay, then he's threatened to print lies that would destroy the company in the newspaper he works for."

"You don't expect me to believe that."

"What lies has he been telling you?" Zeke asked, pounding home the fact that Ace was a liar.

She was quiet for a few moments as Jon took a curve at high speed.

"He said he had proof that Blakemore was involved in illegal activities."

They were on the straight-away again when Ace climbed up their rear with the sedan bumping against them to get them to stop.

"He's crazy!" Jon said, having trouble controlling the car at such high speed.

"Just lose him," Zeke said, impatiently, trying to carry on with Chloe.

"Easy for you to say," Jon tossed back. "Do you see how fast we're going and he's not falling back."

"That's because we've got his hostage and he wants

her back." He turned to Chloe again. "Have you ever seen this proof he claims to have?"

"No, but—"

"What'd I tell you. There isn't any proof. He made a mistake and killed Blakemore's son. That's a sure prison sentence. My bet is that he was heading for the airport to flee the country."

"He wouldn't do that . . ."

"Why, can't you see, he'd do anything. He manufactured evidence and planted it so he could blackmail Blakemore. When Blakemore's son confronted him, he killed him."

The luxury car was bumped from behind again and the car swerved.

"You've got to tell us what you know or you're an accessory. If you tell us, you'll be okay. We don't want to hurt you. We want to help you. But in order for us to help you, you've got to help us."

"I don't know . . ." Chloe wavered.

A second later they were bumped again as they approached a curve in the road and all discussion ended with screams as the luxury car went sailing off the shoulder down a small embankment, flipping over and then settling on its side with the sickening crunch of metal crushing.

Chloe was stunned and disoriented. Her arm was bleeding, and the dust around the car made it difficult to see out from where she had landed near the passenger door which was up in the air. Somehow when the car had flipped, she and Zeke had traded places.

It was so quiet in the car.

She couldn't bring herself to look at her captors. It was everything she could do just to stay conscious. She was light-headed and sick to her stomach. Her mind kept wanting to deny what had happened.

Suddenly the door above her was jerked open.

It was Ace!

"You're bleeding," he said, seeing her bloody arm. He acted quickly, dragging her from the car. Without asking if she could walk, he began carrying her up the embankment and past a pickup truck that had stopped.

"There's two more guys down there," Ace said, carrying Chloe to the sedan.

The two men in the pickup headed down the embankment to help.

Ace ran his hands over Chloe checking for other injuries, but found none that required a hospital visit. "You're going to be all right," he assured her, going around to get in the driver's side.

He started the car as she asked about the two men still in the car.

"Someone went down to see about them. We've got to get out of here. Listen, hear the sirens. Someone must have reported our bumper car game. We can get away clean now because the cops will detain Zeke and Jon for a couple of hours with questions."

"How could you have run us off the road?" Chloe asked as Ace made his way back onto the road.

"I figured you'd rather be a little injured than dead."

"You're supposed to be a hero."

"Look, I didn't have a lot of choices. They were going to kill you."

"That's what they said about you."

"Of course, that's what they said. What did you expect?"

"I don't know. My head hurts."

"Just rest and don't talk. I'll find us somewhere safe to stay in a few minutes."

Good at his word, Ace did just that, pulling into another motel and getting them a room. He carried her to the room after parking the car where it was partially hidden on the lot by a weeping beech tree. He was playing it safe.

Zeke and Jonathon were carted off to the hospital from the crash scene. They were checked out medically and then released.

They placed a call to the chief from the hospital lobby.

Zeke was nervous when the chief came on the line.

"I've got some bad news, Chief," he blurted, in a rush to get it over with.

"What happened?"

Zeke knew that quiet tone of the chief's. Knew it well enough to be unnerved.

"It was an accident." Zeke pondered whether or not to tell the chief they'd kidnapped the girl and then lost her. The kidnapping had been Jon's idea and that was what tipped the scales for Zeke in telling the chief. "Jon insisted we grab the girl."

"You've got Chloe Pembrook?"

"No. There was an accident."

There was silence on the other end of the line and then the chief spit out his anger, "Don't tell me the girl is dead. Don't tell me that Zeke."

"She's not dead, sir."

"Then what the hell are you talking about?" the chief yelled.

Zeke grimaced and held the phone away from his ear. Settling it back after a moment he explained. "Ash Worth saw us grab her. He followed us in his car and ran us off the road. Jon's car is totaled."

"Don't tell me Jon's dead," the chief said, sudden worry in his voice. "I don't want to be having to tell

Peter Blakemore, Sr. his other kid is dead. If I do, I'm gonna kill you."

"No, Jon's here with me at the hospital."

"You mean you're both laid up in the hospital. I don't frigging believe it. Are you both idiots? I sent you to do a job, Zeke. You were supposed to—"

"Neither of us is laid up," Zeke interrupted the chief's tirade to explain. "We're banged up and lucky to be alive," Zeke informed him, hoping to play on his sympathy. Especially before he told him the really bad news. "The hospital just released us."

"And the girl?"

"Ace got her back. We've lost track of both of them, sir."

The chief swore.

Zeke waited for him to calm down and then asked, "What shall we do now? Do you want us to fly home?"

"Hell no, I don't want you to fly home. I sent you up there to do a job. You don't have the evidence and the fugitive still has the girl and both have eluded you. I don't want to see you until—"

"But Chief," Zeke began, "how are we supposed—"

"I'll tell you how," the chief said, cutting Zeke off in mid-excuse. "The two of you get some rest tonight. I'm sure Ash isn't going to do anything until tomorrow. The girl won't be in any shape either. And then in the morning early I want you to rent another car and get that evidence."

"But we don't know where they are, or where they were going," Zeke objected, rubbing his sore leg and wishing he were sprawled on a sofa like Jon.

"But I do."

"You do?" Zeke asked, incredulous.

"I know where they're going. He has a grandmother he's close to who lives in East Hampton. Get a piece of paper and I'll give you the address and directions."

"Get me a paper and pen," Zeke called to Jon. "The chief knows where Ash is heading."

Jon had been about to refuse, but forced himself up at the news.

He was back in a flash with paper and pen from the hospital admissions room, handing them to Zeke.

"Okay, Chief, I'm ready." Zeke copied down the information. "Got it," he said when he was finished.

"Try not to lose it too."

"Don't worry, Chief, I won't."

Zeke hung up the phone and put the folded piece of paper in his wallet. He let out a sigh of relief. The call had gone better than he'd had any right to expect.

Maybe their luck was about to change.

Peter Blakemore, Sr. sat at his desk looking at the picture of his young wife and sons. He hadn't thought about his wife in some time.

Not until he'd seen the red roses laid against their son's tombstone.

Twenty-one

"Will you please put me down. I can walk, you know," Chloe argued when Ace continued carrying her through the motel room to the bathroom.

"Maybe. But you're bound to be shaky. I don't want to take any chances on you falling and injuring yourself any more than you already are."

He set her down on the pastel blue commode in the blue and white bathroom papered with a striped glossy wallpaper. His hands went to lift the hem of her T-shirt.

"What do you think you're doing?" she demanded, pushing his hands away.

"We've got to clean you up and put a bandage on that bad cut on your arm and any other cuts you may have. First we've got to get you undressed and into the shower."

"We've . . . ? I think I can handle it," she objected, thrusting her chin up in determination.

"No way. Most falls occur in the shower. It's a dangerous place to be when you're not feeling steady on your feet."

"I told you I'm fine," she asserted, leaping to her feet to demonstrate, only to feel woozy and sit back down abruptly.

"Okay, so I'm not fine. But I will be in short order.

Just let me sit here a few minutes and I'll be able to take care of myself."

"Forget it. You need my help, accept it. The sooner we get this over with, the better you'll start to feel. Don't fight me on this, Chloe. We've got bigger fish to fry. The danger isn't over."

Chloe sank down into herself, her shoulders slumping, the fight gone out of her as she realized he was telling her the truth. It wasn't over.

"Are you going to cooperate?" he asked, sensing her capitulation.

She nodded.

He pulled off her bloody T-shirt and took a closer look at the cut on her arm. "The bleeding is stopped, but we need to clean it and bandage it. Here, stand up so I can help you out of your shorts and panties."

The fight gone out of her, she did as he requested by rote. When she sat back down, he undid her bra and her breasts sprang free.

Ace acted as if he undressed women every day—which if she thought about it, he probably did—not gawking. Instead he reached to turn on the shower, testing the water with his hand until he got it to the right temperature.

She started to get up, but he stayed her with his hand.

"Just a minute. Since these are the only clothes we have, we need to keep them dry. I'm joining you in the shower to make sure you don't fall, so I'm going to get naked too."

He did as he promised, peeling off his T-shirt and then the snug jeans. Somewhere along the line he must have run out of underwear.

Chloe gawked.

"Close your mouth," he said on a chuckle, helping her up and into the shower where he soaped up a washrag and began washing the dust and blood off her.

She kept her eyes closed.

If her eyes were closed and she couldn't see it happening, it wasn't happening. The only trouble was she could feel it happening. She felt like a harem girl being prepared for a pasha.

She moaned out loud on sensory overload when his hand drew the soapy cloth over her breast.

"Did I hurt you?" he asked, stopping.

"No." She was embarrassed and threw out a lie to cover it, "I'm just tender from being banged around in the car. My whole body aches." That last was true.

"I'll be more gentle," he promised, and he was. The trouble was he took more time with more care and it was pure torture. She was aroused and desperate for him not to know it.

He seemed blissfully unaware.

The spray of water from the shower head plastered Ace's dark hair to his head and dripped in rivulets from his scruffy beard. Wet, his finely honed chest and belly glistened. His naked body was speckled here and there with dabs of soapsuds from where he'd brushed against Chloe as he washed her body, checking carefully for other cuts that would need attention.

She braced her hands on his shoulders when he knelt to do her legs. His hands sliding the soapy cloth over her inner thighs were nearly her undoing even though his touch was circumspect.

"You're doing good," he told her, planting a quick peck on her belly button before he stood and requested she turn around.

Turning only made her more dizzy from the effect of his lips on her belly button, however briefly. She braced her hands against the shower wall while he continued his delicious torture; sudsing her back, bottom and legs.

He stood when he was done with her legs and pronounced the only other cut on her ankle. She'd be fine.

Chloe wasn't so sure.

Showering with Ace had only served to awaken all the chemistry she'd put to bed, or thought she had. How could he be in such intimate circumstances with her and not feel the same effect?

When he reached around her to rinse the washrag, the evidence that indeed he wasn't unaffected grazed her hip.

"Okay, I'll dry off and then do you," Ace said, after hanging up the washrag.

"What?"

"Just wait a minute," he answered, not getting the drift of what she'd thought he meant.

While he covered his head with the towel, to fluff his hair dry, she took the opportunity, however unwisely, to study every tempting inch of him.

He was long, lean and dusted with just enough hair to accent the more intriguing areas of his body. There wasn't an inch to pinch anywhere that she could see. And she definitely wanted to pinch.

What was wrong with her?

She'd just nearly gotten killed and he was the person who'd sent the car she was in over the shoulder of the road. Sure, he was being considerate now, but did he have a vested reason for being so? He needed a hostage to up his chances of escape should his plan go awry.

Was that all she was to him—a hostage?

Were Zeke and Jon telling her the truth?

Or could she believe that he really did care about her safety. And more.

It was easy to believe what you wanted to believe and she wanted to believe Ace felt the same way about her she felt about him.

She looked away when he removed the towel from his head and finished drying off his body. He wrapped the towel around his hips covering the showy interest his body displayed in hers. Grabbing another towel, he announced, "Your turn."

He took her hand then, helping her from the shower so she wouldn't slip.

"I can do this myself," she objected, tugging at the towel in his hand.

"Okay," he agreed, surprising her, letting her have the towel and her way. He busied himself trying to fit "himself" into the snug jeans.

"You go ahead and wear my T-shirt," he offered, remaining bare-chested. "Your T-shirt is ruined with blood. While you finish up getting dressed I'll take a run out to the car to see if I can turn up some kind of first-aid kit in the glove compartment. It figures that a woman would forget to keep a spare tire in the trunk, yet keep a first-aid kit in the glove compartment."

Chloe hurried to get dried off and dressed before Ace returned.

A few minutes later Ace had returned, having lucked out with the first-aid kit. There had been a small one in the glove compartment just as he suspected.

Chloe sat on the bed and Ace applied a large band-aid to the small cut on her ankle. Next he tended to the large cut on her arm, wrapping gauze around it after applying an antiseptic ointment. He tore off strips of adhesive tape with his teeth and taped the gauze in place.

"There you're all better," he said, sitting it down

beside her on the bed and pulling her onto his lap to comfort her. "It's okay to cry you know, you've been very brave."

Well it was all he needed to say. Being sweet to her opened the flood gates and she did cry—like a baby. The stress of the last days since Ace had kidnapped her had been bottled up inside and now there was release.

He held her while she sobbed, stroking her hair, murmuring words meant to comfort and reassure her. Rocking her in his arms, he gave her the freedom to fall apart for a few minutes.

When the initial gush of tears had stopped, he brushed at them with his thumbs against her damp cheeks. Bending to bestow a reassuring peck on the tip of her nose, he met her lips instead when she lifted her head to say something to him.

Both of them were caught by surprise.

Both ignored the danger of deepening the kiss.

Their hungry bodies weren't having any of the reasons why their action was foolish. The emotion of the moment overruled reason, caution. Passion's insurgence took control where they lost it.

The words of comfort on his lips were replaced with words of desire, love words, words of sexual longing . . . coaxing, encouraging words uttered between foraging kisses.

His mustache and scruffy beard scratched against her smooth skin in an erotic masculine manner. He was tough and she was soft. He was man, she was woman.

His hand moved to caress her breast through the soft T-shirt of his she wore. He moved her hand, spreading her fingers to touch his bare chest, encouraging her to explore in like fashion.

While her touch was shy, at least at first, his was sure, expert at getting her response. She clenched her fingers against his chest and she could feel his solid heart beat beneath her fingertips—feel his excitement over her-their embrace.

His breathing was ragged, and he pushed the T-shirt up to reveal a pink-tipped breast, warm and full in his caressing hand. His fingers twisted, pearling the nipple he then took in his mouth, licking. His tongue swirled around it until it was pebble hard and then he opened his mouth over her breast. Its heat compelled her to moan softly.

Sensations stronger and wilder than anything she'd ever felt roamed her body at will, leaving her feeling powerless to deny taking pleasure in them. Her mind was fogged with desire. She couldn't think, only feel.

His hand moved to her other breast while his lips caressed her belly in a slow slide of sensual kisses, open-mouthed, hot erotic kisses that made her ache at the juncture of her thighs.

"Damn, why did we get dressed," Ace swore, tugging then at the zipper on her shorts. "I want you so damn bad, Chloe, it's been driving me mad being with you and yet not—"

For some reason his spoken words broke the spell.

Broke the fantasy she'd allowed herself to slip into when neither spoke, acting only on their desires. On the incredible sexual tension that had been building up between them. Acting on the adrenaline rush of the accident and the danger they were in.

She shook her head.

Clearing it.

And then she stilled his hand, laying hers on his as he worked at the zipper on her shorts. "This isn't a good idea," she said.

"I don't agree. I think it's the best idea we've come up with. The best idea I've ever come up with. And you feel it, too. Don't deny you want me."

"I'm not denying it."

"Okay, then." He proceeded to try her zipper again.

"No, Ace."

He listened. He didn't want to, but he listened, obeying her wishes.

But it didn't mean he was happy about it. Or that he understood. "Why?"

"Because . . . I don't know why. I only know we'll both regret it."

"I won't regret—wait a minute, did I hurt you? Did I do something wrong?"

"Oh, no, you did everything right."

Twenty-two

The following morning, they pulled out from beneath the weeping beech tree and left the motel to head for Ace's grandmother's place in East Hampton. Chloe and Ace avoided talking about what had almost happened between them. The moment had passed. Danger had regained first place on the list of their focus.

Until they solved the dilemma they were in, their personal life would remain on the back burner, by silent agreement.

"How long is the drive to your grandmother's house?" Chloe asked, running the comb she'd found in the glove compartment through her hair.

"It usually takes about two hours, depending on how heavy traffic is." They headed out Southern Parkway to connect up to highway 27.

"What's your grandmother's place like?"

"It's a big old rambling place. You're going to love it. There's a strand of crabapple trees just off the entrance. The compound began with a farmhouse but has long since become quite grand. It's grey-shingled and the gingerbread trim has evolved into a dark green color grandmother settled on years back.

"But even more impressive than the building are the gardens that are grandmother's real love. She's planted everything from bee balm to swamp sunflowers.

"I remember two things from the summers I spent there; ocean breezes and sunshine."

"You make it sound like paradise."

"Almost. Almost . . ."

"So why do you live in Chicago?"

"Because that's where the *Trib* is. It's the best newspaper as far as I'm concerned."

Chloe finished with her hair and tossed the comb back in the glove compartment. "And paradise would lull you into believing all's right with the world," she couldn't resist jabbing.

Ace glanced over, not missing her point at all. "I don't know there are still windmills to tilt in the Hamptons even if their number has thinned considerably through the centuries."

"What about Jane?"

"Jane?"

"Did you call her and tell her why we didn't make it yesterday?"

"Damn, I forgot. Jane's going to have my hide for not calling her. She's bound to have leapt to the wrong conclusion that something awful has happened when we didn't show up when we said we would."

He pulled off southern parkway and stopped at the first available phone they spotted, lowering the car window to make the call.

After dropping change into the phone, he punched in his grandmother's number and waited while the phone started ringing.

"Jane?" he said when the phone was picked up.

"Ace. If you aren't dead, I don't want to talk to you," Jane spouted off, clicking the phone dead in his ear, leaving him with a droning dial tone.

Ace glanced over at Chloe. "Yep, she's pissed, all right."

He put change into the phone again.

"Don't hang up, I'm out of quarters," he said when Jane answered.

She didn't hang up, but she didn't say anything either. She was giving him the silent treatment, and he couldn't say as he blamed her. Not calling had been a stupid, thoughtless thing to do. In Jane's shoes he would have been worried stiff.

"We're on our way now. We'll be there in about two hours."

Silence.

"I'm sorry, okay. We had a little accident, but we're on our way now."

"An accident? Are you all right?" Jane's voice took on a note of concern.

"Yes."

"What happened?"

"We got run off the road—I'll explain when we get there."

"Just get here," Jane instructed. "I've got to run your grandmother by the bank and I want you here before she has me out weeding in the hot sun again. I swear nothing seems to faze her. She has the energy of a woman half her age, hell, half my age."

"Just think of it as a cheap way to get a good tan, that's what I do," Ace informed her as he hung up the phone and raised the window, starting the car to get back on their journey.

"*We* got run off the road . . ." Chloe repeated.

"Don't gang up on me—"

Chloe laughed. Maybe she was going to like this Jane person after all.

* * *

"Are you sure this is the place?" Jon asked.

Zeke rechecked the number on the mailbox after they passed a strand of crabapple trees. "Yes, this is the address the chief gave me. Let's get the lay of the land after we find a good spot to hide the car. A lucky break wasn't it, that you had a pair of binoculars in the trunk of your car? Funny I'd never have pictured you for a bird watcher."

Jon didn't bite on the lure Zeke dangled. He let the remark pass. They were too close to getting what they were after to quarrel. He could always bust up Zeke later if he had a mind to. It was more important right now for him to get what his daddy wanted; to please his daddy for once. To make his daddy not wish it had been Jon that had been killed instead of Peter Jr. . . . as he suspected he did.

Peter had been the one who'd resembled their mother.

Peter had been the one who'd refused to open the presents their mother had sent every birthday and Christmas.

Peter had been the one who was afraid of their daddy, which had pleased him.

Ace and Chloe arrived in East Hampton about two hours after they'd started out. But there was no greeting party when they arrived at his grandmother's house.

If indeed there was a grandmother.

If indeed there was a Jane.

It occurred to Chloe that she hadn't spoken to either.

She'd taken them on faith the same way she'd taken everything Ace had told her. Were Zeke and Jon telling her the truth after all?

Was she being a fool?

The entry to the vast home opened to a large living room done in deep colors and filled with antique furnishings—the kind that weren't bought. They had been acquired by generations of Ellsworths. The dark hardwood floors edged a large printed area rug. The furniture was gathered around in intimate seating arrangements. A bank of French doors framed a view of the magnificent gardens that lay beyond.

Chloe was impressed down to her toes, but launched into her doubts before she lost her nerve to intimidation. This was beyond rich, something money couldn't buy.

"You've been lying to me all along haven't you?" she accused as Ace called out to a grandmother and co-worker who were obviously not there.

"What are you talking about?" he answered, as he was sorting through the mail that had been on the table in the entry as if he were expecting something. Not finding it, he tossed it on the Chippendale tea table and slouched down on the sofa. He glanced at his watch. "They must still be at the bank, or I know, they stopped at the post office. Grandmother is always getting parcels from the catalogs."

Chloe ignored Ace's flimsy stab at explaining away the two women's absence. "You're in on it, aren't you?"

Ace rubbed his beard and looked confused. "In on it?"

"The only thing that's probably true that you've told me is that your family disinherited you. You were trying to shake down Blakemore Chemical to finance the lifestyle you'd grown accustomed to and the shakedown went bad. My first impression was the right one. You killed Peter Blakemore, Jr. in cold blood."

Ace jumped to his feet, hands on hips confrontational. "You can't believe that . . . that hogwash Jon and Zeke filled your head with. You're smarter than that."

She didn't respond, clearly unwilling to continue believing him on faith. He scrambled to make her see she was right to believe him, asking, "What will make you believe I'm telling you the truth—that I am investigating Blakemore's dumping of toxic waste and that I plan to expose it?"

Chloe thought for a moment and then suggested, "Make a call right now to the EPA and report Blakemore. No, better yet, let me make the call while you watch."

If he was lying, he had nerve, she'd give him that, because he held his ground and nodded to the telephone on the desk backing the sofa. "Be my guest."

She called his bluff and dialed information for the number, then put a call through to the EPA.

When the agency took the call, she gave them the information she had, which admittedly wasn't a lot.

The employee took down the information and pronounced it interesting, promising to look into it.

She hung up the phone and looked over to Ace. "Satisfied?"

"I guess."

"Good, then maybe we can get on to more important things like figuring out where the hell Jane has taken grandmother off to, or, knowing grandmother, vice versa."

Chloe turned in a circle checking for the way to the kitchen. "Maybe there's a message on the answering machine?" she suggested.

Ace shook his head no. "Grandmother likes answering machines even less than Jane. She thinks they're rude."

"A note, then . . ." Chloe offered, still looking for

the way to the kitchen which was the heart of just about any home.

"Now that's a possibility. Let's check."

Chloe followed Ace down the short hall on her right to a spacious kitchen framed with sturdy wood beams. A collection of shiny copper pots of assorted sizes hung on a wall, and a tea kettle stood at the ready on the burner of the gas stove. It was a warm, cozy place despite its size.

But there was no note.

"Well, they'll be along shortly, why don't we have us a cup of tea and relax while we wait. Have a seat at the table and I'll fix it for us," he offered and she took him up on it.

After all, relaxation hadn't been a common commodity in the past few days. A cup of tea sounded like a really good idea—as long as she didn't dwell on the reasons why Jane and Ace's grandmother weren't there.

As she watched Ace, she saw that his grandmother had taught him well in the art of brewing a good cup of tea. He began by preheating the teapot by adding very hot tap water. Then he brought a bowl of water to a rolling boil in the microwave oven. After pouring out the hot tap water in the teapot, he took down a box of loose tea from the cupboard and put several teaspoons of loose tea in the teapot. He smiled over at her and added a couple more teaspoons. "Might as well make enough for Jane and grandmother."

"Might as well," she agreed.

He added another minute to the microwave timer so the water he took from it was boiling when he poured it over the tea in the teapot. He checked his watch, then began mucking about the cupboards. "Do you fancy some biscuits with your tea? I know grandmother has some about somewhere. It's always a scavenger hunt though, she tends never to put things back in the same spot—except for her gardening tools, which must always be cleaned and put back exactly in the same spot one found them."

Chloe knew he was parroting a lecture or two he'd most likely gotten on the subject—if there was a grandmother.

"Ah, here we are," Ace said, finding the biscuits. "And just in time too," he added, glancing at his watch.

"A minute longer and the tea would have gone from perfect to bitter. Five minutes, that's the limit."

He poured the tea through a strainer and brought her a cup.

"Were you watching me so closely because I'm so handsome you can't take your eyes off me, or because you thought grandmother kept the rat poison in the cupboard?" he inquired.

Twenty-three

"You're wrong," Ace insisted, shaking his head. "I say the Eagles are hotter. I've been hearing their old tune, 'Wasted Time,' a lot lately."

He was jabbing her purposely, Chloe knew. In effect saying that before he'd brought excitement into her life it had just been wasted time. His ego wouldn't fit in Wrigley Field.

"No you're wrong—" The sounds of a car door slamming echoed loudly.

Hearing them Chloe had stopped in mid-sentence in her defense of her take on adult contemporary music. While Ace had bought Estefan and yielded Etheridge ruling current radio air play, he'd been giving her a tremendous amount of grief over her other choice of Bon Jovi to make up the top three.

"They're back," Ace said, pushing back his chair to stand, ready to focus on the business at hand, the tea party over.

"Or Zeke and Jon have found us," Chloe countered, standing as well.

"Not a chance. I found the tracking device they planted on our car and destroyed it. The only thing the two of them will be chasing is their rolling heads when Jon's daddy lops them off for losing us."

"Do you really think we've escaped?"

"All I have to do is get the documents from Jane,

proving what was really going on in Pleasantville and take them to the authorities to clear myself and nail Blakemore. With any luck at all you'll be winging home back to Chicago tonight."

He didn't have to sound so happy to be rid of her.

"We're in here," Ace called out and in short order the women's voices sounded in the hall heading for the kitchen.

So there was a grandmother, Chloe thought.

And a Jane.

She almost wished there wasn't a Jane when she got a look at the woman with Ace's grandmother. Jane was preternaturally nubile for thirty-five, looking like a Vargas drawing come to life from the pages of *Playboy* magazine.

"I could kiss you," Ace said, swinging Jane into his arms and doing just that.

She pushed him away.

"Please—a small, furry rodent has taken up residence on your face. Don't tell me you haven't noticed."

Ace made a pretense of being wounded. "You don't like my disguise? And I worked so hard on it." He turned to his grandmother. "Grandmother will give me a kiss. She loves me no matter." With that said, Ace pulled a protesting diminutive brunette into his arms, lifted her from the floor and kissed her.

"Ashley Clayton Ellsworth, you behave yourself now," she said when he put her down. "Where are the manners I've drummed into you? Why you haven't even remembered to introduce me to your guest."

Off to one side Jane took in the scene with dancing eyes, and prurient interest in Ace's explaining away the hostage he'd taken.

Ace shot her a look that warned her not to refute any of his impending claim.

Instead of nodding, she let him twist in the wind.

After all, he deserved to be punished for not calling her and letting her know they'd not show up until today. She'd almost gone to the police. And then where would he have been?

Ace nudged Chloe forward. "Grandmother, this is Chloe Pembrook, my ah, traveling companion."

"Is that what they call it these days?" Jane hooted, not helping Ace out at all.

"It's . . . I'm perfectly innocent—" Ace rushed to assure his grandmother while glaring at Jane.

"I'll bet my Pog collection you've been telling your grandmother that since you were seven," Jane asserted. "You haven't been innocent since the day you were born. Since before that probably. No doubt you were making up excuses while you were still in the womb."

"Grandmother, don't listen to her. Chloe and I just met. I hadn't known Chloe more than . . ." He turned to Chloe. ". . . what? a half hour at most, before I found out she needed a ride to East Hampton and I offered one. I was only being a good Samaritan like you taught me."

"Yeah, right," Jane said, rolling her eyes.

"Now, children."

"You have a Pog collection?" Chloe asked Jane.

"She does," Ace answered for her. "How else do you think she attracts those young body builders she takes advantage of?"

"Ace, you take that back—"

"Children—"

"So where is Chloe staying here in East Hampton?" Jane asked, switching the subject and ambushing her fellow star reporter.

"Well, there's been a little mixup." He turned back to his grandmother to keep from murdering Jane. "Chloe was supposed to be meeting a woman who was to bring Chloe up to speed on ribbonwork for Chloe's column in *Chicago* magazine, but there was a sudden illness in the family and the woman had to leave town at the last minute," Ace fabricated from bits of what Chloe had told him and thin air.

"That left Chloe without a source for her column which is due like yesterday. So I suggested she come here with me because my grandmother or someone she knew must have the knowledge she wanted. And because there are so many empty bedrooms I invited her to stay until she got what she needed. It's okay, isn't it, Grandmother?"

His grandmother glanced over at Jane.

"I think it's a capital idea," Jane conceded, letting Ace off the hook at last. Somehow they hadn't ever gotten around to telling his grandmother the two of them were no longer a couple. It was probably Ace's idea. It kept his grandmother from having to invent excuses for all the single women that kept showing up unannounced when Ace was in town.

"Why don't you and Chloe talk about ribbons and bows while Ace and I catch up on the story we're working on. Ace, care to join me upstairs?"

His grandmother beamed her approval at that idea. Chloe beamed her disapproval.

And Ace and Jane retired to an upstairs bedroom where he planned to kill Jane or at the very least steal her Pog collection for giving everyone the wrong idea with willful pleasure in the doing. He wondered where exactly his grandmother did keep the rat poison . . .

He was jerked from that lovely fantasy by Jane when they reached the bedroom she'd chosen upon her arrival; the one with the best view of the gardens.

"Do you mind telling me what in the hell is going on?"

"I'm happy to see you too," he answered, going to look out the window at his grandmother's pride; the English-style rose garden in full bloom.

"You scared me half to death when you didn't show up yesterday. And all the while I had to pretend to your grandmother that it was no big deal, that you'd probably gotten sidetracked by a lead on the story we're working on about the general decline in television programming due to the debut of tabloid television. There are more industry people in the Hamptons in the summer than anywhere else."

"Then grandmother doesn't know any of the details of what's happened . . . she doesn't know about the danger I've been in?"

"No. I've managed to keep her pretty distracted. You can thank my aching back and ruined manicure for that. If I never see another flower, it won't be too soon for me."

Ace turned back to face her, "Thanks for being a pal," he said, meaning it.

She blew off the real sentiment. "Whatever. But you're not keeping me in the dark like your grandmother. Would you mind explaining how you turned into a fugitive with a hostage . . . who by the way looks pretty willing if you ask me?" Jane said with an arched brow over her shrewd green eye.

"It's a long story—"

Jane patted the bed beside her.

"Okay, okay," he said, leaving the window to be grilled by one of the best.

"What do you want to know?"

"I want to know everything. And don't leave out any of the juicy details."

"Tabloid journalism, Jane. I'm shocked!"

"Sure you are. Now give."

"You did bring the documents, didn't you?" he asked, sitting down beside her on the bed.

"I brought them, but first the story—"

"I got an anonymous call . . ." he began.

Peter Blakemore, Sr. was alone in his chemical plant. He was snooping. It was the only way to know what people were up to. You couldn't trust anyone. His wife had taught him that.

While he'd taken her from nothing and given her everything, she'd rewarded him by sleeping with another man.

He was embarrassed to say it had caught him by surprise.

He was proud to say it was the last thing that had.

Now he controlled everyone around him one way or another.

He ran his hand lovingly over a piece of machinery.

No one was going to ever take away what was his again.

No one.

And anyone who tried was going to be punished.

He paid good money to see to that.

"The car is still here. I told you he wasn't going anywhere," Jon said as he drove the rental car past the stand of weeping beech trees again just outside Ace's grandmother's place.

"But there's another car there now, too," Zeke observed.

Jon glanced over. "That's a grandmother's car if I've ever seen one," he said, dismissing the old silver Lincoln town car.

Zeke took the binoculars out of the box to inspect

as they sped past the rambling house with sun-bleached shingles turned grey from the sea moisture.

They'd had to buy a new pair since the pair they'd salvaged from Jon's trunk had been damaged in the crash and were useless.

"What are we going to do now?" Jon asked when they returned to their stakeout place.

"We watch and wait like your daddy wants. What we don't do is act—until we get a shot at getting the evidence they've got on the company."

"I'm really losing patience with all the waiting."

Zeke noticed Jon's hand straying to fondle his gun once again, and his stomach soured. If Jon thought he was tired of the waiting, he had no idea how tired Zeke was. Zeke was waiting for the other shoe to drop.

And that was the most unnerving waiting there was.

You knew in your gut something bad was going to happen.

You just didn't know what.

Or when.

You just knew for certain that it was.

Moving to distract Jon from his tendency to violence he used the only subject he was sure would gain his attention and brought up sex.

"To kill time why don't you do what I do when I'm on stakeout, let your mind wander and occupy it with thoughts that are pleasant. It's a sure-fire way to make the time pass more swiftly."

"You really do that, just daydream while you're on the job?"

"Sure."

"What do you think about?" Jon asked, pushing away a wispy stalk of decorative grass that was tickling his face.

"I fantasize."

"About what?" Jon asked, dense.

"Sex. What else?"

"Oh."

Jon was silent for a moment and Zeke relaxed happy his ploy had worked.

His happiness was doused a few minutes later when Jon asked, "You want to know what I'm thinking about—that woman Ash has with him . . . ?"

Twenty-four

Jane laughed with rich delight when Ace had finished relaying his predicament and how he'd come to be thrust into it.

"It's *not* funny," Ace said, rubbing his beard.

"Not to you, maybe," Jane agreed, mirth still dancing with satisfaction in her eyes. "It's just that I can't feature you with a lifestyle expert. Do you know how anal those kind of people are. Even she must know she's ridiculous. They think they can fix life with a glue gun."

"Chloe's not like that," he lied.

"Uh huh," she disagreed, noting they were not only on a first-name basis, but that there was a softness in his tone when he spoke her name . . . he even pronounced it the French way with the *e* on the end sounding like an *a*. "So, tell me, Ace," she said, making the effort to control her amusement. "What are you planning to do with charming Chloe now that everything is about to be cleared up?"

"What do you mean? I'm going to put her on a plane back to Chicago. I think I owe her that much."

"That much, huh?"

"Why don't you say what it is you're getting at instead of pretending I'm psychic?" Ace jumped up from the bed and went to the window again where he stood watching the goldfish play hide-and-seek between the lily pads dotted with saucer-sized yellow blooms in the fish pond framed with brick walkways laid out in intricate patterns.

"What I'm saying is, you're not going to get rid of her as easy as you're going to get rid of that thicket you've sprouted on your face. You've both been through a traumatic experience together. Sometimes that—"

"And you've been dipping into the romance novels again, haven't you? I thought you went to Fabio anonymous or something to kick the habit."

"Your ass, Ace. You only go to a twelve-step program for a bad habit you want to kick. Hell, romance novels are the only place a woman can find men who—"

"Who say please and thank you . . . ?" he offered smugly.

"Yeah, please, don't stop, and how can I *ever* thank you."

"In your dreams!"

"You know I could help you with getting that scratchy stuff off your face. I think there's a straight razor around here somewhere," Jane sniffed.

"Sorry to spoil your fun, but we've got work to do. Where'd you put the documents on the toxic waste?"

"On the desk downstairs in the library," she answered.

She followed him out of the bedroom to head downstairs. "Speaking of romance heroes, I met one who looked good enough to pose for a book cover. He was on the plane ride out here from Chicago."

"And what have I told you about talking to strangers?" Ace grinned back over his shoulder as they descended the stairs.

"He wasn't a stranger. His name is Erroll. He was drop-jaw gorgeous. He lives in New York unfortunately and has something to do with the arts; dance, I think."

"A man in tights?" Ace raised an eyebrow at her at the entrance to the library.

"Put a sock in it," Jane retorted.

"I'm sure he does—"

Ace ducked the pillow Jane grabbed from the sofa to beat him with.

"Stop it, woman. I told you we've got work to do. Play time is over. Now where's the documents?"

"And I told you on the desk."

"Yeah, but where?" Ace asked, staring at the desk cluttered with mail and newspapers.

"Here let me find it." Jane shoved him aside and began rifling through the clutter that Ace's grandmother had dumped there. It was a week's worth of mail they'd picked up at the post office, the reason the two of them had been late welcoming Ace and Chloe.

Jane began a careful search of the clutter.

First she eliminated the stack of sweepstakes envelopes promising that you were the one like a faithless lover, then the loose utility bills and coupon flyers. She eliminated the newspapers and magazines, shaking them to make sure nothing fluttered from their folds. Then very carefully she sorted through the remaining envelopes of mail.

Ace had been right.

The documents weren't there.

She bit her lip as she looked up at Ace.

"They were here. I put them here myself when I arrived."

"Wait a minute," Ace said, crossing back to the desk and moving her aside. "Perhaps grandmother cleared the desk before she went to the post office with you this morning and she tucked the documents into one of the desk drawers."

"That's probably it," Jane agreed, relieved.

She watched as Ace went through the desk drawers

in search of the documents. He even went so far as to pull the shallow center drawer out and check to see if the documents had gotten stuck.

When it was clear they weren't in the desk, she started to stammer because of the import of their loss. If they didn't have the documents Ace and Chloe were in a lot of danger. "Bu-. . . but I . . . I don't understand. I put the documents there. Where else could they be?"

"Don't panic. I'm sure they're around here somewhere."

"I'm not panicking. *I* don't panic. I'm the one who did the story on gang members, interviewing them when I was the only one present without a gun tucked away on my body, remember."

"And I bet you scared the hell out of them too, like you scare the hell out of me. That's why you got the scoop you did."

"Thank you, I think."

Ace was back to rubbing his beard. "Wait a minute, has anyone else been here since you arrived? Someone could have lifted the documents."

"That's it," Jane said, snapping her fingers for sarcastic effect. "Zeke and Jon dropped by for tea. I just forgot to tell you."

"Don't be cute."

Jane graced him with her dazzling smile. "I try, but what can I say—"

"What I meant was, grandmother was always having single women pop in for me to meet . . ." Ace tried fixing the damage.

"Funny, I guess she just doesn't think of them being my type—"

"Jane—"

"What?"

"Truce, okay."

"Truce," she agreed, her temper banked. Maybe she was just a tiny bit jealous of Ms. Glue Gun.

"Let's have a casual look around the library and then if we can't find the documents, we'll go find grandmother and ask her if she's seen them. You may have noticed she has a tendency to sometimes put things in odd places because her mind is on her roses. Perhaps she picked up the papers and put them somewhere. The only thing is, we have to hope that if she did, that she remembers where she put them."

He laughed. "I recall once I found a puddle of grape popsicle in the bread drawer, and another time my socks were in the freezer."

"No, that was me. And they were your shorts, not your socks."

"Oh. Yeah, right. You were pissed about me scooping you on that corruption story."

Jane knew Ace was just trying to make her feel better. But he wasn't fooling her.

He was plenty worried.

She knew because he was fiddling with that damned mysterious silver bracelet on his wrist he'd always refused to tell her about.

"Can you see anything?" Jon asked as Zeke looked through the binoculars.

"Nah. No, wait a minute. I can see Ash Worth. He and either his grandmother or Chloe Pembrook are talking about something."

"Let me see," Jon said, grabbing for the binoculars in Zeke's hand.

"That's got to be Chloe. She's a blonde and doesn't look like any grandmother to me. Come on Chloe, take off your blouse, you've got killer boobs . . . share the wealth . . . that's it unbutton—"

"Give me that," Zeke said, taking back the binoculars. "She's not taking off her blouse . . ."

"You were the one who told me to fantasize," Jon said with a shrug. "You don't want me getting any more bored or I'm going to shoot someone before we get our hands on the evidence. I say we just go in now and—"

"And I say we wait."

"But—"

"More importantly the chief and your daddy . . ."

"I know, I know. But I'm telling you, if we don't do something soon, I'm going to kill someone."

The photograph was alone on the bulletin board.

It had been there for years and years and years. Bordered in white that had aged to yellow, the photograph was of a young woman smiling from beneath the wide brim of a straw hat, the kind of hat you won at carnivals.

An extraordinarily pretty young woman.

She was blond and had a body that hinted of womanly promise. One had only to look at the photograph to know she was a woman you wouldn't forget.

The woman's name was written in ink beneath her photograph on the yellowed border.

Mrs. Peter Blakemore.

The documents weren't in the library.

"You take the living room and I'll take the kitchen," Ace instructed Jane. "Don't forget not to be logical. If grandmother's misplaced the documents, they could be anywhere."

As Ace made his casual survey of the kitchen his thoughts wandered to Chloe. She hadn't said much after Jane had arrived.

He wondered how Chloe and his grandmother were getting on. Probably like a house afire.

Even though he'd brewed Chloe a perfect cup of tea, he'd known she wasn't fooled. She knew he wasn't civilized, not civilized at all.

He checked the bread drawer—nothing there but bread.

He checked the microwave. It was empty as well. When he leaned forward to check the oven, he caught his reflection in the shiny chrome toaster and nearly jumped. Jane was right, a furry rodent had taken up residence on his face. Maybe if he shaved Chloe would think he was more civilized.

Boy, Jane would get a laugh out of that one. Him thinking of doing anything to please a woman. She thought he was the stubbornest man she'd ever met. And he *was* tenacious.

That's what made him a good journalist.

But he was getting older.

Things weren't so black and white anymore. He'd begun to see the shades of grey.

When they were there.

They weren't when it came to what Peter Blakemore was doing. He was polluting, poisoning the public's land.

Because he could. Because he was powerful. He'd even sacrificed his own son.

Ace hated that attitude that rules didn't apply to him. That he was special somehow, better than anyone else.

He twisted the silver bracelet on his wrist, worrying it. It was an attitude of entitlement he was all too familiar with; an attitude that was buried so deep in his family you almost couldn't smell the stink.

Twenty-five

While Jane and Ace had adjourned to an upstairs bedroom, Chloe had followed Ace's grandmother up an additional flight of stairs that led to the attic. Light spilled across the wooden floor from the dormer windows and played like children amidst the steamer trunks.

"I don't know why the two of them can't see that they are wrong for each other," the older woman said, shaking her head. "But then there's no point in telling Ashley. He's much too headstrong to take advice, even from me."

"Why do you say your grandson and his wiggy friend are wrong for each other?" The words were out of her mouth before Chloe could stop them.

"Call me Sarabeth," Ace's grandmother said, seeing Chloe was having difficulty deciding how to address her. "Well, to answer your question—they can't give each other what they need. Ace needs someone to put bright colors in his life. To decorate it, really." As she smiled at Chloe, her green eyes were twinkling. "Your being a lifestyle expert is in your favor, I'd say."

"Oh, but I'm not—"

Sarabeth laughed. "Ashley may be my grandson, but I'm not blind, even if I am prejudiced to see him in a favorable light. He's quite one of the best catches around."

"But he doesn't want to be caught . . ."

"He thinks he doesn't. He thinks he's so busy saving the world that there isn't time to indulge in a personal life that involves commitment. But what he has to learn is that you can't save anyone until you save yourself."

"Don't you like Jane?" Chloe asked, feeling a little guilty about being favored.

"How can anyone not like Jane? She's a wonderful girl. Stubborn and smart . . . a lot like me, really," Sarabeth said with a wink. "But Ace is wrong for her, too. She needs a man who will balance her, not compete with her every step of the way. Ace and Jane wouldn't have a marriage, they'd have a war. But they have to come to that understanding themselves."

Chloe walked over to a steamer trunk that was open, and filled with rackets. "There certainly are a lot of these trunks," she said.

Sarabeth nodded. "They're the skeletons of generations of Ellsworths' lives. Come over here by the window. I want to show you some of my sister's work. She was the one who liked working with ribbons. I was the tomboy who was always outside with the gardener, bugging the heck out of him. That's why I can't keep one steady, I still bug the heck out of them." She lifted the lid of a steamer trunk and picked up a dress trimmed with plush velvet leaves and rosettes made of French-silk ribbon. "This is some of her work. I wore it when I met Ace's grandfather."

"Why it's beautiful," Chloe exclaimed, stepping closer to study the delicate rosette ribbonwork.

"And this was a birthday gift when I turned sixteen that Marybeth made for me." She handed Chloe a heart-shaped pillow stuck full of antique hatpins. It was trimmed with woven ribbon and seed pearls.

The trunks were a treasure trove of beautiful handwork.

Chloe handed back the items and picked up a small box. The lid was made of lavender woven grosgrain, and the initials SBE were embroidered in one corner.

"That's the box I used to keep love letters from my husband in."

"Oh, I'm sorry," Chloe said, quickly handing it back.

"That's okay. It's empty now. I burned the letters."

At Chloe's curious look, she explained, "Sometimes you can kiss a prince and he turns into a toad— not right away, but . . ." Sarabeth set down the box and shifted a few items in the trunk before withdrawing an old book. "Now this is what will help you with your column. It's a ribbon book that was Marybeth's with instructions on how lampshades and decorated quilts and herb-filled dream pillows were made using ribbonwork."

Chloe let out a delighted squeal despite her usual reserve. It was exactly what she needed; a real find. But before she opened it she had to ask, "Ace has told me he was disinherited and that everyone in the family shuns him except you. I know this isn't proper for me to ask but . . ."

Sarabeth slipped her arm through Chloe's and drew her to the dormer window. "You'll see better here in the light," she said.

Chloe thought she was being dismissed, that her question was rude and would go unanswered. She should never have let her curiosity get so out of control that she forgot her manners. Ace had a way of making her forget her manners.

Chloe was even half expecting a reprimand, and that Sarabeth would leave her alone in the attic to look through the book she'd unearthed on ribbonwork.

Instead Sarabeth surprised her.

"I'll make you a bargain," Ace's grandmother said, finding a pillow and putting it on the old cane chair by the window where she sat down. The offer was made with the echo of bargains she'd made in the past—no doubt with Marybeth in this very attic. There was a tone of youthful conspiracy in her voice.

"A bargain?" Chloe repeated.

Sarabeth nodded, and laid a hand on Chloe's knee as if she were a young child. The sunlight caught the sparkle of the round diamond ring in a platinum filigree setting on the frail hand. But the gem's glitter was no match for the lively sparkle of curiosity in Sarabeth's eyes as she said, "I'll tell you what you want to know about my grandson, *if* you'll tell me just what's really going on."

"What's going on . . . ?"

"Yes. I may be eighty and forget where I put things sometimes, people tend to do that as they age, but I know when something is afoot and I'm not . . . how is it you kids say . . . in the loop?"

Chloe smiled. She liked Sarabeth.

A lot.

"You'll tell me about the silver bracelet your grandson wears . . ." she bargained, seeing that Ace and Jane were being overprotective of Sarabeth. A woman who could run an estate at eighty and cajole grownups to spade her garden did not need coddling.

"Yes. I'll explain the bracelet," Sarabeth agreed.

"Deal," Chloe said, waiting.

Sarabeth began then, a far-away look in her eyes. "You've noticed that Ashley is a curious sort. He has been that way since he was a young toddler. I don't think a child has ever asked 'why' more. He doesn't like secrets.

"And when he can't get an answer to something

that's puzzling or troubling him he's like an IRS agent after a cheat, willing to dig as far as he has to, to get the information he needs. He won't be dismissed, or lied to or handled. You can imagine how popular that made him in a family with plenty to hide.

"The Ellsworth family fortune comes from tobacco investments, paper mills and Wall Street. The interest of Ace's grandfather and father was making money, not doing what was right. If the two things clashed, there was never any question which was sacrificed.

"When Ace chose a career as an investigative journalist both his grandfather and father tried to put pressure on him to change his mind. It was the worst thing they could have done. They threatened to disinherit him.

"He told them he didn't care.

"Both men pulled out that old chestnut about everything they'd done being for him. Of course that's never true, and Ace was too smart to buy it. He told them he'd investigated the family fortunes and wasn't proud of how they'd been gotten. In the confrontation he'd had them dead to rights with the facts he'd dug up, but the two men wouldn't accept blame for the lives they'd ruined in the name of profit and greed.

"They told him he was a fool—an idealist who didn't understand how the world worked.

"He told him he understood it all right, but he didn't like it so he planned to change it. And the first thing he was going to do was expose the skeletons in the closet he'd unearthed.

"Show the world that a family who posed for charity balls was a lie. A charity ball couldn't cover up the back-room deals and swindles they called 'just doing business.'

"Of course he'd said the words in anger. When he

cooled off he realized he'd have written the story for spite and so he didn't.

"But the damage had been done. He'd shown so much disgust for his heritage. When he'd dared to cross them.

"Papers were drawn up for the disinheritance the next day leaving Ace without a cent.

"Though the two men were older they were not wiser and they didn't change their mind.

"They've never forgiven him because they know he's right and they are wrong. His presence only reminds them that their money is ill-gotten. Having him around is like having your mistress around when you've sworn to your wife you're faithful.

"And the sad thing is I believe the only one really hurting from all this is Ashley."

"And you broke with the family over this didn't you?" Chloe said, understanding.

"I'd been as guilty as the others, turning a blind eye. Ace's stand gave me the courage to be the better person I wanted to be."

"And so you divorced your husband?"

Sarabeth looked down at her hand and fiddled with the diamond wedding rings on her marriage finger, smiling sadly. After a moment, she gazed out the windows of the dormer at the gardens she so obviously loved, no doubt seeing a half century of ghostly memories that escaped Chloe's vision.

"We're not divorced. We're still married."

"Oh, but I thought—Ace said . . ."

"A divorce would mean scandal, something to be avoided at all cost. He calls me a silly old woman for insisting on separating. Do you know how incredibly sad it is to find that after fifty years of marriage the love of your spouse's life is his business?

"It wasn't an accidental meeting the night I wore

Marybeth's creation. I was picked out in advance and plucked. I blame myself that I was too busy gardening and daydreaming to notice I was being married for my dowry. Marybeth tried to warn me, but I didn't hear her. I guess I didn't want to.

"Do me a favor Chloe—don't marry my grandson until you're sure you love him.

"And do yourself a favor—make sure whoever you marry marries you for love as well."

Chloe squeezed Sarabeth's hand. "I promise you."

"And now you were going to explain—"

"Before I do, you haven't said why Ace wears that silver bracelet," Chloe prompted.

"He wears it as a reminder. Sometimes I think it more than anything is what drives him to excel at what he does. Because he never takes it off, its presence is a constant push to uncover the truth, to right any wrongs that he finds.

"Have you ever looked at it closely? Do you know what kind of bracelet it is?"

"No, I haven't seen it up close. But it looks like one of those POW or MIA bracelets for the soldiers that fought in Vietnam."

"That's exactly what it is. You see it's one of the family secrets Ace uncovered, perhaps the one that bothered him most of all."

"I don't understand . . ."

"The Ellsworth men have since the Civil War used their money and privilege to avoid going off to war. They pulled the necessary strings and paid the necessary money to have another man go in their place."

"Do you mean—"

"My son was no different. Ashley's father avoided the Vietnam war the same way the men in this family have for generations. The young man who went in his place never came back. He was listed missing in action."

"And his name is on the bracelet Ace wears . . ." Chloe said, with tears in her eyes.

"Yes," Sarabeth said softly. "Of course Ashley couldn't let it go at that. He had to dig deeper and find that the poor young man had been a reporter and that he'd never had a chance to have a son."

"And so Ace tries to be—"

Sarabeth finished for Chloe, ". . . the son he never had."

Twenty-six

"Did you find anything, Jane?" Ace called out as he headed for the living room after his casual perusal of the kitchen.

"Nothing," she answered, looking up from replacing a pillow she'd checked behind on the sofa when he entered the room.

"Then I guess we haven't any choice but to ask Grandmother if she remembers seeing the documents, and if she does, if she recalls straightening up and putting them somewhere. The main problem being where that somewhere might be. Let's head up to the attic. I think she's up there showing Chloe some stuff that's packed away in trunks that she thinks Chloe might be able to use for her column."

"Tell me something, Ace. What in the hell is a life-style expert anyway?"

Ace explained as best he could while they went to the stairs. "You know how we want to expose all the ugliness in the world?"

Jane nodded.

"Well, Chloe wants to make it pretty . . . correction to show *everyone* how to make it pretty."

"Then she's a decorator."

"I think it's more than that."

"Whatever. Listen, I just had a thought. Maybe your grandmother picked them up with the mail she took to the post office when I drove her there today. She could have dropped them in the car or something. You go on upstairs and I'll run out to the car to give it a thorough check, just in case."

"Good idea," Ace agreed, bounding up the rest of the stairs while Jane went to check the car.

When he entered the attic, he didn't see Chloe and his grandmother at first. Chloe's sniffle caught his ear and he turned to see the two of them at the dormer window.

"What's wrong," he asked, hurrying over to join them.

"Nothing," Chloe assured him, wiping her damp cheeks with the backs of her hands. "Your grandmother told me a sad story, that's all."

Ace looked at his grandmother. "You haven't been talking about me, have you?" His tone said he wasn't going to be pleased if her answer was affirmative.

"Why would we be talking about you? Really, Ashley. Chloe and I were looking at the ribbonwork Marybeth's skilled hands made and I got to reminiscing . . ."

Ace wasn't entirely sure he believed his grandmother.

And it was the look in Chloe's eyes that shed doubt on his grandmother's story. Chloe was looking at him much more kindly than she'd been heretofore predisposed to. That look had been inspired by his grandmother he'd bet money—if he had any.

His grandmother was a strong woman who knew her own mind.

And she doted on him.

So much so that she'd bucked her husband and her son when they'd disinherited Ace from the family fortune. The threat of divorce was one she'd made good on for all intents and purposes. His grandfather had moved out, even if he wouldn't give her a divorce.

Ace hadn't liked putting her in such a position and when he'd said so, she'd insisted that he hadn't—that this was a stand she should have taken long ago. Still he felt responsible, and guilty enough to shovel manure and attend high tea because of it.

He knew that while his grandmother liked Jane, she didn't think Jane was the right woman for him. She didn't push her opinion on him, she didn't have to— they were that attuned to each other . . . sympatico. They were kindred spirits though forty-five years spanned the difference in their respective ages.

As a young woman she'd been stifled by the confines of her sex, unable to pursue her independence in ways she might have if she'd been born with the options men enjoyed. Ace chafed at the tradition of corruption and greed which was his heritage. He and his grandmother had not fit into the circumstances. Rebellion had been the only eventual answer for either of them.

Looking at the two women, Ace wondered if he'd failed to notice how selfish he was in his own way. Being focused on his career and getting the story to the exclusion of all else had gotten him awards, but it hadn't won him many friends, or much of a personal life.

And now his choice had put everyone in danger; Chloe, Jane and even his grandmother.

The documents had to be found and the killing resolved before it dragged on any longer, because as long as the documents eluded him, the game was in play and the bad guys could show up . . . take everyone out and walk away—their criminal behavior would go undetected and unpunished.

He took his grandmother's hand. "As long as you're

remembering things, I have something to ask you. Do you remember seeing some paper documents on the desk in the library?"

"That's where I always put the mail."

"I know. But think—did you see any documents?"

She turned Ace's question over in her mind and then gave him the answer he didn't want to hear. "Maybe."

"They aren't there now. Jane and I looked for them and we couldn't find them."

"What kind of documents were they?"

"They were from a chemist verifying that Blakemore has been dumping toxic waste in metal drums that are rusting and leaking into the ground water."

"That's terrible . . ."

Ace asked the hard question. "Grandmother, do you think you might have picked up the documents and put them somewhere else?"

His grandmother's eyes were shrewd. "You mean lost them, don't you, Ashley?"

"No. I'm only suggesting that you might have straightened the desk, had an interruption like a phone call, and then put the papers somewhere other than the desk."

"Let me think. We can retrace my activities. How long were the papers on the desk?"

"Jane put them there when she arrived. The documents are for a story we're working on." In no way did he let on about the murder, kidnapping, etc.

Sarabeth glanced over at Chloe, who'd told her very little before Ace had come upstairs to interrupt.

"Jane went out to check the car just in case they got misplaced on the seat—"

"No, they aren't in the car," Sarabeth insisted. "I'm certain I didn't take them along."

"I'll just go put this book in my room," Chloe said,

sensing Ace wanted time alone with his grandmother, "and then I'll help you search."

As Chloe left the attic, she could hear Ace reassuring Sarabeth that if the documents were truly lost, it wasn't a big problem.

The sincerity in his voice gave her pause.

"Let me have the binoculars for a while," Jon said, wrenching them from Zeke's hand.

"Fine, I'll eat." Zeke reached into the paper bag beside them and took out a pack of chocolate cupcakes and a carton of milk they'd bought at a small market when they'd gone to buy the new binoculars.

"What's going on?" he asked after a few minutes when Jon didn't volunteer any information.

"Chloe Pembrook's in the living room I'm guessing. And she's looking for something, or doing exercises. Her blond head keeps bobbing up and down."

"Is Ash Worth with her?" Zeke asked, polishing off one of the cupcakes and licking the chocolate crumbs from his fingers.

". . . Maybe he is and I just don't see him. Maybe it's not exercises she's doing."

"Oh, for Pete's sake," Zeke said in disgust, wadding up the cellophane wrapper he'd taken off the other cupcake, and tossing the wrapper in the paper bag.

"Well, you're the one who told me to put my mind on sex. I'll just follow your orders. Wow, would you look at that—"

At Jon's salacious comment, Zeke took back the binoculars to see what he was missing. He was missing nothing. The room they'd decided was the living room appeared empty. The afternoon was clouding up so it was getting harder to see with the overcast shadows.

There was a hint of rain in the air and he hoped they weren't about to be soaked.

Stakeouts were the pits when you were uncomfortable and dry. He didn't even want to think about what it would be like to spend time with Jon when he was uncomfortable and wet.

"Tell me something, Francis—how come you never got married?" Jon asked, not at all interested but bored enough to make inane conversation while he peeled the wrapper off a stick of beef jerky.

"I did get married. Once was enough for me. I've never met a woman since, worth making that kind of sacrifice for. I like my life just fine the way it is."

"You were married?" Jon repeated in surprise. "Hell, there's even been rumors you were gay . . ."

"What?"

Jon shrugged, putting down the binoculars since the house seemed to be quiet. "What do you expect? Pleasantville is a small town. You aren't a heavy dater to put it mildly. So the logical conclusion is . . ."

"I'm *not* gay."

"Glad to hear it, since we're stuck out here in the bushes together," Jon said, polishing off the last bit of his beef jerky stick. "Though I do think Cletus at the barbershop is going to be disappointed to hear the news."

"What?"

Jon took great delight in taunting, "Haven't you ever noticed the way he looks at you?"

"You tell Cletus and anybody else who has funny ideas about me to go see Becky Ann at the truck stop. She'll verify I'm not gay by a long shot."

"Becky Ann—you've been dipping into that. I gotta tell you I'm impressed."

"Yeah, well I like women who are just passing

through town. I don't ever want to get hooked up with one again who'll drain me broke."

"Hell, what did your ex-wife do to you?"

"She bankrupted me is what she did. Caught me sleeping with my eyes open with one of her friends. At first she let me apologize. I thought it would blow over after she enjoyed making me crawl on my belly for a while. The bitch was only getting even. She maxed out all my credit cards, ruined our credit and left me high and dry with all her debt to pay off."

"Women are all alike, just after what they can get from a man. Just like my mother. She had everything she could ever want and it wasn't enough for her. I don't know why she even bothered to send those stupid packages for our birthdays and Christmas. I hate her for—"

"Wait a minute . . . who's this . . . ?" Zeke interrupted, raising the binoculars to his eyes.

"What? Where? Oh there, holy shit, look at the tits and ass on her. That is definitely not our lifestyle expert. What happened to Chloe Pembrook? Where'd this babe come from?"

"Damn if I know. She sure ain't the grandmother either."

They both watched Jane walk to the grandmother's car nonetheless. She opened the Lincoln door and Jon took his gun from where it was stashed at his waist.

"I'm not letting her get away. Come on let's go find out who she is and what she knows . . ."

Ace, Chloe and Sarabeth stood at the desk where Jane had left the documents upon her arrival while Sarabeth tried to recall where she might have put them.

"You know where I might have put—" Sarabeth began when there was a loud noise.

"What was that?" Chloe asked, startled.

"Either a car just backfired or that was a gunshot," Ace answered, turning in the direction of the noise which had come from the outside in front of the house.

The two women looked at each other at the same time Ace came to the same conclusion. *"Jane!"* He took off running for the front door, ordering them to stay put.

Twenty-seven

Ace was only a few feet down the drive when he spotted Jane. His heart sank with a painful thud at what he saw.

Jane was sprawled unmoving beside his grandmother's Lincoln with a stream of bright red blood running down her pale cheek.

"Oh, God—Jane! No!" he cried out, running toward where she lay.

"Ping."

Ace dove for the ground and started trying to make his way toward Jane, but every time he tried to move forward someone fired at him. Moving back toward the house was his only option as he was pinned down.

It was probably the best thing he could do for Jane as well. She needed an ambulance. He could call one when he called the police.

He wasn't going to be of any use to any of the three women trapped here alone with him if he was dead. Though his heart cried out for him to get to Jane, to help her, he made himself do the rational thing and made his way back inside the house.

Chloe stood at the entry with her arm around Sarabeth, both of them wide-eyed with fear. "Someone was shooting at you," Chloe accused. "Jane, did they—"

"She's shot and I can't get to her. They had me

pinned down so that the only thing I could do was come back to the house. Did you call the police?''

"I didn't know—" Chloe answered, clearly uncertain what she should do, with Ace being a fugitive from the police.

"Call them," Ace instructed. "And tell them to send an ambulance. That someone's been shot."

As Chloe went to make the call to 911-emergency, Ace insisted Sarabeth go to her room and stay there until it was safe.

"The phone is dead," Chloe said, stopping Ace in his tracks when he'd been about to escort his protesting grandmother to her bedroom.

"What?"

"There's no dial tone. It's dead," Chloe repeated, holding the phone out.

Ace crossed the room and took the phone from her.

"Damn it!" he swore, "They've cut the phone lines so we're trapped."

"We can't just let Jane lie out there bleeding. We have to do something to help her," Chloe vowed.

"There's a phone in my car," Sarabeth offered. "If you can get to the car, you could use it if you know how. I still haven't learned the hang of it since Ace made me have it installed," she added for Chloe's benefit, when she saw the look of surprise on Chloe's face at her having the trendy appliance.

"Where's your gun?" Chloe asked, turning to Ace.

"You have a gun?" Sarabeth was shocked.

"It's upstairs in the satchel," Ace answered Chloe.

"Get it. *And load it.* I'll try to cover you while you make your way to the Lincoln. It's our only chance to get a call out for help."

Ace ran for the stairs.

"What is going on?" Sarabeth demanded to know of Chloe while they waited for Ace to retrieve the gun.

"There's no time to explain now. I think Ace is right and that the best thing is for you to go to your bedroom until the coast is clear. Ace could get hurt if he's worrying about your safety."

Sarabeth didn't argue, only insisting she be told what was going on when everything was over. She went to her room and Ace returned with the gun.

He handed it to Chloe and she took it like he'd handed her a snake.

"You've never fired a gun before, have you?" he demanded, knowing what her answer would be. She was about as comfortable with a gun as his grandmother was with an answering machine or the cellular phone he'd had installed. Sarabeth always acted as if mechanical things would bite her if she got too close to them.

Chloe shook her head no. "But I'm sure I can—"

"You'd probably shoot me more than likely while you're trying to cover me. Or get yourself shot. I'll keep the gun and do my best to try to cover myself. You just stay put and yell out any warning you happen to see."

Chloe gave up the gun reluctantly, and Ace opened the door to venture back out, pausing to throw a brief kiss on her lips.

He'd only taken a few steps on the drive when Chloe heard the *ping* and saw Ace drop.

"What the hell is going on?" Zeke asked as he and Jon heard the gunshot and simultaneously watched the stacked blonde beside the Lincoln crumple to the ground.

"What the hell do you think. Someone is shooting and it isn't us. Let's get the hell out of the line of fire before we get our asses shot."

From their fallback position, Zeke and Jon watched Ace venture outside in response to hearing the gunshot. "Maybe he shot her from the house," Jon suggested as they watched him start down the drive.

The *ping* of another gunshot had Ace diving for the ground.

"I think we can rule him out as the shooter," Zeke said dryly.

"Then who the hell is it?"

"Damned if I know," Zeke answered watching Ace try to crawl to the stacked blonde who was down only to have someone fire at him every time he tried to move forward on the drive.

"Do you think she's dead?" Jon asked.

"She sure as hell ain't moving."

"What a waste if she is."

Zeke knew it wasn't the blonde's soul Jon was talking about.

"He's making a run for the house," Jon said. "Want me to take him down?"

"Hell no, I don't want to announce to whoever's doing the shooting that we're here. Are you crazy? They'll shoot us, soon as not."

Zeke kept his binoculars trained on the entry door until it opened again several minutes later and Ace came out again.

"Do you think whoever was shooting is gone?" Jon asked.

Ace started down the drive this time at a half crouch. He still drew a duo of pinging bullets making him dive to the cover of the car.

"Does that answer your question?" Zeke said.

"Maybe we should go around and creep up to see who the shooter is. Maybe it's the local cops."

"And what are we supposed to do if it's the local boys in blue? We're not even supposed to be here. In case you haven't noticed we've crossed more than a few state lines. I'm so far out of my jurisdiction—"

"What's he doing?" Jon demanded when Ace circled around the Lincoln.

"I don't know, but this time he's got a gun," Zeke said, seeing it through the binoculars. "Keep your head down if you don't want it air-conditioned. I don't want to have to even think about having to go back home and tell your daddy his only remaining son is dead."

"Then tell me what he's doing now," Jon bargained, unable to see from their fall-back position.

"He's getting in the car."

"He's leaving?"

"No. He's got his head down on the seat. I can't see what he's . . . wait a minute, I bet you there's a cellular phone in the car. The phone lines to the house must be cut. I bet he's calling 911. The sonovabitch is going to have cops crawling over this place like ants."

"He's not going to call the cops, he's a fugitive himself. He's wanted for murder, remember."

"Better to be in jail than to be dead like the blonde on the ground. In his shoes, I'd call the cops too. Come on, we got to get."

Ace frantically punched 911.

Nothing.

He swore and tried it again.

Still nothing. A trickle of sweat dripped from his forehead into his eyes. He squinted at the cellular phone in his hand and saw the star button. That was it. He had to hit star 911.

He stabbed in the symbol and numbers.

Nothing.

He felt like throwing the damn thing through the

windshield. No wonder his grandmother didn't like fancy phones. They were a pain in the ass.

Think, Ace, think. Why isn't it working? What's wrong. This is no time to screw up again. His screw-up at Zimmerman's garage had gotten Chloe here as his hostage. A screw-up now could get her dead, like Jane. And his grandmother—shit.

It was hot in the car and adrenaline was flowing through his veins like water through a colander, all in a rush. And then it hit him. Idiot, it's not star 911 on a car phone, it's star 311!

He punched in the numbers and got an emergency operator right away.

"Can I help you?"

"What the hell do you think. Get an ambulance and cops out to the Ellsworth place right away, there's been a shooting. And we're trapped here, damnit. Hurry."

"Now calm down sir, I need the exact address."

Ace gave it to her, or rather swore it at her. "Get somebody out here now or we're all going to be dead."

"I'm sending someone right now. Can you stay on the line while I—"

"No, I'm in the line of fire and I've got women trapped in the house to protect. Just do your freaking job and get me some help." Ace switched off the phone and threw it on the seat.

He knew he'd been rude, but he wasn't feeling any too polite at the moment, nor did he have time to follow some rule book written up by some desk jockey.

Jane. He didn't want to look.

He didn't want to know.

But he knew.

If Jane had gone this long without bitching, she was dead.

He picked up the gun from the seat of the car and

cracked open the car door fully expecting the *ping* of bullets again.

But it was quiet.

Too quiet.

He cracked the car door a little wider and gulped back bile as he saw a section of Jane's blond hair caked with blood. Her hand lay limp just to one side of it on the drive.

His cheeks were damp, as tears leaked from his eyes. It was his fault.

He couldn't see her face, her head was turned away from him. But he could see it in his mind. Could see her laughing at something outrageous she'd said to shock him. She loved trying to shock his cold blue blood as she used to call it. She delighted in labeling him yuppy scum because she knew it ticked him off.

She was the best friend he'd ever had.

And he'd gotten her killed.

He was a selfish bastard.

Why had he involved her? And Chloe? And his grandmother? Was saving the world worth sacrificing those he loved? Was he no better than his father and grandfather and those that had gone before them making the end justify the means?

He heard the sirens then in the distance.

Too late for Jane.

He knew the sirens would scare off whoever was shooting at him. Pushing the car door open, he got out and went to Jane. The least he could do was carry her inside, not leave her face-down on the drive for strangers to pick up.

He was carrying her in his arms when the cops arrived with the ambulance on their bumper.

Twenty-eight

The call had been answered by one blue uniformed policeman in a police car with its siren now off, but red light still flashing. Behind it came the ambulance and a backup police car and officer.

The first young officer drew his gun as he got out of the car and leveled it at Ace, ordering him to stop, which Ace did.

"Who are you? Identify yourself," the officer said, as the paramedic and other officer got out of their vehicles.

"I'm Ashley Ellsworth. I called in the shooting."

The policeman and ambulance driver came forward. While the policeman patted Ace down to make sure he wasn't using Jane for a shield, the paramedic checked Jane.

"She's dead," Ace said with quiet grief. "Some cowardly bastard ambushed her and killed her."

"Let's get her in the ambulance," the paramedic said to the police officer who'd patted Ace down and found nothing. "She's unconscious, but there's a faint, thready pulse."

"Oh God, hurry—" Ace handed over Jane and the police officer and paramedic rushed her to the ambulance which pulled out of the drive with its sirens wailing a minute later.

"Why'd you do it?" the police officer accused.

"I didn't do it, I told you. The same person who shot Jane has been shooting at us, too."

"Us?"

"My grandmother and another woman are inside the house." Except they weren't any longer. They came out of the house together at that moment, with Chloe holding the older woman's arm.

At that minute the police officer's supervisor showed up, and assessing what had gone down, radioed for a detective.

Ace and the two women were shepherded back inside the house for questioning.

First they were asked their names and dates of birth. The policeman who wrote it down went to check it out.

The other policeman took Sarabeth's statement first, and when he was finished two detectives arrived.

The detectives began questioning Ace and Chloe about the shooting, separating them.

The policeman who'd run the three witnesses' names through NYSPIN returned inside the house and told his supervisor they had a hit. NYSPIN had linked up with NCIC to find there was a warrant out for Ace's arrest for felony murder in Illinois.

"Is the warrant active?" the grey-haired supervisor questioned.

"It's active—only a few days old," the officer answered.

The supervisor pulled the detectives aside and relayed the news about the outstanding warrant on Ace.

The supervisor ordered the arrest based on the outstanding warrant and the police officer went to read Ace his rights as he put the handcuffs on him.

"Wait a minute, officer, you can't arrest my grandson," Sarabeth said, outraged.

"I'm afraid we can, ma'am. We have a warrant faxed for his arrest for a violent felony."

"It's okay, grandmother. There's been a mix-up. I didn't do it. It'll be straightened out. Don't worry, okay. Just stay here with Chloe and I'll get back as soon as I can."

"Miss Pembrook is coming along for a statement as well. We need to take a written statement from her about the kidnapping."

"Kidnapping! Ashley, what's going on?"

"It's a mistake. We'll get it all taken care of at the station," Ashley assured her as the police officer led him away to the police car outside, while the other police officer escorted Chloe.

The detectives remained behind to check out the scene of the crime and went to survey the area outside where the crime had taken place.

Down the road from Ace's grandmother's, Zeke and Jon watched from their parked car as first the ambulance flew by with its sirens wailing.

"Do you think they shot him?" Jon asked.

"They shot someone besides the woman. She wouldn't be in the ambulance. They'd call the coroner in to pick her up."

"Now what do we do?"

"We wait."

"I'm sick of waiting—"

"Then go home . . ." Zeke suggested hopefully.

His suggestion was cut off by the police car that went by as both men saw Ace in the back seat cuffed and stuffed.

"It musta been the hostage then who got shot," Jon reasoned. "Do you think . . ."

"I can't think with you talking all the time. I don't know what the hell is going on."

Another police car went by, this time with Chloe inside.

Both men looked at each other, puzzled at seeing Chloe in the police car. "Musta been the old lady who got shot," Zeke said. "That leaves the house empty. We can get in and have a look around for what evidence Ace had on Blakemore."

They drove back down the road to Ace's grandmother's house, but were stopped by the detectives still investigating the scene.

"Shit!" Zeke kept driving past the house and turned around a mile or so down the road to head for a telephone.

The news he had to tell the chief was all bad.

They didn't have what they'd come for and they weren't going to be able to get it. But he had to make the call.

He made the call from the same market where they'd picked up the cupcakes and beef jerky.

"Don't tell me this, Zeke," Darrow Smith said, yelling into the phone.

"What do you want me to do? The local cops have arrested Ash and taken Chloe Pembrook in, too. The grandmother's been shot and taken to the hospital in an ambulance."

"Did you do the shooting, or Jon?"

"I keep telling you neither of us fired a shot," Zeke repeated in frustration.

"Then who in the hell did?"

"I don't know. We didn't see anyone, we were too busy getting out of the line of fire, if you know what I mean. Someone just started shooting all of the sudden and picked off the blond woman."

"You mean Miss Pembrook? I thought you said the grandmother was the one who was shot."

"They both were."

"Both? What are you talking about?"

Zeke tried again, hanging onto his last shred of patience in a day that had been nothing but full of one frustration after another. "There were four people in the house. Ash Worth, Chloe Pembrook, Ace's grandmother, and another woman—a blonde."

"Who was she?"

"We don't know, but it doesn't matter anyway because she's dead."

"Then you're telling me Ace's grandmother's house is empty—so get into it and search for the evidence Ace claimed to have."

"I already thought of that. But when we drove back to attempt it, we found the house and grounds crawling with cops. There's no way we're going to be able to get anywhere near it.

"I'm telling you, Chief, the whole thing has gone to hell in a handbasket. We might as well come back home. I don't think Ash had any evidence. If you want to know what I think, I believe he's been bluffing and that's why he killed Blakemore's son. If he had the evidence, he would have already contacted the authorities here."

"So you think we can start extradition proceedings to bring Ash Worth back here for the murder without anything blowing up in our faces, is that what you're saying?"

"That's what I'm saying," Zeke agreed.

"Okay, then you two come back home and that will take Jon out of the equation before he does something stupid. I'll have tickets waiting for you at JFK. Then we'll fly you back up there alone for the extradition."

"What do you think Jon's daddy is going to say about what's happened?"

"He's not going to be happy, but he's going to have to accept that it'll work out, even if it wasn't his way. I'll handle him, you just concentrate on getting Jon back here before there's a development I can't handle."

"We're on our way."

Zeke hung up the phone and turned to Jon. "We're going back home," he announced.

"What? Why?"

"Because there's nothing more for us to do—"

"I'm staying here," Jon insisted.

"Your daddy wants you home," Zeke lied, knowing it would work.

Sarabeth paced back and forth in her kitchen trying to decide what to do. She couldn't go to her grandson's aid because he was at the police station, as was Chloe. The only way she could help him was to call up the family lawyer, something Ashley probably wouldn't like, but she decided to do it anyway.

After making the call to the lawyer, she decided to go to the hospital and check on Jane. The poor girl wouldn't have anyone there for her, and it was what Ashley would have wanted her to do. He'd want news on Jane and she could get it to him.

After freshening up, Sarabeth went outside to ask one of the policemen to drive her to the hospital. It wasn't that she couldn't drive, she could. But since she was so nervous about what had happened, she thought it better to have someone drive her.

The long history of the Ellsworth name in the community had her on the way to the hospital without argument. She checked with admittance when she arrived at Southampton Hospital, and she took the elevator upstairs to the room assigned to Jane Talbert.

On the ride up in the elevator, she let out the breath she'd been holding for fear the news would be tragic when she arrived at the hospital. Ashley had thought Jane was dead and only the paramedic had found her weak pulse. There was a good chance Jane hadn't made it anyway. But since she'd been assigned a room, she was at least hanging on and putting up a fight to stay alive.

And knowing Jane it would be some fight. The girl had spunk in bushels and pecks to spare.

When the elevator reached Jane's floor, Sarabeth got off and asked for directions to Jane's room from a nurse's aide hurrying down the corridor.

If Jane wasn't down from surgery for removing the bullet from where she'd been shot, Sarabeth decided she'd wait in the lounge until she was.

When Jane felt well enough to talk, she'd find out from her just what Ace was involved in, just what was going on.

She heard Jane before she saw the room number outside her door.

Jane's loud voice carried down the hall. "It's your own damn fault. I told you, but you wouldn't listen to me. And I'm warning you I may do it again. I'm still feeling kind of queasy. If I were you I'd get out of my way. I can make it on my own to the bathroom. I'm not an invalid."

Sarabeth stuck her head in the door.

"Jane?" she inquired.

Jane looked over to the door where Sarabeth stood.

"Hello, come on in, but keep your distance if you don't want to get puked on like I just did Florence Nightengown here," Jane said, nodding to the nurse trying to assist her.

"Are you all right?" Sarabeth asked, coming into the room.

"I've been better. I feel like I got wasted last night on too many micro-beers."

"Ace said you'd been shot," Sarabeth said, surprised to see Jane up and walking, even if with a nurse assisting, or rather trying to assist her.

"I got shot at. The bullet grazed my skull. I got a concussion either from it or from falling. All I remember is everything going black. I kept praying no white light was going to show up and beam me aboard. I'm too young to die."

"Too mean to die," the nurse muttered beneath her breath.

"I heard that. Isn't there some sort of hypocritic oath you people take?"

Sarabeth interrupted, trying to smooth over the cranky Jane's bad mood. "Ace will be thrilled to hear you are all right."

"So why isn't he here?"

"He's been arrested, I'm afraid."

"What!"

"The police took him away in handcuffs."

"I've got to get out of here," Jane vowed, pulling free of the nurse.

"Oh no, you're not going anywhere," the nurse said, making good on her promise.

"I've got a lawyer taking care of everything," Sarabeth assured her. "You just need to rest and get your strength back."

"He doesn't need a lawyer, he needs me," Jane insisted.

"Now, Jane," Sarabeth coaxed.

"You don't understand. I'm the one responsible for him being in jail. I'm the one who lost the documents."

"No, I am," Sarabeth said softly.

Twenty-nine

"So you're both in on this, is that right?"

Chloe didn't answer the young officer who was so preppy, good-looking and clean-cut she was sure there was a mother's stamp of approval on his body somewhere, immediately.

She took a moment to think what would be the best way to handle the situation.

After going over the limited options, she decided to tell the truth. It wouldn't help Ace in the short term, but it would in the longer run. No matter what, they were going to hold him because they had the warrant for his arrest from Pleasantville for the violent felony.

If she tried to make the officer see the gray area of what he'd done, there was a good chance she'd be detained too. She had to make them think she was a victim in all this. Which she was, but Ace had his reasons for doing what he did.

Good reasons, she believed.

"I'm sure you already know I wasn't in on anything. That I was just an innocent victim who was kidnapped because I had the misfortune to be in the wrong place at the wrong time."

"Then what you're claiming is that you didn't go willingly with Ashley Ellsworth, but that he took you forcibly as his hostage."

She nodded.

"I need an answer," the officer prompted, taking down the information.

"Yes. He took me forcibly as his hostage. I was kidnapped, okay?"

"How did he take you forcibly?"

Chloe didn't like the way she was having to make Ace sound. But it was necessary if she was going to get the cops to trust her and let her go. So she said, "He had a gun. He said if I didn't come quietly, he'd shoot me. So I went."

"Shoot you like he shot Jane Talbert?"

"What?"

"You don't think he shot Miss Talbert?"

"I know he didn't shoot Jane. Jane was a co-worker. He—"

"Did you see someone else shoot Miss Talbert?" the officer asked pointedly.

"Well, no. But—"

"Ashley Ellsworth is the only one going around shooting people. He's our killer."

"Then Jane's . . . Jane's dead?"

"Maybe. She was close to it when they took her in the ambulance. Why would he want to shoot Jane Talbert, do you have some idea? Did they have a plan? Were they in on this together? And then they had a fight maybe? Maybe she was going to come to us and spill where he was hiding out."

"I don't know anything. All I know is she writes for the *Chicago Trib* the same as Ace."

"Are they lovers? Maybe they had a lovers' quarrel and he popped her? Has Ashley Ellsworth got a bad temper?"

"I don't know."

"You were with him night and day for days and you don't know if he has a temper? I find that hard to believe, Miss Pembrook. He didn't get angry while on the run? That's a pretty stressful situation. Surely you saw him lose his temper sometime."

"Once," she agreed.

"Did he hit you?"

"No, he kicked the flat tire."

The officer looked at her. "That's it? He kicked a flat tire."

The officer tried another line of questioning.

"Why was he going to his grandmother's?"

"Jane was meeting him there."

"Why?"

Chloe decided it was time to fudge the truth a little, not tell them exactly what she knew, just enough to make it sound authentic. "She had something that he said would help him get out of the mess he was in."

The officer's guess was sarcastic, "Yeah, I'll bet, something like a plane ticket out of the country."

"Look, I've told you everything I know. I walked in on him killing someone. I panicked and ran, driving straight to the police station where I reported the murder. The police stashed me, but he saw where I was and in the confusion he snatched me. I'm innocent, why can't you just let me go?"

There was a knock on the door and a tall blond female officer stuck her head in to say that Pleasantville had faxed a request for extradition and Ashley Ellsworth was refusing it . . . the grandmother had sent over a lawyer for her grandson.

"Who's the lawyer?"

"Dickson."

"Shit."

Chloe inferred that Ace's grandmother knew her lawyers and had sent one who was going to be trouble.

The blond officer left them alone.

"Tell you what Miss Pembrook, I'm going to let you go. But don't leave town."

Chloe tried not to let her joy at the news show on her face. "Uh officer . . ." she said when he got up to dismiss her.

"Yes?"

"I can't go anywhere. I don't have a purse, or a credit card or anything."

He got up and called the blond female officer back to the room. He explained the situation to the other officer and then turned to Chloe, "Officer Haley will see to it that you have a motel room."

"Thank you, sir."

"One more thing, you will testify against Ashley Ellsworth won't you?"

"Yes, sir," Chloe replied, continuing to fudge.

"I want to get out of here, right now. Do you understand me? Where are my clothes?"

"Calm down Miss Talbert. You're not going anywhere until the doctor releases you and he's not going to release you until tomorrow at the earliest. You've suffered a bad concussion. The staff will watch you overnight. Then in the morning you will be sent up to x-ray."

"I'm not going to be here in the morning. Why won't anyone listen to me? I want to see who's in charge."

The nurse with red hair and a dusting of freckles left the room muttering.

"Are you sure they didn't put me in a lunatic asylum?"

Sarabeth smiled at Jane's crabby-bitching. "I know you don't like hearing it, but there is nothing you can do, Jane. You have to abide by the doctor's orders.

Heavens, you came very close to being killed today. In fact, Ace thought you were dead."

"Where is Ace. Oh yeah, he's in jail. Why did they put him in jail? Surely they don't think he shot me? I've got to help him."

"You'll help him by staying here until the doctor says you're ready to go."

Jane got up from the bed to offer evidence that she was fine, but the action defeated her purpose when she got dizzy and had to grab the edge of the bed to remain standing on her feet.

"Do you know what they feed you in these places?" Jane asked. "I'll tell you. Jello and broth. Yeech. It's disgusting." And then Jane brightened. "I'll tell you what, if you promise to smuggle me in some of your skillet cornbread tomorrow, I'll be good and eat my broth."

Sarabeth knew Jane was trying to save face at the unexpected spell of weakness when she'd tried to get out of bed. "I promise. I'll make my special recipe of skillet cornbread up in the cast-iron skillet for you and bring it in."

A nurse's aide came in the room pushing a cart in front of her.

"I don't want any magazines, I have a headache," Jane called out, shooing the woman.

"I think I'd better go now and let you get some rest," Sarabeth said, seeing what was on the nurse's cart.

"I'm afraid to take a nap in this joint, I'm afraid I'll wake up strapped down."

"Oh now, Jane. Try not to give everyone so much trouble. Take care and I'll bring you some of my fresh cornbread."

Sarabeth got up from her chair to let the nurse through with her cart.

As she was walking down the hall she heard Jane's bellowed objections to the nurse's intentions.

"And I'm telling you that no one has bathed me since I was a baby. Get away from me with that. Nurse, nurse. Somebody come in here and get this lesbian away from me."

Ace sat in his cell alone.

Well now he had plenty of time to think.

Think about the havoc he'd wreaked in the name of doing good.

And to worry.

About Jane.

They wouldn't tell him how she was. He sent up a silent prayer that she was alive and well and giving everyone in the hospital an ulcer.

Another for his grandmother who didn't deserve to be paid back for all her faith in him with the danger he'd placed her in.

And a final one for Chloe.

At least she was out of jail. He'd corroborated her story that he'd indeed kidnapped her because he needed a hostage. He didn't know how he was going to get out of the mess he was in, but he didn't want to involve her any more.

And then the thought surfaced that struck terror in him.

Chloe was out there alone and the killer was too. There was nothing to stop Zeke or Jon from trying again. They probably had mistaken Jane for Chloe as both women were blondes.

His grandmother was safe because they'd stake out the scene of the crime just in case anyone returned to the scene.

But Chloe was alone. They didn't suspect her so they wouldn't assign a cop to watch her.

And Chloe wouldn't go back to his grandmother's because she'd stuck to her story that she was an unwilling hostage.

He had to protect Chloe.

And to do that, he had to get out of jail somehow.

Thirty

Chloe woke up to find herself alone the following morning in a strange bedroom. While it was cozy, with a printed yellow flowered wallpaper, she knew she was no longer on Lily Pond Road where Ace's grandmother lived. The police had put her up for the night at a quaint little inn after they'd allowed her to retrieve Julie's car.

It was strange waking up without Ace being there, stranger still that she'd gotten so accustomed to his company in such a short span of time. She wondered how Ace had slept, if he'd slept at all, in the holding cell at the jail. Due to the excitement of the previous day, she'd slept a solid ten hours.

Stretching, she rolled her neck from side to side. Then she moved her legs over the edge of the bed, and got out of the soft, warm cocoon. Crossing to the window, she looked outside. A stiff wind was helping two pheasants cross the road.

Dorothy I don't think we're in Chicago anymore, she muttered with a shake of her head.

The police had ordered her not to leave town, so she'd called her lawyer collect before going to bed and instructed him to wire her money that was to be messengered to the inn. Her lawyer had agreed to wire the money after giving her a lecture about waiving her right to have an attorney present when she'd been questioned by the police.

Using the personal size toiletries in her private bath, she showered and dressed in the shorts and T-shirt she was sick of, then went downstairs to see if the envelope from her lawyer had arrived.

The envelope had arrived, but she'd overslept breakfast and so decided to eat when she shopped for something else to wear.

A light rain began to fall as she slowed her car on the Sunrise Highway where it narrowed into two lanes then veered to the right onto Main Street where the chic shops were located. A bicyclist darted past her in a hurry to get out of the rain.

Window boxes in vibrant bloom gave the shops a profusion of color. The shop she entered had a combination of lamb's ears, incana, lychnis, and santolina, in white window boxes.

The shop was nautical in decor with a navy and white color scheme. A huge old scarred painted produce table held an array of silver jewelry.

A young girl with a dark bob and bow-shaped lips approached to wait on her.

After making her selection of a choker necklace and two bracelet bangles, Chloe handed them to the salesgirl and moved on to the rack of dresses.

On the glass circle above the rack, a tableau of wooden windmills and lighthouse miniatures reminded her of the sea air that she still couldn't get used to.

"Are you looking for a particular color or style?" the young clerk asked.

Chloe smiled and shook her head. "I shop on instinct. So I never know what I want until I see it." She saw it a few seconds later. A sleeveless, tailored long

white linen dress that buttoned up the front from hem
to neck.

"I'll take this," she said, slipping the hanger from
the rack. "And this," she added, selecting a beige cotton open-holed crocheted sleeveless sweater to throw
over it.

"Will that be all?"

Chloe gave the clerk her size in hose and then paid
the damage.

After two more shops, Chloe had added underwear,
a pair of sling-back pumps and white capris to complete her shopping. Anything more would have to wait
for the arrival of her replaced charge card.

It was past time for lunch when she'd finished her
shopping. The sun that had risen over the Atlantic to
shine into her bedroom and wake her, was now high
in the sky.

She opted for health food in light of her fast food
repast for the week. At J. L. Bean Cafe, she ate a new-
age vegetarian Hot Lick Cone, selecting the BBQ tofu
version.

While she ate she scanned one of the Hamptons'
free sheets reading about the Hampton Classic, the
equestrian event of the summer for the Northeast.
Perusing the ads for residential rentals she saw that a
two-bedroom house or condo rented for anywhere
from $1,300.00 to $1,700.00 in East Hampton, one of
the priciest of the local communities. That was a lot
to pay for laid-back ambiance, if you asked her. More
than she could afford at this stage of her career, but
not impossible if her career continued to expand as
she planned.

What was she thinking? The Hamptons were hardly
a summer home when you lived in Chicago. Even Ace,
who had a family compound at his disposal for nada
visited infrequently.

Thinking of Ace brought her round to thinking of what she'd been trying to avoid; her situation.

She couldn't go and visit Ace in jail. That would be suspicious.

She couldn't go and visit Sarabeth, that would be suspicious as well.

That left Jane.

A call to the Southampton Hospital netted her the information that Jane was improving and that made Chloe wonder if that meant the nurses had washed her mouth out with soap. And then she felt guilty for her thought.

Jane had almost been killed because someone had mistaken Jane for her. There simply wasn't a reason for someone to shoot Jane no matter how she turned the idea of it over in her mind. That bullet had to have been fired by Zeke or Blakemore's son because they didn't want to take a chance on what she might have overheard about their shady business practices at Zimmerman's Garage.

Under different circumstances, Jane had, like Chloe, been at the wrong place at the right time.

Since Ace couldn't visit Jane, she should.

And best-case scenario, she might run into Sarabeth visiting Jane. Sarabeth might have information on what was happening with Ace.

After another call to Julie that didn't go through because no one appeared to be at home, Chloe drove back to the inn to change clothes before going to visit Jane at the hospital. She was relieved the call to Julie didn't go through because she wasn't looking forward to trying to explain just what had happened. Let's see . . . she was kidnapped by a gorgeous guy who'd just killed someone as she watched. Bad guys were chasing them. She was sure they were the bad guys because her kidnapper had told her so.

Oh yeah, and she'd fallen in love with her kidnapper, who was in jail and who was possibly in love with a knock-out blond reporter he worked with at the *Chicago Tribune*.

Chloe shook her head at her reflection in the full length oval mirror on a stand in her bedroom at the inn. Even she wouldn't buy that storyline in her favorite soap opera.

You had to be there, she told her reflection.

Smoothing the white linen dress, she pivoted to see her reflection front and back. Satisfied that she looked refreshed, she headed for the hospital, stealing a sunflower from the vase of fresh flowers on the table in her room.

In the elevator at the hospital she took a deep breath, uncertain of the reception she would get from Jane. After all they had barely had a chance to speak to each other. And if Jane was sleeping with Ace, well, Chloe knew how she felt about another blonde being in the picture.

The sunflower in her hand shook as she entered Jane's room.

The room was empty.

Chloe's heart fell in a panic.

Surely nothing terrible had—

"Can I help you?" a passing nurse's aide inquired.

"Yes, the patient in this room. Is she—is she ah—"

"She's up in x-ray," the nurse's aide replied matter-of-factly moving on down the hall.

Chloe sank down into a chair.

"Why Chloe, what are you doing here?"

Chloe opened her eyes and looked up to see Sarabeth entering Jane's room. "And where's Jane?"

"Jane's up in x-ray. I was hoping I might run into you here." Chloe stood and took the vase of flowers

Sarabeth had in her hands, offering Sarabeth the chair.

While Sarabeth sat down, Chloe placed the vase of flowers on the windowsill, adding her sunflower to it.

"These roses smell heavenly, are they from your garden?" Chloe commented, unsure of how to approach Sarabeth.

"The flowers are from my garden," Sarabeth said with a nod. "But we've more important things to talk about than gardens right now. My grandson is in jail for murder. And they think he shot Jane. Can you imagine such a thing? No one will talk to me. I didn't want to upset Jane with it last night, but I want to know what's going on."

While they waited for Jane to return to the room, Chloe filled Sarabeth in on everything that had happened before they'd come to East Hampton.

"You know my grandson is innocent. He's not a murderer," Sarabeth stated unequivocally.

"Yes, I believe him," Chloe said, squeezing Sarabeth's hand for reassurance. "The bullet that knocked Jane unconscious was meant for me, I'm sure. We're both blonde and . . ."

"Oh, you mustn't blame yourself," Sarabeth comforted. "I've got the family lawyer working to get Ashley out of jail. Everything will be all right, you'll see."

Chloe didn't bother to explain that even if the family lawyer could get the charges against Ace for shooting Jane dropped, Pleasantville would be extraditing him back to Illinois to stand trial for the murder of Blakemore's son, not that Ace would ever live to get to trial.

She needed time alone to talk with Jane. Perhaps between the two of them they could come up with a plan to help Ace.

But it didn't look good.

"Did I die and no one told me?" Jane said, entering the room. "If the two of you came to cheer me up, it's not working. I think you have to smile at the very least. Is it cold in here? I feel a draft all the time. I swear some pervert designed these damned hospital gowns."

"Hello, Jane," Sarabeth said. "How did the x-rays come out?"

"It's a secret. They won't tell me. All the people in white coats around here think they work for the secret service. I tell you this is a lunatic asylum."

"Sarabeth brought you flowers," Chloe said, inanely nodding to the vase on the windowsill.

"Thank you. It'll make a hell of an improvement smelling roses over the antiseptic. Hello, Chloe. I was wondering if you were going to have the nerve to show up."

"Jane!" Sarabeth exclaimed.

"Oh not because I took a bullet for her. I meant because she thinks I'm sleeping with your grandson."

"I—ah . . ." Chloe stammered.

"Oh for heaven's sake, Chloe. Even Sarabeth can see the two of you are smitten and that you were pea-green with envy when you thought Ace and I went upstairs to frolic while you and Sarabeth were in the attic. I admit I got a kick out of leading you on. Ace wanted to strangle me for giving you the wrong impression.

"It's true we were lovers. But now we're only friends. I know you're as relieved to hear it, Sarabeth, as Chloe is. The only reason we hadn't made it clear to you before, Sarabeth, was because you were always bringing maiden ladies for Ace to court."

"I was not . . ."

"No hard feelings, Sarabeth. I know you like me.

And I like you. But you're right, Ace and I are wrong for each other and we figured that out. We'd probably kill each other trying to get the scoop on the same story. So, he's all yours, Chloe. You just have to get him out of jail."

"Easier said than done," Chloe said glumly.

"Sarabeth, I hope you brought me that fresh skillet cornbread of yours you promised me. I'm starving."

"Oh, dear, I forgot. I took my sleeping pills last night so I'd get a good night's sleep. And this morning I forgot about making the cornbread. I'm going home right now to make you some."

Sarabeth made good her escape, leaving Chloe to deal with Jane.

When Jane was sure Sarabeth was gone, she sat down on the bed and looked at Chloe.

"I suppose you've figured out Ace isn't the only one in danger," she warned.

Thirty-one

Ace felt like hell.

Sleep had eluded him.

He'd spent the night in the holding cell going over ideas for ways to escape. He had to get to Chloe and protect her.

His first plan had been to attempt his escape when he made his appearance before the first district judge. When the cops took him from the police car to the courthouse he could have head-butted the one cop and kicked the other in the groin, taking the cuff keys.

He'd discarded that plan when he realized it could take up to forty-eight hours before he was brought to appear in Riverhead before the judge.

It was imperative he get to Chloe before then.

The plan he settled on was illness.

His nonexistent ulcer was about to act up—and so was he.

He began moaning softly at first. When he got the guard's attention he increased the volume, adding an agonized groan.

The guard came over to the cell, peering in. "What's wrong in there?"

"Nothing," Ace answered by way of diverting suspicion that he was trying to gain attention. "I just don't feel so good."

"You want an aspirin or something?"

"No. No, I can't take aspirin. I've got an ulcer. Ohhhh . . . damn, it hurts. It hurts all the way through to my back. I hope it's not bleeding again."

"What?"

"Sometimes when I get really stressed my ulcer acts up and begins bleeding. Look if I . . ." Ace began weaving on his feet. ". . . get me to a doc . . ." He fell to the floor.

The guard bought it.

Before he knew what had happened, Ace was loaded in the back of an ambulance wearing cuffs with a police officer chaperon sitting beside him.

The siren sliced through the quiet day, and Ace continued his act for the police officer's benefit. He couldn't afford a screw-up.

Once they were at the hospital and the handcuffs were off he'd make good on his escape.

In his mind it had been a lot easier.

But in reality the police officer guarding him was a tough cop. There was no way Ace was going to escape while he was with him. It would have to be while Ace was with the doctor and hopefully uncuffed.

So Ace stayed "in character" keeping himself curled into a fetal position and moaning until the doctor was ready to see him.

After checking him and listening to Ace's description of his pain, the doctor ordered x-rays, which meant Ace had to be uncuffed.

The x-ray technicians were still talking about a patient they'd had earlier in the day. The woman had turned the place upside down with her determination not to be x-rayed. When Ace heard the description of her as a ditsy blond broad, his heart leapt—Jane!

The woman who hadn't wanted her head x-rayed sounded like Jane. Was it possible . . .

But to ask might arouse suspicion and he couldn't

risk it. Instead he told the technician he had to go to the bathroom and couldn't wait. He didn't, however, go to the bathroom the harried technician indicated.

Picking the room next to it, Ace slipped into it and out the window. Knowing he had only a few minutes before his absence was detected, he made his way to the parking lot by climbing across and then jumping down from the air-conditioning unit.

He couldn't believe his luck when he saw Chloe on the parking lot about to get into her car. It gave him even more hope that Jane was alive, and it told him he wasn't too late to save Chloe from harm.

Since he was still in street clothes, no one paid any attention to him as he hurried to the end of the parking aisle Chloe would have to drive through in order to leave the parking lot. He crouched down until she was almost upon him, then stood, flagging her down discreetly.

She braked sharply and he pulled open the unlocked passenger door and dove inside, yelling for her to "get the hell out of here, fast."

"Are you kidnapping me again, Ace?"

"Yes, now will you please go, before they discover I'm gone and they arrest both of us."

She did as he instructed and sped out of the parking lot.

"Where are we going?" she asked when they'd gone several blocks and he was still keeping out of sight below the window.

"Head to my grandmother's, but don't stop. Keep going past it, I'll tell you when to stop," he instructed. "We've got a good head start. I don't hear any sirens yet. Either they don't know I'm gone yet, or they still think I'm on the hospital premises."

Chloe placed her hand on her chest, continuing to drive with her other hand on the steering wheel. Her heart was pounding beneath her left hand as she looked in the rear-view mirror.

She braked when the car in front of her stopped suddenly. Ace was thrown against the dash.

"Sorry."

"Just try to get us back to East Hampton in one piece." He rubbed his head where it had banged into the dash hard enough to raise a bump.

"Can I ask you a question?" Chloe asked as she maneuvered around the slow driver ahead of her.

"What?"

"Why are you barefoot?"

"They took my shoes at the police station when they put me in the holding cell. I guess they were worried I was going to hang myself with my shoelaces or something weird."

"Oh."

"What were you doing at the hospital?" he asked hopefully.

"Seeing Jane."

"Then she's going to be all right."

"I wouldn't go that far," Chloe said dryly. "I think that might take years of intense therapy."

"Then she is going to be all right. You wouldn't say anything that mean unless she was feeling good enough to drive everyone crazy. In x-ray they were talking about a blond patient doing just that. I was hoping against hope it was Jane. What happened? I thought she was almost dead, actually I thought she was dead until the paramedic found a pulse."

"The bullet just creased her skull knocking her unconscious. The blood you saw was only a scalp wound. Sarabeth said Jane threw up all over the nurse when she came to."

Ace laughed. "That sounds like Jane."

On highway 27 they got behind the green Hampton

Jitney carrying New York's social elite from Manhattan.

"Ace," Chloe said when they'd rode in silence for a while.

"Yes . . ."

"You do have a plan—"

"I'm working on one."

"What's all the excitement?" Jane asked the nurse who came in to take her blood pressure. "Why is everyone running around? Is there a fire you aren't telling me about?"

"Yes, I think you should jump out the window," the petite brunette nurse said, not the least bit intimidated by Jane.

"What kind of remark is that? You're making my blood pressure rise. Come on, tell me what's going on that's got everyone so excited. Have the Harlem Globetrotters come to visit? Clowns? What?"

"Someone escaped," the nurse answered taking off the blood-pressure cuff.

"See I knew this place was an asylum and they were making up stories about why I couldn't leave. You aren't a nurse at all, are you. You're an attendant, right?"

"Yeah, I'm an attendant. At night I'm a bouncer at a dockside bar," the nurse said dryly, alluding to her size.

"Someone really escaped?" Jane said, sitting up with interest. "From what? Do you have a psych ward here or something?"

"This is the Hamptons, Miss Talbert."

"What? So there can't be any crazy people here? They all come from New York, how could they not be crazy? There are too many people in your face all the time."

"He was a prisoner," the nurse explained, on her way out of the room. "They brought him over here from the jail in East Hampton."

East Hampton. Jane's brain began buzzing. Could it be?

"Was he good-looking?" Jane asked, trying to sound casual.

"Why, do you need a date to the prom?"

"That's some bedside manner you've got there."

The nurse smiled smugly. "Thanks, I try to tailor it to my patients' individual needs."

"Are you saying that I'm—"

"Charming? What do you think?"

"Are you going to tell me if this guy was good-looking or did you stash him in a linen closet for yourself?" Jane persisted.

"Who knows? They said he had a full beard. I suspect he was trying to hide a weak chin. Now if you don't mind I do have other patients, you know."

"But none as charming as me," Jane said, waving her off.

Instinctively Jane knew there was no weak chin under that beard. Ace's chin was anything but weak.

"Where am I going?" Chloe asked as they passed Ace's grandmother's.

"Three houses down on the left," he instructed.

"Okay," she answered a few minutes later. "We're there. Now what?"

"Pull off the road and follow the drive down to the cottage in back. It's the guest house and it isn't wired for intruders. The family goes to Scotland every sum-

mer during August. We can park the car in the garage
and hide out here until it gets dark.

"No one will think to look for us here especially
since it's so close to Grandmother's. They'll think I
headed back to Manhattan."

Chloe stopped at the end of the drive and waited
while Ace went and opened the garage for her to pull
the car inside.

When she'd parked it and gotten out, he'd closed
the garage door.

"How do you know about this place?" she asked,
following him outside to where he found a buried key
under a rock.

"I used to be friends with their son when we were
in school together. He used to throw some wild bache-
lor parties here in the summer before he went to live
in New York, where he works as a stockbroker."

"Aren't you afraid he might show up?"

"No, he had some kind of falling-out with his parents and he hasn't been back in years. My grandmother keeps me up with the local gossip. How is she
holding up?"

"Okay. She said she's having trouble sleeping, so
she's been taking sleeping pills to help her sleep at
night."

"Good."

"Good?"

"We have to break into grandmother's tonight and
I'd rather not wake her. We have to find those documents."

Thirty-two

The cottage mirrored the wealth of the main house but was casual and comfortable in style. It had been planned to take advantage of the view, with lots of windows for light.

Pale yellow walls and white woodwork gave the rooms a warm, sunny friendliness. Window seats invited curling up to enjoy the view or a good book from the bookshelves crammed with hardbacks that were worn and seemingly well read.

A 1920s gilded iron bed sat on an angle in the bedroom facing a fireplace that was filled with candles for the summer. A club chair was upholstered in mattress ticking. Beside it was a floor lamp. The odds and ends that made up the wooden bedroom furniture were painted white.

After their quick tour of the cottage, Ace went in search of a shower while Chloe went in search of food in the pantry in the small kitchen.

In the tiny kitchen she found a couple of cans of chili in the cupboard, and a box of soda crackers dated for September expiration. The refrigerator didn't hold much bounty, however. There wasn't a cold beer or soda to be found. Just ice in the ice-cube trays and a bottle of catsup.

Resourceful, Chloe kept rummaging.

The last guests to visit must have had kids because

she found a packet of Kool-Aid in some ghastly color and a box of animal crackers they could split for dessert. With the canister of sugar, she made up a pitcher of Kool-Aid and set it in the refrigerator to cool. While she stirred the warming chili she let her mind think about what she had deliberately avoided.

Who would believe Ace had kidnapped her twice?

This time she wasn't going to get off with a hint of suspicion and a warning. If they caught them before Ace and she located the documents, the jig was up. Her career was up.

And it was worth the risk.

Because Jane and Ace weren't lovers after all. They were friends as Ace had claimed. He hadn't played her for a fool. She could trust him.

As well as love him.

In the shower Ace thought about Chloe.

Had he done the right thing? What if Zeke and Jon had high-tailed it back to Pleasantville when the cops had arrived after they'd shot Jane? What if he'd involved Chloe again and she hadn't been in any real danger?

She had been alone since her release from questioning and there hadn't been any attempt on her life.

He leaned his head against the tile wall of the shower and let the rushing water from the shower pound down on his head as if the water would clear it.

Maybe he should have told the authorities the truth, on the hope that he'd be believed. All they had to do was call the Environmental Protection Agency to see what the result of their follow-up on Chloe's call had been. But it was probably too soon for the bureaucracy to have acted yet.

If Chloe hadn't stood a chance of being in danger,

he probably would have gone that route. It was just that he wasn't prepared to take any chances where Chloe was concerned. He'd involved her, so he owed her his protection. He had promised that if she did as he asked, she wouldn't be hurt.

That wasn't true. Even if they got out of this unscathed, her career would be touched by it. Scandal would touch her.

And he was to blame.

After he'd scrubbed the germs of the holding cell from his body, and rinsed away the suds, he stepped out of the shower and toweled off with a beach towel that had the Harvard insignia on it. Confronting his reflection in the mirror, he decided to come out of hiding.

Finding a can of citrusy shaving cream and a pack of toss-away razors in the medicine cabinet, he scraped off the several days' worth of beard he'd encouraged while they were on the run.

The man who looked back at him from the mirror looked much younger without the beard. He hoped he was much wiser.

The pair of jeans from his friend's closet were a size too large and rode dangerously low on his belly. The loafers were too small as it turned out so he gave up on them, getting used to wearing nothing but jeans and his skin.

The aroma of spicy chili led him to the kitchen and to Chloe, who was bending forward over the table she'd set. She was lighting a candle she'd taken from the fireplace to add a hint of atmosphere to the funky dinner.

All of a sudden Ace's mouth was watering.

* * *

"Let me get this straight," Peter Blakemore said to the three men sitting in the library of his home.

"Someone, not you, Zeke or Jon, was shooting at Ash Worth and a blond woman who wasn't Chloe Pembrook? Whoever it was hit the blond woman and the cops swarmed the place."

"That's right," Jon assured his father. "We think the blond woman might be Jane Talbert, a woman who works with Ash at the *Trib*. He went to her apartment when he stopped in Chicago on the way to the coast, but the woman wasn't there. We think she arranged to meet him at his grandmother's with something he could use against us."

"Us?"

"The family," Jon explained hastily.

"I see." Blakemore's long fingers played with a large silver paper clip. "But you don't know who the someone doing the shooting was?"

Jon and Zeke shook their heads no.

Blakemore looked to Darrow Smith. "And you?"

"Only a guess—since both Ace and the Talbert woman are investigative reporters, maybe they hacked someone else off real good. Maybe it was an old score being settled by a hit."

Blakemore looked from his son to Zeke and back, saving the contempt for his son. "So you went all that way and found out nothing. Is that what you have to tell me?"

Jon didn't say anything at first. Then he allowed his anger to bubble up to his lips. "You're the one who ordered us not to—"

"That isn't what I asked you, now is it?" Blakemore's dark eyes were cold and unforgiving.

Jon stomped from the library, slamming the door behind him like a teenager who'd been told he couldn't have the car.

Blakemore looked from Zeke to Darrow, unembarrassed. "I wonder how my son is going to like driving a compact four-cylinder instead of the luxury car you boys totaled," he asked, not expecting an answer.

"You've put through the paperwork for the extradition to bring Ash Worth back to Pleasantville . . ." Blakemore verified looking to Darrow.

Darrow nodded.

"And there won't be any problem with the woman being shot? I want Ash Worth."

"There shouldn't be any problem. The woman turns out to have only a flesh wound, nothing to compete with a violent felony like we have a warrant out for him on. We should have first and best dibs on Ash Worth. I wouldn't worry about it, sir."

"I will worry until he's here. And this time there had better not be any screw-ups. Who's going to bring Ash back here?"

"Zeke will as soon as—"

"That's not good enough." Blakemore stood and walked over to the window. His grey striped double-breasted suit was tailored to perfection and showed off his elegant carriage. "I want you to go."

"Instead of Zeke?"

"No, with him. I don't want any slip-ups. Ash Worth is not going to take me down with him. Do you understand me?"

"Yes, sir." Darrow wished he'd just said no when the opportunity to double dip had been presented to him. He hadn't thought the price would escalate the way it had. He should have known better. The minute he'd seen who was writing the checks he should have known better. How in the hell had he gotten so stupid? First he let a woman take advantage and now this bastard . . .

"Is that all?" Zeke asked when neither man spoke for some time.

"No. I want to know for certain if Ash Worth was bluffing. I don't want someone calling me with a blackmail scheme. I don't want this to come back to haunt me when we've dealt with Ash Worth. Do you understand? I want to know."

"I understand," Darrow answered. Though he wasn't sure it was possible to do what Blakemore requested. All he knew is that he'd better hope that if he didn't find anything, there was nothing to be found.

Blakemore turned a few minutes later and seemed surprised to find them still there.

Taking their cue, the two men left his company, both wanting to keep going until they were out of town. When they were out of the house and in the police car, Zeke voiced his dislike of the wealthy man.

"Why is it some people never have enough, Chief? He didn't need to do anything crooked to get what he has. He's got the biggest house in town, the most expensive cars, and that suit he was wearing would cost me a month's wages. He could afford any woman he wants, he does want women, doesn't he?"

"He's straight, if that's what you were wondering. But he likes married women, that's why you never hear who he's seeing even in this small a town. The women he sees are well paid and have too much to lose by talking. There's no way he'd marry any of them and they know it. To talk would cut off the presents," Darrow said, in a talkative mood. "As to why he does what he does, the answer is simple. It's greed. Money buys power. And power is what's important to men like Blakemore. He'd die being a small fish in a big pond."

"Go figure, to be miserable with all the money he has. Hell, if I'd be."

"Amen, to that Zeke."

* * *

Jane was in a much better mood.

When Ace had escaped they'd put a cop on her door. Every woman should have one. Especially one like hers; he was a hunk and a half.

She sat propped up in her hospital bed no longer threatening to sign herself out of the hospital. In her hands was a wonderful new Bonnie Jeanne Perry romance titled, *Naked Truths*. The petite tough nurse who'd taken her blood pressure had turned out not to be such a bad sort. She'd lifted the paperback for Jane from the nurse's station, practically tearing it out of a nurse's aide's hand.

The further she got into the novel, the better the policeman stationed at the door to her room looked. She wondered what he would look like in purple tights. And then she smiled, recalling Errol Mills. The policeman probably wouldn't look as good as Errol. And most likely would slug anyone who suggested he don them.

Oh well, some men had no imagination. There the good-looking young stud was with a pair of shiny silver handcuffs at his disposal and no imagination. What a waste.

Maybe she'd just have some fun with him.

She *was* feeling better, only a little dizzy when she got up too quickly. But no one said she had to get up—he was the one who had to get up!

"Hey officer . . ." she called out in her best Mae West imitation; a young virginal coo wouldn't float, she knew.

"Yes, ma'am."

"That's good. Remember to say that. I like a man who—"

". . . says please and thank you," the cop guessed.

"My pillow, it needs fluffing. Do you think you could . . ."

Poor thing didn't know what he was getting into

when he approached, if a little apprehensively. The hospital gown really was much more practical worn backwards . . .

Thirty-three

"This was a pretty funky meal," Ace said when they'd finished the chili, Kool-Aid and animal crackers. "How many demerits would a lifestyle expert get for serving a meal like this?"

Chloe blotted her lips lightly with a paper napkin with a purple dinosaur printed on it. "I'd get points, not demerits. It takes resourcefulness and flair to make something from nothing, and make it appealing."

"I'll tell you what will get you points. He pushed his damp hair back from his face. If you can cut my hair, you'll not only get points, I'll give you twenty bucks."

"No deal."

"Not that resourceful, huh?" he challenged.

"I can cut your hair, but I've got money. My lawyer wired me some. I'll cut your hair, if you do the dishes."

She hadn't thought he'd take her up on it. In fact she had thought he was only ragging her about cutting his hair. Evidently he didn't wear it that long all the time, it had only been part of his investigative-reporter disguise.

But since he'd agreed to do the dishes, she was caught. Caught in the web of a more than half naked man whose jeans kept threatening to slide past provocative, all the way to invitation.

She bit her lip.

And saw that he knew his appeal. It was there in

his flashy green eyes. He was bored, with nothing to do until dark, so taunting her was sport.

She steeled herself. He was the one who should be nervous. She was the one with the scissors she took from the kitchen drawer in her hand.

"Where would you like me to do this, Samson?"

"Here's fine. I'll get a comb."

She practiced taking deep breaths to calm her nerves until he returned to hand her the comb and sit down before her.

The deep breaths had been a mistake. She felt light-headed.

"How short do you want it?"

"Leave enough at the crown for a ponytail," he instructed as she parted a section of hair, and dropped the scissors.

"You're kidding, right?"

She reached her hand over his shoulder for the scissors he'd picked up.

"Not any more," he said, hoarsely, kissing, then licking her open palm he'd wrapped in his hand.

She took a sudden intake of breath in surprised response to his flirting.

It was there between them again. The adrenaline rush she couldn't deny or identify as a response to the danger they were in or their sexual attraction or both.

She was about to pull her hand away when he tugged her off balance to land in his lap, wrapped in his arms.

Once again a willing hostage.

"You look good in white," he said. "No wonder the professor married you. I bet you were a beautiful bride."

His coaxing voice was velvet as he reduced her to liquid describing how he'd remove her wedding gown, button by tiny satin-covered button if she were his bride.

It was a fantasy in his mind, she knew.

A potent one because she shared it, but not just the visual image, the emotional one as well.

"And you'd wear the family pearls," he said, fingering the silver choker she wore. "And following the family tradition we'd start, the pearls would have to be restrung after every succeeding bride's wedding night because they'd get broken *somehow*."

A man who talked of weddings? A romantic?

He took her thoughts and breath away whispering and showing her with his reckless kissing assault of seduction what making love with him would be like, his tongue thrusting and parrying . . . sure, expert and coaxing.

"Ace," she said shakily.

"Hmmmm . . ." he pulled his lips away from hers, his eyes glittering with sexy intent, passion unbanked.

"I can't do this and walk away—"

"I came after you, didn't I? I'm here to protect you, not harm you, Chloe." His eyes searched her for understanding, and when he saw it, he threaded his hand through her hair and bent her head back so he could slide open-mouthed kisses down her slender throat.

Her hand moved on his bare chest, caressing his honed muscles while his caress made her tremble with longing.

His lips nipped lower, stopping at the cleavage at the scooped neck of her dress. He looked up at her. His stare was hot as his hand went to push up the wispy beige sweater shell she wore.

"Looky what I've uncovered," he said, laughing softly. "A bridal white dress with the buttons conveniently in front."

He began undoing the buttons slowly one by one.

He stopped at her waist and slid his hand beneath the open front of her white linen dress, his touch warm on her satin-encased breast. He caressed her through the material until she grew impatient and guided his hand inside her bra to splay around her bare breast.

She threw back her head, moaning softly in response to the feel on her bare skin of his hand, tugging, kneading then squeezing gently.

She felt his response—his heart beating wildly beneath her hand, his ragged breathing, his hard arousal where she sat on his lap, no that was the scissors!

"Ouch!" she said, leaping up from the chair.

"What? What did I do?"

She showed him the scissors in her hand.

"Sorry, I got distracted," he apologized.

"Yeah, so did I." She waited.

He waited.

"Hold me," she said softly.

He stood and took her in his arms, comforting her. Protecting her. Loving her.

And they began again.

Only this time they were toe to toe both seducing and being seduced, each taking, giving, not knowing where either left off.

He lifted her in his arms, carrying her to the bedroom. He set her on her feet beside the bed and then he was kissing her again, and again. Breaking his lips from hers, he dragged in a gulp of air. "I keep forgetting to breathe. You're a dangerously exciting woman, Chloe Pembrook."

She found his words thrilling because they validated her feminine power over him. He wanted her as much as she wanted him.

He stepped back, tugging off the jeans he'd unbuttoned when he'd set her down beside the bed. His body announced his desire for her, exciting her.

He pulled her slowly toward him, and then began inching up her dress, up past the tops of her stockings, up past her hips until he could slide his hand inside her panties while he rubbed his hardness against her. The steady rhythm of his hand caressed her intimately until she found herself moving shamelessly toward that rhythm.

They tumbled sideways onto the bed and all teasing foreplay escalated to full-out lovemaking as he urgently pulled her panties to her knees and raised her hips to meet his deep thrust.

He pulled her hips up from the bed to meet his thrusts as he knelt before her. Ecstasy swept them over the edge and he shuddered against her.

Later, in the shower, when Chloe had a somewhat clearer head, she brought up the subject of protection while Ace was soaping up her back.

"Safe sex?" Ace repeated. "You're right, we both—I should have, but we haven't done anything safe since fate threw us together like dry kindling and lit a match. Don't worry, I practice it as a rule. You just have me breaking all my rules. You've got me talking about weddings without stuttering when I should be thinking about the terrible jam I've gotten us in."

"And if there's a baby—" Chloe held her breath. Her professor husband had been phobic about the thought of a child.

"A baby. If there's a baby, you have to make me a promise."

Chloe closed her eyes. Here it came. The avoidance of responsibility and commitment for one's actions. Ace talked a good story about ideals, but his were global, not personal. His integrity was tied up in causes, not effects. A tear slid down her cheek and was washed away by the shower of water sluicing down her body.

When she didn't say anything, Ace took her silence

as acquiescence. "You have to promise to bring our baby to see me in prison."

"Prison!"

"If we don't find those documents, you have to understand prison is a very real threat."

She turned to face him, putting her arms around his neck. "Don't say that."

"It's true. I know the police think I'm the one who shot at Jane, since Zeke and/or Jon eluded them. I tried to tell them, but they weren't going to believe a guy who had a violent felony warrant out on him from another state. And of course, with your statement that I did kidnap you and that you saw me commit the murder—"

"I told them that so they'd let me out. I figured that was the only way I could try to . . ."

"I know," he quieted her explanation with a kiss. "You did the right thing. And you did help me. But now you're involved again."

"I'm involved no matter what," she vowed, returning his earlier kiss with hungry need. "We'll find the documents tonight."

"We have to. At least with the evidence that Blakemore was dumping toxic waste and I was a threat to his operation, I have some proof that his son had reason to lure me out on a wild goose hunt to kill me. Without the evidence, Blakemore will dispose of the drums by the time the case gets to trial. It will be too late to prove my innocence and I'll have to take my chances with my word against a dead man's."

"What's to keep Blakemore from disposing of the drums now?"

"He won't want to draw attention while the spotlight is on him. He'd wait until things settle down."

Chloe shook off a shiver as the shower water grew

cool. They'd been in the shower so long the hot water had run out.

Ace saw her shiver, and he reached for a towel. Wrapping her in it, he lifted her in his arms and carried her back to the bed.

"Do you have a plan . . . ?" she asked, her mind still on the lost documents they were going to search his grandmother's house for, as soon as it got dark.

"Yes."

She heard the sexy rasp of his voice and looked up to see the glint of desire shimmering in his green eyes.

"My plan is to—"

"I'm talking about how we're going to go about tonight."

"Chloe . . ."

"What?" she said, when he leaned over her, raining soft baby kisses on her lower belly.

"Don't think. Just feel. Tonight will take care of itself. You can distract the guard," he said, taking her nipple in his mouth and sucking until she moaned. "And then while he's distracted, I'll slip in like this," his two fingers slipped inside her swiftly, making her gasp with surprise.

"What guard?" she asked, her mind beginning to fog over with lust.

"They'll have a cop watching the house for me to return."

"Oh. Oh!" The second "oh!" was in response to his mouth covering her sex while his fingers worked equal magic.

And then she couldn't think anymore.

Only feel.

Really, *really* good.

Thirty-four

"Well they definitely know you're missing," Chloe said to Ace as they watched the news on television while waiting for dusk to settle into darkness so they could make their way across the land that separated them from his grandmother's house.

The news story had video coverage of the hospital Ace had escaped from, after the police had taken him there in an ambulance from the holding cell at the jail.

The content of the news story stated that he had seemed to just disappear and that he was dangerous, wanted in another state for a violent felony. They showed the gun they'd confiscated from Ace's grandmother's house when they searched it; the gun that had been used to kill Peter Blakemore, Jr., the reporter said.

"But I don't think they know you've disappeared with me," Ace pointed out. "They only said you had not been reached for comment."

They had reached his grandmother though.

The reporter didn't have enough sense not to torment an eighty-year-old woman.

But by the time the reporter was done, Ace was smiling, betting the reporter had wished she hadn't questioned Sarabeth Ellsworth of "the prominent Ellsworth family of East Hampton."

His grandmother had told the reporter that either

she didn't have a lick of sense or she knew her grandson hadn't killed anyone. At least anyone who hadn't
needing killing. She explained that her grandson had
been working hard on a difficult story and that she
was certain that when everything was said and done,
they'd feel pretty foolish for arresting and charging
him. For example, she'd used Jane, explaining they'd
been wrong to believe Ace had shot her.

The next video was of Jane. In her hospital bed.
With a mohair pink sweater on that made her look
sexy and innocent all at once. Ace wondered where
she'd gotten the sweater in August. It certainly wasn't
anything he'd ever seen her in before.

If the reporter had wished she hadn't talked to Ace's
grandmother, that would have gone double for Jane.

Jane didn't let her get a word in edgeways.

"Only an idiot would think Ace had shot her," she
stated flat out. Then, with a twinkle in her eye—Ace
knew it was for his benefit, should he catch the news
report—she added, "Ace wouldn't kill me. He worships
the ground I walk on. Why I practically taught him everything he knows about being an investigative reporter."

"Yes Ace would kill you," Ace said, switching off
the television and wishing he could switch off Jane's
mouth as well. "Now that's what I call tabloid news,"
he said to Chloe.

"It's only news because I'm one of the East Hampton Ellsworths from an old-line pedigreed, spell that
GREED, family tree. They hate the exclusivity of The
Maidstone sitting high on the hill above the golf
course that's Private with a capital P. Every time they
see a station wagon with a country club sticker on the
rear window they want to hit something. You could
see the relish on her face.

"And the funny thing is I belong and I don't care.

Couldn't care less. They *care*. They are the ones who are desperate to belong.

"Oh well, it's a good thing my family isn't speaking to me, because for sure they wouldn't be speaking to me now."

"Are you done?" Chloe asked when he'd wound down his speech.

"Yeah," he said sheepish. She was even able to discern a faint blush beneath his freshly shaven pale skin.

"It's getting dark out," she noted.

"So it is. You're going to have to change into something black if you don't want to be seen breaking in. See what you can find in the closet that will suffice."

When they were both ready, she saw he was dressed in a black T-shirt and dark jogging pants. While normally he had a sort of skewed academic sexiness, in that outfit he looked almost rugged.

"Are we ready?" she asked.

Ace nodded.

"Where's the flashlight?"

"No flashlight. I know all the buttons to push. It's all in the fingertips." He rubbed his together to illustrate his point.

She'd gotten his point and taken it one further. He certainly did know what buttons to push to break and enter. And it was all in his fingertips . . .

"Don't go daydreamin' on me now, woman. This isn't going to be a walk in the park, as easy as falling off a log or any of those inane—"

"How do you want me to distract the policeman they'll have posted," she asked.

"I was kidding about that."

"You don't think they'll have a policeman posted in case you show up?"

"If they do, I don't want you anywhere near him, silly. They'll want to talk to you for sure, detain you for sure. And you have this unfortunate penchant for telling the absolute truth. Tell me before we go off on this dangerous mission. Do you love me?"

She deemed it best not to answer him.

"Okay then, let's get this show on the road so I can get back in time to watch *Baywatch.*"

"*Baywatch!*"

"You shoulda answered my question," he said with a wink. "Now don't go getting all jealous. I watch for the kite flying on the beach. I love the blue sky, not the babes jogging in their red swimsuits on the beach."

"*Red* swimsuits, eh. You really haven't noticed them at all, have you. Maybe you should do this on your own."

"Come on, I was only teasing to make sure you were paying attention. Now here's the plan, listen up."

Peter Blakemore took the call from Chief Smith. A frown appeared on his face as he listened to the new development in what was becoming a never-ending saga. He was not pleased and didn't bother to try to disguise it as he demanded, "What do you mean there's a little snag in the extradition of Ash Worth back to Pleasantville? You told me there wouldn't be any problem."

"Legally, I didn't anticipate any. The problem is Ash. He's not in custody any longer."

"He's *what?*"

"It seems he managed to give them the slip when they transported him to the hospital. He was complaining of severe stomach cramps he claimed were caused by a chronic ulcer he feared might be bleeding again."

Peter bent the paperclip in his hand.

"He escaped, you're telling me he escaped."

"Yes sir."

"And Miss Pembrook . . . ?"

"I don't know, sir."

"Well, I suggest you find out."

The dial tone droned in Darrow Smith's ear.

Well the other shoe had not only dropped, it had rolled under the bed.

Darrow knew it was over. Not the business with Ash Worth. That was still unfolding. And not favorably. He wasn't going to wait around to meet Mayor Whitehouse's fate.

He fingered the badge he laid on his desk next to his gun.

Unlike Billy Whitehouse he knew when to fold.

He went home to pack.

"Are you sure you know where you're going?" Chloe asked, stumbling along beside Ace in the dark, her hand tucked in his.

"Are you kidding, I spent my summers here. I know every nook and cranny between the two places. Just follow my lead."

They skirted a tennis court and nearby swimming pool, circling around the pool cabaña that probably cost more than several pricey German cars.

A large noisy dog sent them scurrying to grass-covered dunes before the animal reached the end of its lengthy chain and gave up on having them for an after-dinner snack. He concluded with several pitiful whines.

The next house provided the shelter of high hedges to prevent them being seen. Nevertheless, Chloe tripped and would have gone flying face first, if Ace hadn't grabbed her up to break her fall.

"What was that?" she asked, looking back to see what she'd tripped over.

"Probably a telephone line. I think there are more phones per person here than lawyers on the Simpson case." It had in fact been a root from a large elm the home owner had moved so he could have a better view.

In the Hamptons no one thought anything of ostentatious ego trips. It was the norm rather than the exception, more especially with the new money rather than the old.

"Are you okay?" he asked, before continuing.

"Yeah, other than feeling stupid for not lifting my feet."

The next house was his grandmother's and he stopped at the edge of the property.

"Wait here, I want to check out the situation and see where they've put the cop."

He left her alone then, disappearing into the darkness. She hadn't wanted him to go, but she hadn't wanted to think she was a wuss, so she'd done as he ordered and waited nervously.

It was funny how many strange noises you heard in the dark. Well not funny exactly, unnerving. She nearly screamed, giving everything up, when a small furry animal—a chipmunk, she later decided—crawled across her foot.

She distracted herself by thinking about her career. And then gave it up, deciding she didn't have one left. The events of the past few days were definitely not going to look good on a resume.

Unless you were applying for an acting job on a movie-of-the-week for television. She tried cheering herself up with a pep talk about celebrity being more important than scandal. It was the 90s not the 50s.

All this had happened to her and she hadn't written on any of the pages of her journal. Her journal to date had been filled with fountain-pen-ink-perfect penmanship about observing life rather than living it.

Maybe when—if—she got back home to Chicago she'd fill in those pages, writing about her most excellent adventure.

Because that's what it was.

She could see that clearly now when she wasn't physically with Ace.

It was just when she was with him that she couldn't distinguish between reality and the fantasies she spun out about the two of them . . . together.

He didn't have a history of monogamy.

Okay, to be fair, maybe serial monogamy.

Okay, to be real, he had a history she didn't want to think about at all.

She hadn't even seen Sarabeth's garden.

She hadn't seen anything really but Ace since she'd first laid eyes on him.

How ridiculous she was. She was the sort of woman who wore a scented cotton ball tucked in her bra. Ace was the sort of man who collected trophy bras.

Whether he wanted to or not.

She lived in fantasy, not reality . . . and had figured out a way to make a fortune at it. Ace lived in reality and didn't care about money. Had given up a fortune.

A noise nearby disturbed her musing, frightening her when she saw a shadow move by the tree in the direction the noise had come from.

She was ready to take flight when Ace called out in a loud whisper that the coast was clear.

That meant to join him.

She didn't need any encouragement.

Thirty-five

Knowing the alarm code, Ace easily gained entry to the house the back way through the kitchen door.

Chloe bumped into a French flower bucket and reached to catch it before it tipped over and fell with a clatter. "Don't turn on the light," Ace warned when she lifted her hand to do just that.

"If we don't turn on the light how are we ever going to find anything?" she whispered.

"Wait a minute," Ace instructed, sliding open a drawer in the cabinet beneath the microwave. He rummaged around in the dark until he came up with a flashlight. He flicked it on and a beam of light shone. "Good the batteries aren't dead."

"First, I need to check on my grandmother to make sure she's not still up. I don't want to give her a scare. She's usually asleep by this hour, because she gets up with the birds."

"She's probably asleep. I heard her tell Jane she was taking sleeping pills to get some rest because she was so worried about you."

"Don't make me feel worse than I already do about this, okay? Just wait here and I'll check to make sure she's asleep."

He left the flashlight with her because he knew his way in the dark from sneaking down to the cookie jar all those years.

Chloe pulled out a kitchen chair and sat down at the table to wait for Ace to return. She didn't even know where to start looking for the documents that gave weight to Ace's claim that he'd killed in self-defense. Because his investigation had been discovered, he was a threat to the whole illegal operation and had to be gotten rid of.

The doorbell rang.

Unprepared for the intrusion, she jumped up, flustered. What should she do?

She sat back down.

And then got back up when it rang again.

Whoever it was, was persistent. Was obviously not going to go away.

Ace couldn't answer the door, even if he'd heard it. No one could know he was there.

And they didn't want Sarabeth woken.

Chloe took a deep breath, picked up the flashlight and made her way to the front door. One way or another she'd have to get rid of whoever it was without drawing suspicion.

The doorbell rang again as she pulled open the door hoping it was a neighbor borrowing a cup of sugar, who could be easily dispatched.

A middle-aged guy stood in the open doorway. He had bad skin and a receding hairline. About five foot eight and thin except for a slight paunch, he was very polite and not the least bit imposing.

"Good evening, ma'am," he said, smiling. He then flashed some identification at her. "I'm Mark Sherman from the Environmental Protection Agency. Someone from this number placed a call about some illegal dumping of toxic waste by the Blakemore Company in Pleasantville, Illinois. I was assigned to the investigation and I have some results of our investigation I'd like to talk to you about if I might come inside."

"Of course," Chloe said, excited. It was about time they got a break and things started going their way.

She ushered Mark Sherman inside. "Sorry about the flashlight, but ah . . . we're having a little problem with the electricity. Why don't we talk in the kitchen."

He followed her lead to the kitchen, offering him a chair.

She was about to offer him a cup of tea when Ace came tearing into the kitchen. "Did I just hear the doorbell . . ."

Ace pulled up short when he saw Mark Sherman. *"Who the hell is he?"*

"Oh Ace, this is the guy from the Environmental Protection Agency. Remember I called them. His name is Mark Sherman and he's going to help us."

"Does the EPA always conduct business this late, Mr. Sherman . . . and how'd you get past the cop outside—"

Ace's suspicions were confirmed and his questions checked by the Glock 17 semiautomatic weapon Mark Sherman pulled from his shoulder holster beneath his dark jacket.

"I'll be asking the questions from now on," he informed both of them. He nodded to the chair he'd just vacated. "Sit down," he instructed Ace.

Ace didn't move.

Mark pointed the weapon at Chloe. "I can shoot her now and get her out of the way."

Ace took a seat in the chair Mark indicated. His body language was telegraphing his unwillingness to cooperate and his frustration at being caught off guard.

"Find something for me to tie him to the chair with," Mark ordered Chloe.

"What?" Chloe's voice was shaky, fear-filled.

"Find me something. Some duct tape, anything. I don't want to have to ask you again. Do it now."

"There's some duct tape in the drawer beneath the microwave," Ace informed her, seeing the indecision in her eyes. "I saw it when I was looking for the flashlight earlier."

Chloe went to the drawer and searched it. She came up with the roll of silver duct tape, crossed the room, and handed the tape to Mark, who refused it.

"You do it," he said, continuing to hold the gun on them. "And do it tight. I'm watching you, so don't get any cute ideas."

Chloe went to the chair where Ace sat, looking confused about how to start.

Mark told her to tape his hands together behind the chair first.

Ace folded his hands together behind the chair and she began loosening the end of the tape from the roll. She leaned down to begin winding the tape around his wrists as Mark instructed.

"Your bracelet . . . your silver bracelet is gone. What happened to it?" she asked, amazed to find it missing from his wrist.

"The cops took it when they put me in the holding cell at the jail."

"Oh Ace, I'm sorry—"

"Cut the chit-chat and get on with it. This ain't no church social, you two."

Chloe finished taping his hands in silence.

"Now his feet," Mark instructed. He picked up the flashlight and went to inspect Chloe's work on binding Ace's hands.

He did the same when she'd finished her job on Ace's feet.

"Okay, now wrap the tape around him and the chair. I don't want him going anywhere while I'm questioning him."

Chloe started, but ran out of tape after going around

his body only once. She held up the empty roll of tape for Mark's inspection, and waited.

"Find something else to finish the job with," Mark demanded impatiently. "And hurry up. I don't plan for this to take all night."

Chloe suddenly found herself praying the cop outside would ring the doorbell wanting a cup of coffee, donuts, anything. She'd even settle for a neighbor borrowing a cup of sugar. Any distraction to give her time to think of a way to get them out of Mark Sherman's clutches. She wasn't an idiot . . . Mark Sherman wanted something, and when he got it both she and Ace would be dead.

Returning to the drawer where she'd found the duct tape, she searched it and came up empty. There weren't any more rolls of duct tape, no twine, no clothesline, there was nothing.

Turning to Mark Sherman she showed her hands palms up to indicate she'd come up empty.

"Not very resourceful are you, honey?" Mark said.

He crossed to the bank of cabinet drawers to the left of the dishwasher and pulled the top one open correctly guessing it was the one that held the cutlery. He withdrew a butcher knife and checked the edge for its sharpness.

"If you hurt her," Ace warned.

"You'll watch," Mark said, pointing out the obvious. Ace was helpless to do anything. He couldn't even help himself.

Turning, Mark swiftly cut the long cord on the wall-mounted kitchen phone and then cut the earphone receiver off the end of the telephone cord. He tossed the length of coiled cord at Chloe.

"Finish the job with this."

Chloe picked up the telephone cord and followed Mark's orders, winding it around Ace's chest and the chair. When her back was to Mark, Ace whispered he'd try to distract Mark so she could escape. He told her she was not to worry about him, just get the hell out when she saw a chance.

Chloe didn't answer him.

"If the cop outside is still alive," Ace whispered, "tell him to get my grandmother out somehow—but you get as far away from here as fast as you can."

"I told you to cut the chit-chat," Mark warned.

Chloe moved to stand behind Ace when she was finished knotting the telephone cord as loose as she felt she could get by with.

"Move away from him," Mark ordered. "Come over here and stand by me."

"Why don't you leave her alone. Just let her go, she doesn't know anything. It's me you want to talk to," Ace said, knowing his request wouldn't be granted, but he'd had to try anyway.

"I don't know, you seem to have some reason for wanting her around. Tell me, is it because you don't want her telling what she knows? Or is it because you like looking at her pretty face, and . . ." Mark reached out and squeezed her behind.

"You sonovabitch!" Ace spit out.

Chloe's reaction wasn't verbal, she just automatically slugged Mark, not even thinking of the gun in his hand.

Mark's reaction was equally physical. He backhanded Chloe, sending her flying into the stove. She bounced off the stove, taking a cooling cast-iron skillet of cornbread with her to the floor with a loud clattering thud.

"You sniveling coward. Does that make you feel like a big man?" Ace's eyes were glued to Chloe sprawled on the floor near Mark's feet unmoving. Cornbread lay in hunks scattered everywhere.

"No, this does," Mark said, stepping forward and punching Ace in the gut.

Ace coughed, then finally caught his breath.

"Got any more smart-assed questions for me, or are you ready to cooperate?"

"At least see if she's all right."

Mark Sherman looked to where Ace's eyes lingered on Chloe, who still lay unmoving on the floor.

"I don't care if she's all right. All I care is that she's not bothering me right now. You're bothering me. I'm the one who's asking the questions and giving the orders. And it's time for you to give me some answers."

Ace was relieved to see Chloe's hand move slightly. He gave Mark his attention then, wanting to draw attention away from Chloe so Mark didn't get any more ideas about harming her.

"What do you want to know?" Ace asked.

"I want to know how you know about Blakemore Chemical. Who told you?"

"Do you really work for the EPA?"

"Yeah, I do."

"Since when does the government—"

"I work for myself as well."

"And Peter Blakemore too, I'll wager."

"Bright boy. You don't have to be a freaking genius to figure out that's why I'm here. You've become a real pain in the ass, you know that."

"I try."

"I warned you about being a smart ass. If I were you I'd tell me what evidence you've gathered and where it is."

"And if I don't . . . ?"

"You will."

Thirty-six

"So I was right," Ace said, stalling for time by trying to get the guy to boast. Ace knew he was a dead man, but he had to give Chloe time to come around and make her escape. She had opened one eye and looked at him, wincing.

Mark Sherman hadn't noticed. He was too busy showing how macho he was, so Ace continued to encourage him to talk. "Just contacting the EPA wasn't going to get me free of the murder rap, was it? It's as I thought all along, I needed the evidence of Blakemore's dumping that toxic waste in those drums verified by an outside source before any action would be taken. Am I right?"

"You're right. It doesn't do you any good, but you're right. We've had tips before, anonymous ones of course, but they always came to me. I'd put them down so no one got suspicious, but I just relegated them to a less important list that never got acted on. We're way understaffed, and government cutbacks keep making the work pile up until some things just don't get got to. Most of these tree lovers are crackpots anyway. You know how it is."

"So Blakemore was paying you off all along . . . you were the guy making it happen for him," Ace coaxed, playing on his ego. Chloe had opened both eyes, listening to their conversation, still not moving.

"I couldn't afford to have anyone find out I was on the take. My pension and all. I had too much to lose—to let a do-gooder like you screw it up."

"So you shot Jane, thinking she was Chloe."

"That's right. Enough talk. I don't want that cop outside coming round and finding me still here. Tell me where the evidence you have is."

"Why should I do that?" Ace asked, knowing that he couldn't even if he wanted to. Wherever his grandmother had put it, she'd tucked it away good. "You're just going to kill me anyway."

Mark Sherman came to stand in front of Ace. He pointed the gun at Ace's crotch. "But I don't have to do it neat and quick—think about that. Where's the evidence?"

"Go to hell!" Ace said, seeing Chloe's hand grip the handle of the iron skillet that had fallen to land beside her. She was crazy! He had to do something to help her.

He shifted his weight and tipped his chair so that he fell toward Mark.

"What the hell do you think you're—" Mark demanded, jumping back just as Chloe rose and swung the iron skillet with all her might connecting with Mark's skull as he stepped back into it.

Mark Sherman went down like a ton of bricks, unconscious before he hit the floor, and Ace ducked the sailing skillet.

"Holy shit, get his gun. Take the, clip out and get rid of it before he comes to," Ace yelled.

Chloe grabbed the gun that had skittered across the floor from Mark's hand, and with Ace's instruction unloaded the clip. She looked around for somewhere to hide it and after several false turns shoved the clip down the garbage disposal.

"Quick, tie him up while he's still out," Ace said,

knowing it was going to take a while for Chloe to un-bind and untie him. They couldn't take a chance that Mark would come around before then.

"What am I going to use?" Chloe asked, her palms plastered to both sides of her head as she tried to think.

"What are you doing?" Ace asked when she began pulling off the dark sweat pants she'd borrowed from the same closet Ace had borrowed his from.

"I'm gonna tie him up," she answered, stepping out of her panties first and then her pantyhose. "This'll work," she explained, pantyhose in hand.

Ace watched in open-mouthed amazement as Chloe walked over to Mark wearing nothing but a navy T-shirt. She stepped around the broken glass from the waist-high glass-doored bookcase Mark had crashed into as he fell, bringing it down with him and scattering the contents. Gardening books and catalogues lay among the chunks of cornbread.

Mark had fallen face down amidst the mess. She pushed at him with her foot.

He didn't move, or respond in any way.

Grabbing his hands, she began trussing him up like a Christmas goose, tying his feet together and then tying his ankles to his wrists. Her tongue's tip was clamped between her teeth as she concentrated.

"Good job," Ace strangled out, taking in the extraordinary vision she made when she stood half naked beside Mark with her bicep flexed. "I couldn't have done it better myself," he complimented.

"Not unless you wear pantyhose—" Chloe said, dryly, bending to look at something that had caught her eye.

"Ah, do you think you could untie me, or at least straighten my chair up," Ace said.

She looked over to where he'd tipped himself on the floor. He did look pretty helpless.

And she kind of liked it that way.

"What do the documents we're looking for look like?" she asked, picking some papers up from between two gardening catalogs.

"Don't tell me—"

"I think so," she said standing, reading the papers in her hand. "Apparently Sarabeth picked the documents up with her gardening catalogs and stacked them in the bookcase."

"All this time they were right here in the kitchen under our noses. I don't believe it."

"Well, believe it." Chloe brought the documents over to the table and set them down. Then it took all the strength she had left to get Ace upright in his chair.

"Let me see those," he said, when she picked the documents up again and began studying them.

Chloe held them out for Ace to read.

He glanced down the cover letter from the chemist Jane had hired to run the tests. The evidence of toxic waste in the samples he'd sent was confirmed.

"Untie me, and we'll go celebrate," Ace said, with a big grin on his face.

"I was thinking I'd leave you tied up and I'll celebrate," Chloe said with an even bigger grin.

She set the papers back on the table, and stood before him with her arms crossed, contemplating him.

"Knock it off, Chloe. Quit kidding around. Chloe, *untie me.*"

"I think I owe you some trouble for all the trouble you've caused me."

"What are you talking about?" he demanded, watching her with apprehension as she walked slowly toward him with a sly grin of mischief on her face. She made a very unnerving, provocative picture dressed in nothing more than the borrowed T-shirt.

His imagination was so fueled, he would have squirmed in the chair if he'd been able. As it was, he was unable to move—either to defend himself or participate.

"What are you going to do?" he demanded, when she reached his side and began trailing her fingertip over his lips while licking her own.

"I don't know—got any ideas, Ace? What would you do if you had me tied to a chair?"

"Untie you, *now.*"

"Oh Ace, I'm disappointed in you. I thought a journalist would have more imagination than that."

"You're the one who deals in fiction, baby. I'm strictly non-fiction."

"Strictly . . . I like that word," Chloe mused. "It must thrill you to give orders. You gave so many to me. I think turnabout is fair play, don't you, Ace?" She leaned forward with her hands braced on her hips. "Why don't you kiss me, Ace."

"Will you untie me if I do?"

"Ummmm . . . eventually."

"Chloe, stop it. You've had your fun, now untie me so we can—"

"But I'm not ready. And besides I'm the one giving orders now. Kiss me."

He did as ordered, swiftly, perfunctorily.

Chloe blinked open her eyes. "You aren't trying to get untied. Come on, Ace. I know you can do better than that."

Ace cleared his throat, trying to clear his mind. "Look, I don't know what your plans are, but that cop outside could show up any minute, Mark could wake up any minute, and my *grandmother* could wake up and come down any minute and find us like this!"

Chloe smiled like a Chesire cat. "I know, isn't it exciting . . ."

"You're crazy, woman."

"Weren't you the one telling me I had no sense of adventure? Isn't that just like a man to tell you one thing and then he wants another."

"I want you to untie me."

Chloe bent forward again and kissed him senseless, a kiss that curled his toes among other things. "My point exactly," she said, playing on his words.

"Are you feeling hungry, Ace. Maybe you're fading, feeling a little weak . . ." Chloe crossed to the cupboard and took out a jar of honey she found.

"I'm not hungry."

She ignored him.

Unscrewing the lid from the small jar of honey, she placed the lid on the table. Walking back toward him she stuck her finger in the jar and lifted the sticky sweet to her full lips. Slipping her finger between her lips, she began to slowly lick and suck. The action was mesmerizingly sexual, commanding his full and undivided attention.

She watched him watch her.

"Your turn," she said, when she had licked every bit of honey from her finger.

"Cute, Chloe. I can't move my finger, much less lick honey from it."

"That wasn't what I had in mind," she informed him, setting the jar of honey on the table. Then crossing her arms in front of her to pull her navy T-shirt over her head, she discarded it.

As she stood before Ace naked, he wasn't saying anything, just swallowing dryly, while watching her dip her finger back in the honey. She began smearing the honey over her nipples in generous dabs. She took her time, stretching out the delicious torture.

Finally she turned and moved to stand before him.

Placing her hands on his shoulders and bending forward, she said, "Lick."

His objections seemed to have deserted him. She only had to ask him once.

And he licked up every speck.

"You did that rather quickly," Chloe said, smiling down at him. "I think I'll have you repeat it, more slowly this time," she instructed, reaching for the small jar of honey again. Only this time she stood and tipped the jar against her golden pubic hair, letting the syrupy honey trickle where it would.

Ace seemed to be strangling in his chair.

"Chloe—for heaven's sake," he sputtered when he finally got his voice. "We can't . . . you can't . . . what if . . ."

"Hush," she ordered. "I need to figure out the logistics of how to do this—"

A few seconds later she was positioned on her knees braced on his thighs.

And this time she didn't even have to ask.

Ace decided to hell with it. He'd go for it. He deserved it.

And suddenly the tables were turned.

Chloe was the one who couldn't move. Who was caught captive. Only it wasn't anything so mundane as duct tape and telephone cord that bound her to Ace.

It was sensation.

Sensational sensation. She trembled against his lips, his tongue, his teeth, as an aching flood of desire overtook her, sweeping her. She reacted to the heat and sweetness of Ace's mouth on her with passion as naked as she was.

Her unbridled response caused her to lose her precarious balance and the chair tipped over backward to send them crashing to the floor.

"Is somebody down there?" Sarabeth's voice floated down from upstairs.

"This time she has to believe I am not to blame," Ace said on a chuckle as Chloe scrambled for her discarded sweat pants.

Thirty-seven

Cold dark eyes burning with the fire of revenge watched unseen as the circus began. The whole town of Pleasantville was abuzz about the U.S. Attorney ordering a task force to dig up the sites where Blakemore Chemical was suspected of dumping toxic waste bombs polluting surface water and soil over time.

If they found what the investigative reporter claimed they'd find—in fact he had shown the evidence—Peter Blakemore was going down.

Not down to hell where he belonged, but down.

He'd be put away in prison for the environmental crimes he'd committed against the community. It had been a long, long quest, but Peter Blakemore was at last going to pay for something evil he'd done.

If the land was polluted, Peter Blakemore wasn't the only one who'd lose. The town would lose because the property would have to be sanitized, at costs that would be prohibitive.

Peter Blakemore's name would never be spoken with any kind of reverence. That more than anything was going to kill him.

Not the Smith and Wesson .38 pointed at his sweaty brow.

The loaded gun that was detaining him from skipping out on the certainty of incarceration for environ mental crimes, even though his bags were packed—one of them with a considerable fortune.

As the crew moved in wearing moon suits to inspect the unearthed drums of waste that had been dumped in Pleasantville, Ace paced the floor at his grandmother's house in East Hampton.

The *Chicago Trib*'s team of lawyers had managed to get him out on bail, but he'd been forbidden to leave town. There was no way after the little trip he'd taken with Chloe after shooting Peter Blakemore, Jr. that the newspaper's lawyers could claim he wasn't a flight risk.

Jane had taken his grandmother to the nursery for some rose food, leaving him all alone in the house raiding the refrigerator. So far he'd gone through some cold fried chicken and several pieces of fruit. He was trying to hold out against the chocolate cake that was to be dessert for dinner. But if he didn't hear some news soon from Pleasantville, he was going to go nuts. Or develop an eating disorder, he thought, finding himself reaching for the lettuce to make a salad.

Looking through the cabinets for some croutons for his salad, he came across the jar of honey. He picked it up, grinning.

Unscrewing the top, he dipped his finger in and brought the thick, sweet syrup to his lips while memories of Chloe flooded his mind.

She'd been wicked and wild and loving every minute of giving him back some of his own. The images of her naked and honey dipped were never going to be far from surfacing, haunting him.

But the following morning had brought a cooler head.

She'd had herself back in check.

He'd argued that they'd found something special together. But she'd dismissed his argument as situational. Dangerous circumstances had made both of them act in ways they might not have otherwise. He was reading something in what had happened that wasn't there.

You didn't just have someone kidnap you, and then fall in love with them.

Not if you were Chloe Pembrook.

And wanted to have any kind of career left as a lifestyle expert. She'd driven Julie's car back to Chicago and set about repairing her image.

And there was nothing he could do about it because he was stuck in East Hampton until his lawyers got the charges against him dropped.

It had to count for something that he was the one who'd gone outside and called an ambulance for the cop on his police car radio. Still he hadn't exactly endeared himself to the East Hampton police by giving one of them the slip at the hospital.

When the police had arrived, they'd removed Ace, Mark Sherman—who'd come around when grandmother had come downstairs to see if anyone wanted a cup of tea—Sherman's weapon, which still had a hollow-point bullet in the firing chamber, to Ace's dismay, and the magazine clip from the garbage disposal.

The telephone rang and he put the jar of honey away.

But it turned out not to be the call he'd been waiting for. Instead of news from his attorneys, it was the carpenter calling about repairing the glass-doored bookcase that had been broken.

He was like a caged tiger, pacing still when his grandmother and Jane returned.

"Any news yet?" Jane asked when she entered the kitchen.

Ace shook his head.

"I'm starved, why don't we have some of that left-over fried chicken—it's *all* gone!" Jane looked from the refrigerator.

Ace had the decency to at least look guilty. In his defense, he said, "I didn't touch the chocolate cake."

Jane picked up the chocolate cake and got a strange light in her eyes.

"Grandmother!" he yelled, backing away from Jane's menacing threat.

"She's not here to defend you. She's out in the rose garden," Jane said.

"If you push that cake in my face, you won't have anything to eat," Ace bargained.

She stopped and considered. "You've got a point, bright boy. But you owe me some fried chicken." She put the cake down and waited.

"I can't leave now and get you some fried chicken. I'm waiting for a phone call."

"So I'll take a message," Jane said, getting a big knife out of the cutlery drawer to cut a slice of the chocolate cake.

"I wouldn't do that if I were you," Ace advised, catching the keys to the Lincoln, Jane tossed him. "Grandmother is planning on serving it for dinner. She baked it to celebrate my getting out of jail."

Jane looked longingly at the chocolate cake, then put the knife away.

"You're in all the papers, you know. I'll bet the rest of the Ellsworth family can't wait for you to go back to Chicago."

"I can't help it. I don't start out to embarrass them. Maybe if they didn't have so much to cover up, they wouldn't be so worried about their public image."

"Yeah, I know it's never your fault. I had to listen to that on the ride to the nursery. You sure have your grandmother snowed. She thinks you're a prince."

"I *am* a prince."

"So how come your princess went off and left you, Prince Charming?"

"She's just a little skittish, is all," Ace assured Jane. "Once this is all over and I can go back to Chicago, I'm sure I can—"

"Your ass, Ace. You're lying and you know it. If you were so certain about Chloe, you wouldn't be wearing a hole in the floor pacing like an expectant father in the waiting room at the hospital."

The subject of babies had him looking a little pale, he could feel it. Evidently Jane could see it.

"You love her don't you, Ace?" Jane clued in.

"Maybe."

"Oh, don't go getting out on the limb of commitment. No wonder she fled back to Chicago. *Maybe.* You don't maybe love someone, you fool."

"Listen to you, Miss Advice for the Romantically Challenged. I don't notice any diamond on your marriage finger."

"That's cause I'm . . . I'm . . . we aren't talking about me. We're talking about you."

"No, we're not," he said, tossing the keys in his hand. "Because I'm outta here. I'm going to get you your fried chicken. Later."

"Where's Ace going?" Sarabeth asked, when she entered the kitchen from the garden.

"He went to get some more fried chicken since he ate everything in the refrigerator."

"He didn't eat the chocolate cake—"

"No. He knew better."

"What's wrong with him? Ever since he got out of jail, he's so restless. You'd think he'd relax now that the worst of what's happened is behind him. The attorneys tell me they believe they will be able to get the charges against him dropped when they prove Ace was telling the truth about the chemicals being dumped."

"What's wrong with him is that he's in love."

Sarabeth took a cup from the cabinet for some tea she was about to brew. "He misses Chloe . . ."

"He won't admit it, but he does. And if he isn't careful he's going to mess up any chance he has with her. His having to stay here is the best thing that could ever have happened to him."

"Why's that?"

"Because," Jane said, handing Sarabeth the tea kettle, "Chloe needs some time to sort through everything that happened to her."

The telephone rang, interrupting their conversation about Ace. "I still can't get over how easy it was to replace the phone that had its cord ruined," Sarabeth said, on the way to answer the telephone. "They even gave me a longer cord when I went to exchange it."

After identifying herself, Sarabeth listened a moment and then turned the telephone over to Jane.

"It's the attorneys for the newspaper. They want to talk to Ace. But since he isn't here, they asked to talk to you."

Jane took the telephone.

She listened as the attorney relayed information for Ace regarding the investigation into the Blakemore dumping site in Pleasantville.

Nodding her head and trying to look normal instead of intrigued as hell, she watched Sarabeth making a fresh pot of tea. Jane's smile when Sarabeth looked over at her was meant to reassure.

The conversation wound down and Jane hung up the telephone promising to relay the information the attorney had given her to Ace.

"Is there some news?" Sarabeth asked when Jane hung up the telephone.

"Yes. The attorneys want to talk to Ace."

"Have they gotten the police to drop the charges?" Sarabeth asked hopefully, pouring boiling water over the dry tea.

"Not yet. But something interesting did turn up."

Ace came into the kitchen, back from his trip to fetch food for Jane. He handed over a box of extra crispy, asking, "Any messages?"

"Sit down, Ace," his grandmother ordered. "We're going to have tea. I don't want the two of you picking any fights and acting like two-year-olds for at least fifteen minutes," she said, pouring the tea she'd made. "We'll all feel better and think clearer when we've had our cup of tea."

"How about tea and chocolate cake . . ." Ace advanced.

"The cake is for dinner," Sarabeth reminded him, not budging an iota.

When they'd dutifully drunk their tea, Jane returned to the subject of the telephone call.

"The attorneys called? What did they want?" Ace demanded, perhaps clearer headed, but not calmer for the cup of tea.

"There's been an interesting new development," Jane answered, biting into a crispy chicken leg.

"Good or bad?" Ace pressed.

"I'm not sure. It seems that no one has seen Mayor Billy Whitehouse lately and Chief Darrow Smith has also dropped out of sight."

"I'm not surprised," Ace responded. "Both of them were involved in what's gone on with the illegal dumping. They knew I wasn't going to let go of the story, so they did."

"Maybe, maybe not," Jane sing-songed.

"What's that supposed to mean, Jane?"

"It's just that the attorney I talked to on the phone told me that in a couple of the first drums they dug up at the site, they found human remains."

Thirty-eight

On the plane back to Chicago, Jane talked the entranced businessman sitting next to her out of his bag of peanuts, regaling him with the exciting life of being a reporter for the *Chicago Trib*. Some of her tales were highly exaggerated. A few, full-blown lies.

While in her professional life she was careful about the truth and the pursuit of same . . . in her personal life, anything went. You just didn't go around telling people the truth. Not only did they not want to hear it, they couldn't be trusted with it. She conducted her personal life like a board game. The only trouble was she'd lost the rules long ago, so she couldn't tell if she was winning or not.

But she was having a hell of a time playing the game.

She and Sarabeth had become friends, now that Ace's grandmother understood that Jane and Ace weren't pursuing a disastrous marriage. Sarabeth had, in fact, given her a standing invitation to come stay any old time she chose.

Jane planned to take her up on it. The seaside villages were only a two-hour drive from Manhattan, so she could do a Broadway play and lie on an untouched beach, all in one weekend.

The guy beside her had taken the hint when she'd gotten out her laptop and began making notes; ideas for future investigative pieces. There was no shortage of interesting people in the Hamptons. Everyone from the old line families like Ace's, to tycoons and movie producers rubbed shoulders at play. Who knew what tidbit would drop into conversation while they were at play.

She might even write that book, *Bound in Leather*, that even Ace didn't know she harbored the desire to write. She wasn't sure what his reaction to her dream of being a novelist someday would be, though he was sure to be intrigued by the title.

It wasn't a book really, but a series of short stories that were erotic and had a Rod Serling twist at the end of each. Sort of a constellation of who she was; wildly sexy and bitingly funny. It wasn't a combination many men could handle.

But she wasn't about to change.

She liked herself.

But with Sarabeth's backing she had entry to such toney A-list restaurants as Sapore di Mare, and who knew what well-heeled Hamptonite might finance a year off to write her best seller.

But for now it was back to Chicago.

Back to work.

Ace was wrapping up his story on Blakemore Chemical. He would be flying back to Chicago as well when the formalities of dropping the charges against him were finalized by the *Trib's* attorneys.

The EPA, without Mark Sherman's duplicity, had verified that Ace's claims were valid. The drums that had been illegally dumped did contain toxic waste. On the strength of the evidence, Peter Blakemore had been arrested and charged with environmental crimes.

It was time to move on.

Time for her to go head to head with Ace again.

Time for her to outmaneuver him.

* * *

"Ace, there's someone here to see you," Sarabeth said, coming into the library where Ace was working on his story on the laptop computer he'd rented.

"Who is it?"

"Jonathon Blakemore."

Ace's head jerked up from the laptop. "Who?"

"He said his name is Jonathon Blakemore," Sarabeth repeated. "Isn't that the same name as the family who . . ."

Ace rose to his feet. "Yes, I just put his father in prison, and his brother tried to kill me. What in the hell is he doing here in East Hampton?"

"He said it was important."

"Did he have a gun?"

"A gun? No. I—"

"Wait here grandmother, I'll get rid of him."

Ace headed for the entry where Sarabeth had left Jonathon to wait, dropping her usual good manners in her confusion at his being there.

"What are you doing here?" Ace demanded upon seeing Jonathon Blakemore still standing in the entry where Sarabeth had bade him wait.

"I need to talk to you."

The need was clear in the tone of his voice. This Jonathon Blakemore wasn't his usual belligerent threatening bully self. The big, blond man was overwrought. Something had gotten him into a distraught state. Ace had difficulty believing it was the arrest of Jonathon's father.

Peter Blakemore hadn't been rumored to be especially close to either son and vice versa.

"Come into the library," Ace invited, making a judgement call he hoped he wouldn't regret.

Jonathon followed him into the library and Ace indicated the sofa for Jonathon, while Ace took a seat at the desk.

"What is it . . ." Ace prodded, waiting.

Jonathon wouldn't look at him. The big blond man's shoulders were slumped, his whole posture one of dejection and resignation. Staring at the floor, Jonathon began.

"I suppose you've heard about the bodies that were found at the site they investigated."

"I heard. I also heard Mayor Whitehouse and Chief Smith are missing. Are you responsible? Is that what you've come here with— a confession?"

"Mayor Whitehouse was gone on a toot. He sobered up and surfaced. The chief's still missing, that's true. But I'm not here to talk about them."

Ace rubbed his chin. His curiosity was piqued. What was Jonathon so desperate to tell him, and why?

"I'm going to tell you a story and I want you to just listen until I'm finished, okay?"

Ace leaned back in the chair. "Okay."

Jonathon took a deep breath, let it out, wrung his hands together and began. "I suppose you know I hate you for killing my brother. But I hate my father even more for being the one who was responsible for you pulling the trigger."

Ace was surprised to see a tear slide down the big man's cheek.

Jonathon didn't bother to wipe it away, he just went on with the story he was determined to tell Ace.

"I thought I hated my father all my life because he was so cold and strict. Because he seemed to hate us. I could never understand why he hated his own sons. And then as I got older, I decided it was because we were a daily living reminder of the woman who'd dared to cross him. The woman who hadn't bowed to his absolute power to control everything and everyone around him.

"I decided her leaving him had made him a sick man.

"The fact that she left him for another man had to have galled him. She'd made a fool of him in front of the entire town.

"And the ultimate betrayal had been her not wanting my brother and I. She'd rejected my father *and* his sons.

"Not that he wanted us."

Ace sat silently listening as Jonathon had requested, but he couldn't help wanting to ask Jonathon what all this had to do with Jonathon's wanting to tell *him*. It was old news. And it wasn't even news. It was common knowledge in the town.

Ace hadn't stopped to think how the events of twenty years ago might have shaped Jonathon, making him into the unsavory person he was. It was hard to feel sympathy, even knowing the family's history. Ace was more inclined to feel sympathy for Peter Blakemore's wife.

While he might not respect her choice to leave her children, he did believe women should get out of abusive relationships. And he believed the society they lived in needed to provide more support for women to be able to leave without the very real danger of risking their lives. The story he'd won his most-prized award for had been on the very subject.

While gossip had it that Peter Blakemore's wife had suffered mental abuse, not physical abuse, either was deadly, as far as Ace was concerned. One killed your body, the other killed your soul.

Jonathon looked up at him.

"You mentioned the bodies that were discovered in two of the drums. They weren't actually bodies. What they found was skeletal remains. Bones. Whoever was in those drums had been in them a long time."

Jonathon looked away, into the past really, as he began telling Ace what he'd come to tell him.

"When you managed to escape a second time, it enraged my father. I happened to be there when he got the call from Darrow Smith telling him of your escape when you'd slipped away at the hospital in Southampton.

"The fury on his face triggered a memory.

"One I'd repressed.

"The memory was of another of my father's rages."

Ace leaned forward, listening intently as Jonathon's voice was soft, focused on what he was *seeing*, as he was recalling.

"My father did not like to be thwarted.

"By anyone."

Jonathon took a deep breath trying to swallow the half sob that escaped his lips. He put his hand over his mouth.

"Would you like a drink?" Ace asked, thinking it might make what Jonathon had to tell him easier.

Jonathon shook his head and continued.

"I had come home from school sick, that day. When I arrived, I heard voices yelling upstairs. One of the voices was my father's. My mother was crying.

"I crept up the stairs, afraid, yet wanting to protect my mother.

"They were in the master bedroom.

"And there was another man there as well. He was naked and standing beside the bed struggling with my father. My mother was in bed with a sheet wrapped around her, begging my father not to hurt the young man he'd found her with.

"My father didn't listen. He hit the man and the

man fell forward hitting his head against the marble seat in front of the fireplace.

"My mother screamed when the man didn't move, she accused my father of killing him, which of course he had. Though it could have been construed as accidental since the blow that killed the man was dealt to his head when he fell.

"But my father wasn't satisfied that he'd avenged his wife's unfaithfulness. He couldn't let the woman who'd shamed him live. In a jealous rage, he strangled my mother with his bare hands.

"His rage was so great that he didn't notice a young boy standing in the open doorway witnessing the murder.

"I ran and hid in the closet in my room. He never saw me. Never knew that I knew.

"*I* didn't even know that I knew.

"Until I saw that murderous rage at being thwarted on my father's face again when you escaped.

"I had blocked it all out because it was something so horrible my mind couldn't accept it.

"All these year's I let myself believe my mother had abandoned my brother and I. The birthday presents through the years I refused to open—hadn't really been from her at all—and on some level I guess I knew it.

"The bodies never turned up. Gossip said my mother had run away with her lover.

"My father had gotten away with it.

"I don't want him to get away with it any longer.

"I want the world to know he killed my mother. I want you to write the story, and include it when you expose the whole sordid mess.

"I want my father to pay for what he did.

"To my mother.

"To my brother.

"To me."

"Are you going to the police with your story?" Ace asked.

"Yes, I'm willing to testify in a court of law against my father."

"I have to ask you this, Jonathon. Are you sure you really remember this. It could be your mind's way of allowing you to get revenge on your father for what he's done to you over the years." Ace wasn't sure of the legal standing on spontaneous recollection of repressed memories. And he didn't trust Jonathon Blakemore.

"The skeletal remains they found in the drums at the site Blakemore Chemical was dumping will verify the truth of my memory. The skeletal remains are of a man and a woman."

Thirty-nine

It was good to be home.

Chicago.

Although bar food had taken a strange twist.

Jane had told him about Lucille's with its atmosphere of exposed-brick walls, a high tin ceiling and fabulous-looking back bar. She'd recommended the black peppercorn-encrusted salmon with three sauces.

She hadn't told him about the hard-back chairs used for seating, as well as polished wooden booths. He seemed to have developed something between a phobia and a fetish for hard-backed chairs, so he chose a booth.

After placing his order for the salmon, he pulled out the newspaper to read his story on the Blakemore Chemical scandal.

He felt comfortable reading in the casual atmosphere of loud music, fun-seeking groups and cigarette smoke.

With the arrival of his Samuel Adams from the tap, and some crusty bread to dunk in the bottles of herbed olive oil, he began to relax and unwind.

Getting the story out had been difficult at best. There had been delays and surprises. But he'd gotten the truth of it. There was something very satisfying in that.

It wasn't any good to live in the age of information

if most of the information was misinformation; un-truths, half truths, and biased truths.

His story exposed the danger of power being seated too strongly in any one place or person. That old saw that power corrupts and absolute power corrupts absolutely was one he found truth in.

The other truth was that power often kills.

It kills people.

Ideas.

Thought itself.

America was a nation getting lazy when it came to thinking. He blamed it on a school system that encouraged learning by memorizing. A school system that served to train wage slaves for major corporations.

If his stories served to make people discuss, exchange and create ideas and opinions which they could back up with good thought processes, he was happy.

His grandmother would translate that to say Ace loved a good argument.

His story and Jonathon's testimony along with the evidence would serve justice. Peter Blakemore would pay for his crimes. As would Mark Sherman.

When he finished reading, he folded the newspaper just as his meal came. Radicchio cups held the three sauces for the salmon. Pretty fancy stuff. Even the pizza those around him were enjoying was yuppiefied.

As he ate, a pretty brunette with a waist Scarlett would have envied flirted with him from across the room. It was a one-sided flirtation and she gave up after a while.

He was sick.

But there was no use taking his temperature when he got home. There was no thermometer around that could read what he had.

He was love sick.

Chloe Pembrook had dipped his mind in honey.

He had it so bad, even good-looking brunettes didn't register. *Willing* good-looking brunettes.

But he had his pride.

Chloe had made her choice; making it clear she didn't want him involved in her life. He didn't fit her freaking *lifestyle*.

She'd gone back to being all style and no life.

It was what she preferred.

Angry at being dumped, Ace tried to focus on a judicious set of ta-ta's at the end of the bar that were probably Wonderbra inspired. But he was such a sick puppy that all they made him think of was Chloe's . . . honey dipped.

Ace rubbed his wrist. He was still getting used to the silver bracelet not being there. In its place was a self-winding chronograph navigator-like watch. It was time he'd decided he lived his life for himself.

He'd already begun.

An atheist, he'd started exploring religion. There was nothing like almost dying to make you hope you weren't the only thing running the show. And that there was some sort of encore planned.

One thing, though, probably wouldn't change, he thought, watching a woman walk by in a pair of red tango shoes. High heels were always going to turn him on.

Too bad he'd never gotten to see Chloe in a pair of them. He wondered if she'd ever wear them. You couldn't count the pair of dignified sling-backs she'd worn with that prim, yet sexy white linen dress she'd bought.

He liked the kind that said, "Come fuck me."

He liked a woman with balls. It was what had first attracted him to Jane. Unfortunately, he'd not seen that Jane's testosterone level rivaled his own.

Chloe on the other hand only played dirty when he needed to be pulled up short, when he deserved it.

Chloe played fair.

Or had, until she left him standing at the altar so to speak. Of course he hadn't asked her. When had there been time?

But she had to know how he felt about her.

How could she not know?

His grandmother knew.

Jane knew.

He rolled his eyes. Great, now probably the whole world knew. He picked up the newspaper again and checked the personals. You could never tell with Jane.

He was almost surprised not to find some embarrassing poem or announcement in the personals that would make him the hit of the Larry King Show.

He was safe.

If only he weren't so sorry.

Mary Martin folded the newspaper.

It was over.

She walked to the bulletin board and took down the faded photograph of her best friend.

She'd known all along something had happened to her. Known she wouldn't have left her sons behind. Known she would have heard from her.

Known Peter Blakemore hadn't let his young wife leave town.

She'd evened the score for her best friend.

Now Peter Blakemore wasn't leaving town either. She'd seen to it. Had held the gun to his head.

When the police had come to arrest him.

Peter Blakemore had been there waiting, despite all his money, despite all his power . . . a woman had brought him down.

* * *

Chloe stretched.

And "ouched."

Yoga was the latest thing and supposed to be relaxing she reminded herself. She was taking a class so she could write about it in her column. She planned to do one that encompassed all the 90s methods of relaxation; everything from yoga to aromatherapy.

She'd tried them all and none of them had worked for her yet.

But then she was a hard case.

In her heart, she didn't really want to relax. She craved the excitement Ace had brought into her life. It was a foolish craving. An obsessive one.

One she had wisely put a stop to.

She was like her antique MG.

Stylish, temperamental and needed someone willing to give her tender loving care. Not someone who'd take her out and see how fast she could go.

The ride might be thrilling, but . . . she'd regret it. Wouldn't she?

Julie had told Chloe that she knew everything about women and nothing about men. Was Julie right?

Or was Julie just trying to pay her back for stealing her car and her clothes? She'd returned both, and Julie had been a good sport—fascinated about "this Ace person" to her husband's pique.

Julie thought she'd acted too hastily. That she ought to have given Ace a chance.

But Julie didn't know Ace. He was like Jane. Give either of them an inch and they'd have your underwear off with your zipper still up; sort of like the magician's trick of removing the tablecloth without disturbing the dishes. Maybe that wasn't a good analogy. Her dishes had been plenty disturbed.

True to her promise she'd filled up her journal pages and that was probably why she was lingering over what had happened.

Lingering over Ace.

She should move on.

S-t-r-e-t-c-h, as the instructor kept repeating.

Ace did have one good thing to recommend him. Sarabeth.

She'd adored Ace's grandmother and her gardens. The column she'd written on ribbonwork inspired by the book Sarabeth had given her had turned out to be one of her favorites.

While she had thought the scandal of the kidnapping was going to ruin her career, it had had the opposite effect, juicing it. It had cinched the television spot. Now she was going to need more material than ever.

She didn't have time to moon over men she knew better than to.

And yes, she was a coward after all.

She might have survived being kidnapped—twice. She might have survived Mark Sherman's deadly intentions.

But she was still a coward.

She had this strange phobia and fetish for Ashley Clayton Ellsworth.

He confused her.

She didn't know who she was when she was with him.

Maybe if he'd made the grand gesture and skipped bail to kidnap her a third time . . .

There was something to be said for Dustin Hoffman racing to steal Katherine Ross from the arms of her yuppie groom before she said, "I do."

There was a certain appeal to Richard Gere carrying Debra Winger from that factory in his dress whites.

Patrick Swayze coming back from the dead to save Demi Moore. Now that was romance.

But stuff like that didn't happen in real life.
Men weren't that romantic.
Shame.

Forty

Nothing could ruin this day.

Chloe Pembrook was so jazzed she could have climbed the stairs to the television studio without breathing hard. She'd hadn't. She'd taken the elevator. She was jazzed, not crazy.

She wore a velvet trouser suit she'd bought especially for her first television show. She wanted to look professional, feminine and stylish. Festive even.

Because it was a day to celebrate.

A day when she'd won the prize, accomplished one of her long-held goals. Her audience would widen considerably with television.

For today's show she was going to demonstrate how to make garlands of magnolias—the flower that had supplanted the sunflower in the spotlight.

She'd checked the set to make sure everything was ready while the producer gave the crew a last minute shake down.

And then with dizzying speed she heard her name announced, and she was on.

Live.

Before a live audience.

And suddenly nervous.

But she managed to hide her nerves as she got into the show, demonstrating her skill at making things beautiful. She was confident of her ideas and her sense of style.

The audience applauded with approval when she'd completed the first garland.

She gave some ideas of how a garland might be used: to decorate the top of a tall armoire, to use as a valance at a window, even a swag along a fireplace mantel.

A woman from the audience was selected to make a garland with Chloe and she came up on the stage. As they began, the show was interrupted by the delivery of a huge bouquet of flowers. The bouquet was so big it came to Chloe's waist when she set it on the floor beside the table where she was helping the audience participant assemble her magnolia garland.

"Who are the flowers from?" the young girl asked, obviously smitten with the idea of getting flowers.

"I'm sure they're from a sponsor, who's possibly even a florist," Chloe said, getting a laugh from the audience.

"Aren't you going to read the card?"

The girl had put her on the spot as the audience began applauding for her to do just that.

Chloe slipped the card from the small white envelope and read Ace's message, blushing bright red.

"Is it from a sponsor?"

"No," Chloe answered, wishing she'd chosen someone less curious from the audience. Although that was probably not possible, as the same audience was chanting, "Who, who, who?"

"The flowers are from someone I once did a favor for. They're a bread-and-butter gift. Now can we continue with the garland?"

The audience settled down, but only until a big box of candy was delivered onstage.

Chloe was speechless.

Unfortunately the young girl beside her wasn't.

"W-O-W! Is that from the same guy?"

Chloe didn't want to read the card.

The audience had other plans, chanting, "Who, who, who?" again.

Chloe was forced to open the card accompanying the heart-shaped box of candy and read it.

"He's grateful, okay. I'm sure that's all we're going to hear from Mr. Ellsworth now. Can we get on with our show?" She glared off-stage at her producer, who was beaming, absolutely delighted at the audience's fascination with Ace's gifts.

The audience settled down with watchful anticipation, their attention more at the stage entry where the gifts had come from than on the garland Chloe helped the young girl complete.

Their watchful attention paid off for yet another gift arrived. It came in the form of an envelope.

Chloe gave up and opened the envelope without prodding from the audience.

"It's the bill for the flowers and the candy," she quipped and the audience roared.

Chloe laid the envelope down.

"What's really in the envelope?" a blonde in the audience called out.

"It looked like airplane tickets," the young girl beside her said, thoroughly enjoying herself. In fact, Chloe was beginning to smell a frame. Not only did the young girl and the producer seem in on it. The voice from the crowd had sounded familiar.

"Who are the airplane tickets from?" the same voice called out again. This time Chloe recognized the voice.

It was Jane Talbert.

She had been set up.

The young girl slipped the tickets from the envelope, winked and read off the name, "Ace."

"Isn't that the guy who kidnapped you?" Jane called out.

Chloe saw her career flash before her eyes. It didn't take long. There was the television show that—

"Ace, Ace, Ace," the audience began to chant, encouraged by Jane.

Applause broke out becoming thunderous as Ace crossed the stage to Chloe.

"I'm going to kill you," she muttered beneath her breath.

"You won't get away with it, you're live with a studio audience of witnesses."

When the audience settled down again expectantly, Ace grinned, all smooth sexy operator. "Do you mind if I whisk Chloe off to England? I have something to ask her," he said, making the audience part of his wildly romantic gesture.

"Go, go, go," they chanted.

"I can't just walk off my first television show," Chloe sputtered.

"Think of the ratings . . ." Ace coaxed.

"Bye," she said, waving to the audience as Ace swept her off-stage and off her feet.

Epilogue

The city editor walked into the deserted newsroom of the *Chicago Trib* and laid the news release he'd just ripped off the API on her desk.
"You're it."
Jane scanned the news release.
"Oh, fuck!"

TELEGRAM:

TO: ASHLEY CLAYTON ELLSWORTH
    LONDON, ENGLAND

    Have you seen the news? STOP
    Story breaking STOP Come home STOP

                JANE TALBERT
                CHICAGO, ILLINOIS

TELEGRAM:

TO: JANE TALBERT
    CHICAGO, ILLINOIS
    Handle it STOP

                ACE
                LONDON, ENGLAND

TELEGRAM:

TO: ASHLEY CLAYTON ELLSWORTH
    LONDON, ENGLAND
    But I need you STOP

                        JANE TALBERT
                        CHICAGO, ILLINOIS

TELEGRAM:

TO: JANE TALBERT
    CHICAGO, ILLINOIS
    Sorry, I'm all tied up STOP

                        ACE
                        LONDON, ENGLAND

Dear Reader:

I wanted to write a heroine who would rather be baking cookies. A heroine who wants life to be prettier than it is. I wanted to put her with a hero who craves excitement. A hero who wants to shatter the illusion of perfection to expose the truth.

I really enjoy working within the "Man in Jeopardy" format, so I matched lifestyle expert Chloe Pembrook with investigative reporter Ashley Clayton Ellsworth III, or ACE as he prefers to be called.

It all begins with Chloe's really bad day when she gets lost, witnesses a murder and is kidnapped. Chloe and Ace are thrown together, and reluctantly drawn to each other. She loves the excitement he brings to her quiet life. He loves the beauty and serenity she brings to his messy life. They fight the attraction every step of the way, until they come to learn the world needs both truth and beauty . . . as they need each other.

I love hearing from my readers. Please address your correspondence to:

Anna Eberhardt
1515 N. Warson #106
St. Louis, MO 63132

I hope you enjoyed *Something Wild!*

Anna Eberhardt

**If you liked this book, be sure to look for others
in the *Denise Little Presents* line:**

*Available wherever paperbacks are sold, or order direct from the
Publisher. Send cover price plus 50¢ per copy for mailing and
handling to Penguin USA, P.O. Box 999, c/o Dept. 17109,
Bergenfield, NJ 07621. Residents of New York and Tennessee
must include sales tax. DO NOT SEND CASH.*

FOR THE VERY BEST IN ROMANCE—
DENISE LITTLE PRESENTS!

AMBER, SING SOFTLY   (0038, $4.99)
by Joan Elliott Pickart
Astonished to find a wounded gun-slinger on her doorstep, Amber
Prescott can't decide whether to take him in or put him out of his misery.
Since this lonely frontierswoman can't deny her longing to have a man
of her own, who nurses him back to health, while savoring the glorious
possibilities of the situation. But what Amber doesn't realize is that this
strong, handsome man is full of surprises!

A DEEPER MAGIC   (0039, $4.99)
by Jillian Hunter
From the moment wealthy Margaret Rose and struggling physician Ian
MacNeill meet, they are swept away in an adventure that takes them
from the haunted land of Aberdeen to a primitive, faraway island—and
into a world of danger and irresistible desire. Amid the clash of ancient
magic and new science Margaret and Ian find themselves falling help-
lessly in love.

SWEET AMY JANE   (0050, $4.99)
by Anna Eberhardt
Her horoscope warned her she'd be dealing with the wrong sort of man.
And private eye Amy Jane Chadwick was used to dealing with the wrong
kind of man, due to her profession. But nothing prepared her for the
gorgeously handsome Max, a former professional athlete who is being
stalked by an obsessive fan. And from the moment they meet, sparks
fly and danger follows!

MORE THAN MAGIC   (0049, $4.99)
by Olga Bicos
This classic romance is a thrilling tale of two adventurers who set out
for the wilds of the Arizona territory in the year 1878. Seeking treasure,
an archaeologist and an astronomer find the greatest prize of all—love.

ROMANCE YOU'LL ALWAYS REMEMBER...

A NAME YOU'LL NEVER FORGET!

Receive
$2 REBATE
With the purchase of any two
DENISE LITTLE PRESENTS
Romances

To receive your rebate, enclose:
+ Original cash register receipts with book prices circled
+ This certificate with information printed
+ ISBN numbers filled in from book covers

Mail to: DLP Rebate, P.O. Box 1092
         Grand Rapids, MN 55745-1092

Name_____

Address_____

City_____State_____Zip_____

Telephone number ( )_____(OPTIONAL)

COMPLETE ISBN NUMBERS:

0-7860-_____ 0-7860-_____

This certificate must accompany your request. No duplicates accepted. Void where prohibited, taxed or restricted. Offer available to U.S. & Canadian residents only. Allow 6 weeks for mailing of your refund payable in U.S. funds.

OFFER EXPIRES 5/30/96